# FULL CONTACT

A MILES JACOBY MYSTERY

# FULL CONTACT

## ROBERT J. RANDISI

A MILES JACOBY MYSTERY

— ST. MARTIN'S PRESS —
*New York*

Library of Congress Cataloging in Publication Data
Randisi, Robert J.
Full contact.
I. Title.
PS3568.A53F8   1984      813'.54      84-13273
ISBN 0-312-30966-X

First Edition

10 9 8 7 6 5 4 3 2 1

*for Anna and Christopher*

I would like to thank the following people for the support and friendship they have supplied over the years: Chris Steinbrunner, Max Allan Collins, Michael Seidman, Loren D. Estleman, and Warren Murphy.

I would also like to thank Billy and Karen Palmer for allowing Jacoby and his creator to become part of their lives, and part of Bogie's.

Thanks to all of the above I can no longer count all of my "good" friends on the fingers of one hand.

Thanks, too, to the entire membership of PWA, without whom a dream could not have become a reality.

# FULL CONTACT

A MILES JACOBY MYSTERY

# — one

I had just come out of the shower in the back office at Bogie's, which was doubling as my apartment for a while, when the intercom buzzer sounded. Billy Palmer, the owner of the restaurant, was out front, so I knew it couldn't be for him.

"Yeah, hello?" I said, picking up the receiver.

"Jack, you've got company up here," Billy's voice informed me.

"A client?"

"She says she's a friend of yours," Billy said. "I put her at your table. Want me to get her name?"

"No, that's all right," I said, drying my hair with a towel. "I'll be right out. Thanks, Billy."

"I'll tell her."

"Give her whatever she wants, okay?"

"Sure," he said, and hung up.

Billy Palmer was a good friend. I had moved out of my apartment some months back—temporarily, I thought—and he had kindly extended to me the hospitality of his back office, which was actually an apartment. Then, when somebody blew up my place—and my brother with it—Billy had told me I could stay in the office as long as I liked. I hoped to be ready to move out before he regretted his decision.

The office/apartment was actually part of the next building, so to get to the restaurant I had to go out the back door and enter Bogie's through the kitchen. When I descended the short stairway into the restaurant proper, I knew who my visitor was.

"My table," as Billy had called it, was the one against the

wall in front of the mirror, and I was treated to a double view of the lovely face of Tiger Lee, who was Knock Wood Lee's "bottom lady." Wood was a Chinese bookie whose real name was Nok Woo Lee, and Tiger Lee, whose real name was Anna, had been one his "girls" back when he was running girls. He still has some of them on tap for special occasions, but Tiger isn't one of them.

"Lee," I said, approaching the table.

She turned her head at the sound of my voice, and I could see the worry in her beautiful, almond-shaped eyes.

"Jack," she breathed, relieved to see me. "Oh God, Jack."

"What's wrong?" I asked, taking her hands in mine. Her fingers were cold and clammy. There was a glass of amber liquid in front of her. It could have been cream soda or scotch, among other things.

"It's Wood, Jack," she said. She had to fight to get the words out.

"Relax, Lee."

"There's no time," she replied. "We need your help, Jack."

"Then I guess you'd better tell me what's happened."

"It's Wood," she repeated. "He's been arrested."

"Wood's been arrested before, honey."

"I know, but not for murder!"

"What?"

"He was arrested this morning for murder, Jack," she said. "You've got to help him."

"All right, Lee," I said, cradling both her hands in mine, "but before I can do that you've got to tell me everything you know."

"All I know is that he called me from the police station and told me to find you. He said you'd help."

"You know I'll help, Lee. You didn't need Wood to tell you that."

"No," she agreed, and now her hands clung to mine, "you're right, I didn't. Jack—"

"Who is he accused of killing?"

"I know that he left home this morning to see a man named Alan Cross. Cross owes Wood a lot of money, and is way behind on his payments."

"And now Cross is dead?"

She shook her head and said, "I don't know, I don't know. . . ."

"All right, take it easy," I said, wanting to touch her again but refraining. "Even if Cross is dead, the fact that he owed Wood money is a motive for Wood to want him alive, not dead. The cops will see that."

"I hope so," she said, not sounding very confident.

"Where did he call you from?"

"The Seventeenth Precinct."

"Don't tell me, let me guess. The arresting officer was Detective Hocus?"

"He didn't say, Jack. All he said was to get hold of you. I went to your office first, but when I saw you weren't there I came here."

"Okay, I'll get up there and find out what the story is. When I know something I'll call you."

"I want to come with you," she said.

"I think you better go home, babe," I said, gently. "I'll have Billy get you a cab."

"But—"

"I'll call you as soon as I find out anything," I said again. "I promise."

She stared at me for a few seconds, then released my hands reluctantly and said, "All right."

"Trust me, Lee," I said, touching her shoulder through the dark curtain of her hair, "I'll take care of it."

"I knew you would, Jack."

I went over to the bar to ask Billy to call a cab for her.

"What's up?"

"Her man just got locked up for murder," I explained. "I told her not to worry about it, that I'd handle it."

"That was nice of you."

"Yeah," I said with a sour feeling in the pit of my stomach. "Now I only hope I can deliver."

My brother had been arrested for murder once, before he was killed by a bomb that was meant for me. That had been the first time I'd gone to the Seventeenth Precinct. There had been many times since then, but this trip was the only one that made me think of Benny again.

It felt the same and, in one way, I hoped it would be. My brother had been innocent.

The desk man knew me, so I waved and went right upstairs to the squad room. Hocus was seated at his desk—he always seemed to be at his desk when I came around. If I didn't know what a good cop he was, I might have gotten the wrong idea by now.

"I hear you collared Knock Wood Lee for murder. Can you tell me about it?"

He looked up at me in surprise and then said, "No, I can't."

"Why not?"

"Because it's not my collar."

"Oh. Then whose is it?"

"Vadala."

"Oh, shit."

Detective Vadala and I had never seen eye to eye. I don't think it was me so much as it was the fact that I was a private investigator. He hated P.I.'s.

"Shit," I said again, "it would be him."

"Sorry, pal."

"Well, what can you tell me about it anyway?"

"Not much, and I shouldn't be telling you anything at all."

"I appreciate that fact."

"Okay," he said. "Wood was arrested for beating a man named Alan Cross to death."

"With what?"

"His hands. You and I both know, Jack, that's all Knock Wood Lee would need."

That much was true. Wood was a third or fourth degree

black belt in karate, and he could easily tear up someone twice his size.

"This guy was supposed to owe Wood money, Hocus," I said. "You know Wood wouldn't kill for money."

"Tell that to Vadala," Hocus said. "He's the one sitting on the evidence, and if there's anyone he dislikes more than you, it's Knock Wood Lee."

"Damn," I swore, softly but with feeling. "Where is he?"

"Wood's in the lockup," he said, "and Vadala is talking to the A.D.A."

"Can I get in to see Wood?"

"I doubt it," he said. "You're not family and you're not legal counsel."

"No, I'm not," I said thoughtfully, "but maybe we can fix that."

"How? You gonna adopt him?"

"No, but I can get him a lawyer." I picked up his phone and started dialing, still talking. "Once I get him a lawyer, he can get me in to see Wood."

"Going a little out of your way, aren't you?"

"Maybe," I said, listening to the ringing at the other end of the line, "but Wood's gone out of his way often enough for me."

Hocus shrugged and the phone was picked up at the other end.

"Mr. Delgado's office," a female voice said.

"Hi, Missy, it's me."

"Jack? How are you? We haven't seen you—"

"I've got to talk to Heck, Missy," I interrupted her. "It's urgent."

"Hold on," she said, without asking a bunch of questions first. A few seconds later, Hector Domingo Gonzales Delgado came on the line.

"What's the matter, Jack?" he asked. "Missy said it was urgent."

"It is, Heck. A friend of mine has been arrested and is being held at the Seventeenth Precinct."

5

"What is he charged with?"

"Murder, I think. I haven't been able to get in to see him, or to get all of the particulars. The arresting officer is not a fan of mine—"

"—and you need some sort of official status to be allowed to see him," he finished for me.

"Right," I said. "I need a favor."

"I'll be there as soon as I can," Heck said, "but this doesn't mean that I'll take the case once we've heard all the facts."

"I understand," I said. "Thanks, Heck."

"See you soon."

When I hung up Hocus was looking at me. He said, "Vadala's not going to like this."

"That's tough," I said. "Once Heck is here to represent Wood, I can go in with him as his investigator, and there's nothing Vadala can do about it."

"That's what I mean," Hocus said, nodding. "He's not going to like it at all."

## — two

Heck made it from his office on Madison and Twenty-third Street to the precinct, which was on Fifty-First Street between Lexington and Third, in just under twenty minutes.

"Had trouble finding a cab," he apologized, unnecessarily.

"No problem," I assured him. "I appreciate this."

"Where's the arresting officer?"

As if on cue, Vadala walked into the squad room and pulled up short when he saw me.

"What do you want, Jacoby?"

"I understand you have arrested a client of mine," Heck said in his fine Ricardo Montalban-accented voice.

"Who would that be?"

"Nok Woo Lee."

Vadala made a face and said, "Yeah, I've got him."

"My associate and I would like to see him, please."

"Your associate?" Vadala said. He fixed a glare on me and said to Heck, "I don't want him—"

"Mr. Jacoby is my investigator on this case, detective," Heck said, cutting him off. "He has as much right to see my client as I do."

Vadala looked past me at Hocus, as if it was his fault, and when Hocus just shrugged, Vadala looked at Heck and said, "Follow me."

"Would you care to explain to me just what evidence you have against my client?" Heck asked, playing the game to the hilt.

"Why don't you talk to him first?" Vadala said. "Afterward, come back to the squad room and I'll give you what we have. Just do me one favor," he added.

"What's that?"

"Leave your 'associate' behind."

We followed him down to the lockup and he had Wood taken from his cell to a room where we could sit and talk.

"Knock when you're finished," Vadala said. "I'll be in the squad room."

"Have a nice day," I said, but he ignored me and left.

Wood was seated at a long table, dressed in his own clothes, althought by now they had a rumpled look to them. Other than that, he looked as he always did, cool and totally inscrutable.

"Wood, this is Heck Delgado," I said, making the introductions.

"Ah yes," Wood said, "you've mentioned him several times."

"I'm flattered," Heck said.

"Are you going to be my lawyer?"

"It was the only way I could get in to see you," I explained. "Whether or not he'll be your lawyer will be up to the two of you."

"I see. You spoke to Lee?" Wood asked me.

7

"Yes, but she didn't know much."

"I didn't tell her much," he admitted. "Is she all right?"

"Reasonably," I said. "We'll all feel a little better once you tell us what happened."

"It's very simple," he said. "I'm being framed."

Heck closed his eyes and said, "I was hoping he wouldn't say that."

"How about running it down from the top, Wood?"

"Alan Cross owed me money," Wood said, "and he was way behind on the payments. I'd given him enough chances already."

"So you sent someone to see him?" Heck asked.

"Wood doesn't use knuckle-dusters," I explained. "When somebody is that far behind, he goes to see them himself."

"Ah, the personal touch."

"It's so impersonal the other way," Wood said.

"I can see that."

"So, you went to see Cross this morning," I said, "and . . . ?"

"And found him dead."

"How?" I asked.

"His door was open. I just walked in—"

"No, I meant, how was he killed?"

"Oh. He was beaten to death," Wood said. "Good job, too."

"You sound like an expert," Heck said.

"Black belt," I said, "in judo and karate."

"Oh," Heck said. He didn't look particularly happy about that little piece of news.

"Yeah," Wood said, understanding.

"Is that on your sheet?" Heck asked.

"Oh, yes."

"I see."

"Means and motive," Heck said gloomily.

"What motive?" I asked. "Cross owed Wood money. That's a motive *not* to kill him."

"Not to the police, I'm afraid," Heck said. "They have an odd sort of intellect."

Wood smiled for the first time since we'd arrived and said, "I like this friend of yours, Jack."

"Thank you," Heck said. "Tell me, how did they catch you?"

"They got there a couple of minutes after I did."

"And you were still there?"

Wood looked sheepish and said, "I was looking for my money."

"I can imagine," Heck said. "Weren't you shocked by what you'd found?"

"I've seen death before," Wood explained. "I would have been gone in another minute or so, money or no money."

"But they got there first," I said.

"How convenient," Heck said.

"I was set up," Wood said, again.

"It would seem so," Heck said in agreement, "if your story is true."

"You don't believe me?"

"Actually," Heck said, standing up, "I don't have to believe you, I just have to get you off."

Wood smiled again and said, "All right!"

Heck looked at me and said, "Let's go talk to Vadala."

"Sit tight," I said to Wood. "We're on it, now."

"Tell Lee how much of a retainer you need," Wood said to both of us.

"Heck will need a retainer," I said. "I owe you a couple of favors."

"Ha!" Wood said, derisively. "A couple?"

I clapped him on the shoulder, said, "I'll see you later," and followed Heck out into the hall.

In the hall I grabbed Heck's arm and said, "You'd better go up and see Vadala alone. He'll talk more freely without me around."

"You're probably right."

"Thanks for taking this one on, Heck."

"A man has to make a living, my friend."

"You'll make a good one off Wood," I said. "Pad your bill, he can afford it."

He laughed and we started up the stairs together. When we reached the ground floor I stopped him again and said, "Don't let Vadala know how smart you really are."

"What's his story?"

"He's not very hard to get a handle on," I said. "He's a smart cop, but he doesn't like anybody but other cops."

"I'll remember that," he said. "What will you be doing while I'm talking to him?"

"I've got another little problem to take care of."

He frowned and asked, "It won't keep you from working on this, will it?"

"Oh, no," I said. "As a matter of fact, it's the reason I *can* work on this. See you later, after your meeting with Vadala. I'll be dying to hear all about it."


# — *three* —

The "little problem" that would enable me to work on Wood's case—for free—was a paying client.

Robert Saberhagen had come into my office a week earlier, wanting to hire me to find his missing daughter.

"Where are you from, Mr. Saberhagen?"

"Detroit."

"Your daughter came here from Detroit on her own?"

"Yes."

"How old is she?"

"Melanie is seventeen."

"That's a little young to be coming to the Big Apple all alone, wouldn't you say?"

"I sent Melanie here to attend the International Institute of Martial Arts. It's up on Lexington Avenue and Eighty-Third Street."

I knew the place was considered one of the finest martial arts studios in the world, according to Billy Palmer, who was a fourth degree black belt himself. In fact, for the past eight months or so, I had been working out with Billy, in karate, getting myself back into shape following an embarrassing sparring session where I had been unable to go three rounds for the sparring fee.

"Your daughter is interested in martial arts?"

"Yes," he said, "karate. She started taking lessons three years ago, when some boys in school starting bothering her."

Saberhagen was a large man, very tall and powerfully built, but he had the demeanor of a gentleman. His voice, soft and a couple of octaves higher than you'd expect, belied his size. The thought of his daughter being involved in something as physical as karate seemed repugnant to him. He had small hands, with almost delicate looking fingers, and they were well cared for. He was missing the thumb on the left one, probably the reason he took such good care of the remaining nine fingers. Nervously, he dry-washed them as we spoke.

"When her mother died last year," he went on, "Melanie took it very hard. We became sort of . . . distant, and when she asked me to send her to New York to study—well, I'm ashamed to say I jumped at the opportunity."

"It must have been expensive."

"The cost was enormous, but I can afford it."

I was glad to hear that. It's always nice to hear that a client can afford your fees, even if you double them.

"Well then, if she's in Manhattan attending this institute," I asked, "what's the problem?"

"She hasn't been to a class in two months," he replied.

"Where was she staying? Not alone?"

"No, she was living with my sister, but about the same time she stopped attending classes she disappeared from there. Just packed up one day and moved out without a word."

"Didn't your sister call you?"

"Not right away," he said. "She thought Melanie would come back. When she didn't, Ida called me."

"Ida is your sister?"

"Right."

"What did you do then?"

"I came to New York to look for her. I spent weeks wandering the streets, hoping I wouldn't find her on a street corner in Times Square turning . . . what do they call them, tricks?"

I didn't have the heart to tell him he'd have been more likely to find her along Eighth Avenue if she was doing that.

"You didn't find her, I take it?"

"But I did," he said, surprising me. "That is, I saw her one day."

"Where?"

"In front of Madison Square Garden, with a group of people."

"And what happened?"

"I was across the street, and by the time I made my way to the other side, she and the others had gone."

"Did she see you?"

"I really don't know," he said, shaking his head bleakly. He leaned his forehead on his right hand and said, "I kept looking after that, but I never saw her again. That's when I decided to hire a private investigator."

"How did you decide to come to me?" I asked. "There are an awful lot of private detectives in New York."

"I wanted the best," he said, and before I could get too pumped up he said, "so I went to Walker Blue."

"I see."

There was no arguing the fact that Walker Blue was the best P.I. in the business. In fact, Heck Delgado used him more than any other investigator.

"And Blue couldn't take the job?"

"No, he couldn't, so he recommended you."

"Really?" I said, before I could stop myself. In spite of myself, I felt a certain amount of satisfaction with the fact that Walker Blue had recommended me.

"He said you'd probably have the time to do it," he added.

"Oh," I said, but I refused to let myself be shot down

that easily. "Well, luckily, I've just wrapped up a case, so I do have the time," I lied.

"Wonderful."

Actually, there *was* something wonderful about it. Saberhagen had been all set to pay Walker Blue's fee, so even if I did double mine, it would seem like a bargain to him.

We discussed a fee and retainer, and he wrote a check without so much as an extra blink.

"Shall I stay in New York—" he started to ask, but I cut him off and told him no. I didn't need him looking over my shoulder.

"There's really no point to that, Mr. Saberhagen," I said. "I'll call you in Detroit when I've found out something."

"I'll give you my card," he said, digging into his pocket. "It has my home number and my business number."

"Fine," I said, taking it from him. Calling him in Detroit wouldn't bother me, because it would all go down on the expenses. Actually, it was worth it to me not to have him in New York, where he might be demanding progress reports every day.

"Go back home, Mr. Saberhagen, and don't jump everytime the phone rings. I'll do my best to find her."

"I hope so," he said, rising.

"Did you bring a picture of your daughter?"

He reached into his jacket and brought out two photos, one three by five and the other five by seven. The smaller one looked like a head and shoulders high school photo, while the five by seven was a full length job, showing a pretty, well built girl in her late teens.

"Pretty."

"Yes, she's very pretty," he said, "but she's changed quite a bit since those photos were taken."

"I'll remember that."

I walked him to the door and he asked, "What will you do first?"

"Well, I guess I'll just have to brush up on my front kicks."

*　　*　　*

Actually, my first step had to be research, and to research the karate scene there was no better person to go to than Billy Palmer at Bogie's.

After Saberhagen left my office I walked to Bogie's and got there in time to miss the lunch rush. Good timing is everything in the detective business.

Billy was in his customary position at the end of the bar when I walked in, and he waved.

"Can I have a beer?" I asked him.

"You're in training," he reminded me. "You have the nerve to ask me that?"

"Just one?"

"All right," he said, "a light beer . . . and just one."

I had gotten out of shape, the result of retirement and a large appetite, and Billy had offered to help me get back into shape—through karate. He wouldn't let me pay him, but we had made a deal, and I was about to cash in on it—or, more to the point, he was.

"What's up?" he asked, when I had my beer and he had another glass of coffee. I don't know what it is about him, but he always has to drink his coffee from a glass. I'm always waiting for the damn thing to crack. It never does.

"Remember the deal we made?" I asked. "You get me back into shape and I'll let you work on a case with me?"

"I remember," he said, and then his eyes widened and he said, "Are you about to pay off?"

"I am," I said, "and that ought to be worth another beer."

"You can't change the deal now," he said, "and besides, you're not even half through with that one. Come on now, pay up. What's the case?"

"A missing girl," I told him, and proceeded to tell him the whole story.

"Her old man must be loaded," he commented when I was done, "or have some pretty good connections."

"Why do you say that?"

"The institute doesn't take just anybody, Jack," he answered. "You've either got to be connected—"

"Connected? Are we talking—"

"—Mafia?" he asked, laughing. "No, not that kind of connected."

"You mean connected in the karate world," I said. "Her teacher in Detroit must be a heavy hitter, then."

"Maybe," Billy said. "It might be a good idea to find out his name. I could tell you if I ever heard of him.

I checked my watch.

"Her old man's probably on a plane right now, and if I call him too soon he'll get his hopes up. If it starts to seem important, I'll ask him."

"Okay," he said. "What do you want me to do?"

I'd had one thing in mind when I first went to Bogie's, but at that point, another idea struck me.

"How am I doing, Billy?"

"In karate?" he asked. I nodded and he said, "You've progressed more in eight months than any other student I've ever seen."

"Could I get into the institute?"

"Not on my say-so," he admitted candidly.

"Do you know anybody who could get me in?"

"Why?"

"What would happen if I went over there and started asking questions?"

"We're talking New York people here," he said. "It wouldn't matter if it was a karate school or a sewing school. They'd clam up."

"Exactly. I need to get in as a student. Do you think I could hold my own?"

"For how long?"

"Long enough to find out if Melanie Saberhagen made any friends there. I don't know how long that will take."

"You're going to run into some rough characters, Jack," Billy warned me. "Some of them grew up that way, and some of them got that way because of the confidence karate has given them. They're all tough, though."

"Thanks for caring, but can you get me in?"

"There's somebody I know who might be able to," he said, "if he wants to."

"You'll ask him?"

"I'll ask him, and let you know . . . but this isn't exactly what I had in mind when we made our deal."

"I'll see if I can come up with a blond for you to tail," I promised.

"Whoa, don't say that too loud," he said, looking around, "Karen might hear you."

I finished my beer and said, "There is something else you can do."

"Name it."

"I'm sure you know a few other instructors in New York with their own dojo."

"Sure," he said, "in Manhattan, Brooklyn, even Staten Island."

"Check with them, will you, but do it discreetly? See if they have any new students, someone who might have joined during the last couple of months."

"You think maybe she just changed schools and her old man's jumping to conclusions?"

"No. She might have changed schools, but there's got to be more to it than that. She left her aunt's house without a word. She wouldn't have done that if she was just changing schools."

"What are you going to do?"

"I'm going to talk to her aunt and see if I can't find out what happened to make her leave."

I got down off my stool to leave, then turned back.

"When will you get a chance to talk to your, uh, friend?"

"I do have a business to run," he said, reminding me.

"A deal is a deal, oh assistant to the great detective," I said, remining *him*.

He saluted and said, "I'll get right on it, sir."

"While you're at it, Watson," I called out on my way to the door, "have my violin tuned!"

# — four

Written on the back of one of Melanie Saberhagen's photos was the address of her aunt, Ida Saberhagen. I went to see her and found a bitter, spinsterish woman who seemed to take Melanie's disappearance as just another of life's slaps in the face.

Ida Saberhagen lived in an apartment building on Thirteenth Street between University Place and Fifth Avenue.

She appeared to be in her mid-forties, but the lines around her eyes and mouth might have made you think she was older. She was wearing a shapeless one-piece shift that hung on her bony, angular frame. Still I had the feeling that with some makeup and decent clothes, she wouldn't have been bad looking. Wearing her dark hair in some fashion other than a tight bun wouldn't have hurt, either.

"Miss Saberhagen?"

"Yes," she said. She pushed away from the door frame, unfolded her arms, and said, "You might as well come in."

"Thank you."

I followed her into the apartment, which was oppressively stuffy.

"Is my brother still in town?"

"I'm afraid he's gone back to Detroit."

She laughed shortly and said, "He was so worried about his daughter that he rushed right back home after hiring you."

The lines around her mouth deepened and she folded her arms across her breasts again.

"He returned at my request, Miss Saberhagen," I said. "I really didn't feel it would do anyone any good for him to stay around. Besides, I'm sure he has business to attend to back in Detroit."

"Hmph," she said, and then added, "he could have stopped in to see me just once."

So that was the source of her anger. Saberhagen had not

stopped in to see her before leaving, but he must have stopped in when he first arrived. . . .

I asked her if that was the case, and she laughed bitterly again, a habit that was going to get on my nerves very quickly.

"Why should he have?" she asked. "His daughter wasn't here anymore, right? And now I'm sure he'll stop sending—" she started, and then broke off abruptly.

"Stop sending what?"

She hesitated a moment before answering, then shrugged in a "What the hell?" manner and said, "Checks."

"Checks?" I said. "Mr. Saberhagen was sending you money to look after Melanie?"

"Well, why not?" she demanded defensively. "She was eating my food, wasn't she? Using my electricity? I was entitled."

"I'm sure you were," I said, trying to appease her. "Miss Saberhagen, I'd simply like to see the room where Melanie slept, and ask you a few questions."

"Ha," she laughed, and I gritted my teeth, "you're in it."

"In what?"

"The room she slept in," she said, opening her arms to encompass the living room.

"She slept here?"

"On the couch."

"I see."

"And it was damned inconvenient, I tell you."

I'm sure it was, I thought. I was also sure that this woman must have let Melanie know, too.

"Did she leave anything behind?"

"Nothing. She had one suitcase when she came, and she left with it."

"During the time she was here, did she ever bring any friends home?"

"Home," she said, in a tone just as bad as her short laugh. "No, she never brought anyone up here. I forbade it."

That figured.

The small apartment was becoming more and more op-

18

pressive by the minute, and it was having less and less to do with the heat.

"Has she called you since she left?"

"Why should she?"

"Has anyone called for her?"

"I forbade her to give out the number."

"I see."

"There's really nothing else I can tell you, Mr. Jacoby," she said, pronouncing my name incorrectly. I didn't bother correcting her, because I was hoping I'd never have to hear say it again.

"No, I don't suppose there is, Miss Saberhagen."

I allowed her to show me to the door, which closed decisively behind me.

I hadn't even been on the case a day and although I didn't know why Melanie was missing, I had a pretty good idea why she had left her aunt's apartment.

I couldn't wait to get out myself.

My office is not the cheeriest looking place in the world, but after Ida Saberhagen's apartment it looked pretty inviting.

I walked behind my desk and accidentally kicked the trash can. Looking down I saw its scorched bottom, which reminded me of a letter I had burned in it months ago. I was going to have to buy a new can. I didn't need reminders of an unread letter from my dead brother's wife. I didn't need reminders of Julie Jacoby, because I thought of her enough as it was, even after almost a year.

Sitting behind my desk I thought about what Billy had said about Melanie's teacher in Detroit. I knew a P.I. in that city and it wouldn't take much to call him and ask him to check it out for me. At the same time he could run a check on my client, just so I'd know something about the man who hired me.

I took out Eddie Waters's phone book, which I still used a lot, and looked up Amos Walker's number in Detroit. Eddie—who had been my teacher up until the day he was killed—had P.I. contacts in a lot of cities around the country, all of whom were listed in that book. Some of them I knew and some I didn't; Amos Walker was one of those I knew. We had met during a trip I'd made to Detroit for Eddie.

When Amos answered his phone we went through the usual amenities and then I asked him if he had some time to do a little legwork for me.

"In New York or Detroit?"

"Detroit, pal," I said. "I haven't reached the level of success where I can afford to import talent."

"Well, I guess I could make some room in my busy schedule. What exactly can I do for you?"

I ran it down for him, giving him Roger and Melanie Saberhagen's names, telling him I wanted a check on Roger, and that I wanted him to find Melanie's martial arts sensei and check him out for me, as well.

"That's all?"

"That's it," I said, "and Amos, I'm not calling in any favors here, so make sure you send me a bill."

"That's okay with me, since I don't remember owing you any favors. Besides, making out my bill is the one part of this business I've got down pat."

That was a lie. He was a damned good investigator, and we both knew it. His natural talent for it put me to shame.

"Thanks, Amos."

"I'll be in touch, Jack."

We hung up. Getting ready to leave, I looked down at the metal trash can again. On impulse I picked it up and carried it out into the hall for the trash pickup. By the time I returned, any physical reminder of that letter would be gone forever.

 — *five*

After a week of working out at the institute without endearing myself to a single soul, I called Saberhagen to give him a report.

"It's been a whole week—"

"I'm afraid I'm still trying to get myself accepted by these people, Mr. Saberhagen," I said, cutting off his complaint. "I'm afraid they're not a very trusting bunch. If you're dissatisfied—"

"No, no," he blurted out, "you've invested all of this time, you might as well continue."

"I'll call you again, soon," I promised, and hung up.

Billy Palmer had gone to his old sensei, his teacher, and arranged for the man to give me a recommendation for the institute. John Olden did it as a favor to Billy and, I think, because Billy told him that he saw something in me. My boxing ability—or what was left of it—had enabled me to adapt to the rigors of karate training very well. I just hoped that I'd adapted enough to pass muster at the institute.

Later that week, Amos Walker had called back with the rundown on the Saberhagens.

Saberhagen was a heavyweight in Detroit industry who had little or no time for anything outside of his business. His wife had been killed in an automobile accident the year before, apparently driving while intoxicated.

"She was driving back from a big party after a nice, public battle with her husband. Apparently the daughter blames him for her death."

"That's a little more than he told me."

"Yeah, well there's more. He couldn't get away from a business meeting to attend the funeral, so the girl had to go alone."

"No other relatives showed?"

"None."

"This kid's got some family. What did you get on her teacher?"

"His name's Kinoshi and he's very highly respected in martial arts circles—if that's what you call it."

I thanked Amos and reminded him to send me his bill.

"First order of business when I hang up, Jack."

I didn't make any positive contact at the institute until early the second week, in the locker room when I was dressing to leave.

"Hey, Jacoby," someone said, touching me on the shoulder from behind. When I turned I saw that it was one of the students, Greg Foster.

"Foster, right?"

"That's right. Listen, a few of us are going out to get something to eat. We wondered if you'd like to come along?"

"Sure," I said, trying not to seem too anxious. "Let me get my shoes on and I'll meet you out front."

"We'll wait for you."

He left and I sat down to put on my shoes. More than a week without so much as a hello nod to the new kid, and now they were inviting me out to eat with them. I wondered if they were suspicious of a new face, or if it was just some sort of snobbery. Greg and his friends were brown belts, while I was still a green belt.

When I got out in front of the institute I was surprised to find Foster waiting alone.

"The others go on ahead?"

"No, one of the girls had to go home and since they all share the same ride, the others went, too."

"How many is all?"

"There would have been six of us, with you," he said, shrugging. "Now there's just us. Mind?"

"Hey, man, I've been treated like a leper since I got here. Any attention is welcome."

"Come on," he said, laughing. "There's a place up the block, what I call a two-handed eating joint. They give you so much food you've got to eat it with two hands."

Foster was a few years younger than I was, and if he'd been a fighter he would have been a light heavyweight.

He took me to a place called the Swiss Palace, and we got a table on the lower level. They didn't spend much on furnishings—Early American patio set—but the food was good, and there was plenty of it, as Greg Foster had said.

"So tell me," I said, when we had our food in front of us, "why the sudden invitation?"

"You've got to excuse us, Miles—can I call you Miles?"

"Be my guest."

"We're all New Yorkers, you know, which I guess makes us naturally standoffish towards new people. The institute is kind of exclusive and although we do get new students now and then, most of them can't cut it and fade out of the picture pretty quick. But you're different."

"Because I'm still here after a week?"

"Naw, it's not just that," he said. "You've got the moves, Miles. I know the instructors are impressed, and the rest of us are, too."

"The rest of you? Who exactly is that?"

"Some of us work out together outside the institute and I hope that after you meet the others you'll agree to work with us."

"As long as the others don't mind."

"Well, that's what we'll find out tomorrow night. If you can come then, too, we'll go out and eat afterward and you can meet them."

"I appreciate that, Greg," I said, my disappointment at having missed the others fading. Foster seemed friendly enough and with his endorsement, I didn't anticipate any trouble being accepted. All I had to hope for at this point was that one of them had known Melanie.

I didn't bring up her name with Foster because I didn't want to rush things. I was going to have to work my way into their confidence before I broached the subject of Melanie Saberhagen with any of them.

I asked him why they had decided to work out together and he said, "I think we're the most devoted students at the institute, and the extra work has to pay off in the long run, don't you think?"

"I'd say so, yes. Serious training is the key to success." I was thinking back to my boxing days, not so long ago.

"Exactly!" he said with great pleasure. "You're going to fit right in with us, Miles. I can tell."

"I hope so."

When we finished eating we split the tab down the middle and left.

"Where are you headed now?" he asked.

"Chelsea," I said. "I've got an apartment there."

"I'm going through the park," he said. "I live on West Eighty-first. I'll see you tomorrow night, huh?"

"Sure."

As Foster walked down the block to a parking garage, I was feeling pretty pleased with myself. At least this was a start. I'd been accepted by one of the students after only a week. Maybe now I'd really start to make some progress on the case.

I went back to Bogie's and took a shower, then in the morning took another to wake myself up. That was when Tiger Lee came in and put a crimp in my plans for progress.


— *six* ————————————————————————

After leaving Heck at the precinct I went back to Bogie's to pick up my karate gear and head uptown to the institute. I was in the locker room getting into my gi—that pajama type outfit they wear in martial arts—when Greg Foster came in.

"Hey, Jacoby!"

"Hi, Greg."

"All set for tonight?"

"I've got nowhere else to go."

"Good," Foster said, whipping off his jacket. As he was unbuttoning the cuffs of his shirt he said, "I should also tell you that there are one or two people we work out with who aren't from the institute. You won't mind that, will you?"

"Hey, they're in the group, right? It's up to them to accept me."

"Nice attitude, Miles."

I started to leave and said, "See you after class."

There was very little fraternizing during class. They frowned on that at the institute.

"You come highly recommended, Mr. Jacoby," the director had said that first night. He was a black man named Bayard who had calluses like rocks on his hands and feet, a bullet-shaped head and a squat body that wouldn't ordinarily have seemed suited to the sport. He was, however, a fifth degree black belt, and was considered a top man in his field.

"Thank you."

"Have you studied with Sensei Olden long?"

"Not very long," I said. "I'm a relative newcomer."

"I understand you were a boxer."

"Yes."

"I suppose your athletic ability has enabled you to progress more rapidly than others might."

"You would know that better than I."

Bayard regarded me in stony silence for a few moments, then said, "I will formulate an opinion soon enough. Please, all we ask is that you obey the rules of the institute, one of which is no socializing while in the dojo. Please save that for the locker rooms, or outside."

"Understood."

"Very well," he said. He had a slight accent, possibly Jamaican. He closed the folder he had been studying while we were speaking, and I had wondered at the time if it said anywhere in there what I did for a living.

I had expected him to say something else but when the silence became awkward, I realized I had been dismissed.

Now as I walked out onto the dojo floor I was aware of Bayard's eyes on me, watching me warm up. I wondered what was going on inside that bullet head of his.

Bayard worked us hard for almost two hours, and then we had to clear the floor for what the students called the "killer class." It was made up solely of black belts and although no one had actually been killed, things had been

25

known to get rough. You were expected to be able to protect yourself, and if you got hurt nobody felt sorry for you. It was your own fault.

Some of the earlier students stood around and watched the black belts; Greg Foster and others headed for the showers. So did I.

I met Foster outside the locker room and he said, "The others are waiting outside. I thought before we went out, though, I'd warn you about Brown."

"Brown?"

"Yeah, he showed up tonight."

"Is he part of your workout group?"

"Yeah. He used to be here at the institute, but he washed out."

"Not good enough?"

"Oh, Brown's good, all right," Foster said, "real good. He just doesn't react well to rules, and discipline."

"I thought discipline was a must around here."

"Brown is trying to prove the exception to the rule," Foster said. "He's got all the physical skills, and he's trying to get by on that."

"Why do you want to warn me?"

"Well, Brown's not exactly the sociable type."

"Then why is he in the group?"

"I've wondered about that myself," Foster said. "Look, just don't pay any attention to anything he says, okay?"

"I'll try."

"Let's go and meet the others."

When we got outside there were five other people waiting for us, two girls and three men.

"People," Foster said, "meet Miles Jacoby."

Four of them greeted me cordially enough, but one of the men said testily, "Who's he?"

"He's one of us, man," Greg said, frowning. "Chill out."

The man subsided, grumbling to himself, and I correctly assumed that this was Brown.

On the way to the Swiss Palace Greg Foster and I walked behind the others. He told me that Brown was the oldest of the bunch at thirty-eight. If he was a fighter he'd have been what they were calling these days a super heavyweight. Greg said that Brown was a black belt, but confided that he'd only received it before the others because he was now in a school with lower standards.

The other men were Dan McCoy and J.C. Smith. Both were tall and slender, in their early twenties. Greg Foster himself was of average height, but solidly packed. I had never seen Brown in action, but Foster was the best of the others I'd seen. He seemed very committed to the sport.

The girls were Fallon and Ginger, a study in contrasts. Ginger was plain and chunky while Fallon was pretty and slender. Both girls appeared to be about eighteen or nineteen—not much older than Melanie—and each was attractive in her own way. I wondered if Melanie might have made friends with them.

I noticed that on the way Brown seemed to make a point of walking with the girls, but when we arrived, and after a shuffle of chairs to make a small table accommodate more people, I ended up sitting next to Ginger and across from Fallon. That didn't endear me to him.

"You must be something pretty special," Ginger said, pressing her thigh tightly against mine. She smelled good after her shower, but I didn't need the extra problem.

"Why do you say that?"

She smiled, showing pretty white teeth. It transformed her plain face. She had a mass of curly red hair, and a sprinkling of freckles on her nose and cheeks.

"Well, I understand you haven't been at it as long as some of us," she said, "and Bayard let you in."

"I had a good recommendation."

"Oh yeah?" Brown asked. "Who from?"

"John Olden."

Brown shrugged and said, "Never heard of him."

"I have," Fallon said.

"So have I," Dan McCoy said.

Brown shrugged again and said, "So what? Let's get some food."

Some of the others looked at each other, then everyone started studying the menus. Ginger still had her thigh planted firmly against mine, and in shifting my feet to avoid her I accidentally kicked Fallon, who was sitting across from me. She looked up, smiled a friendly smile, and then went back to her menu. My luck, Brown caught that, too, and frowned.

It was over coffee that Foster told the others that he had invited me to join their group.

"What for?" Brown asked immediately.

"He's got good moves, Brownie," Greg Foster said.

"So what? You heard what Ginger said, he ain't been at it as long as we have. What do we need him for?"

"Brownie—"

"Look," I said, interrupting Foster, "if anybody's got any objections there's no problem."

"Hey, nobody's got any objections, man," Foster said. He was seated on my other side and put a hand on my shoulder to reassure me.

"Yeah," Ginger said, smiling, "especially not me. You're cute." She pressed her solid thigh even more tightly against mine to bring her point home.

"Thanks," I said, avoiding Brown's eyes.

"What do you people think?" Foster asked them all. "You've seen him work out."

"I haven't," Brown said loudly. "I think I should see him before I make up my mind."

"Why can't you just take our word for it, Brownie," J.C. Smith said.

"Why the hell—"

"Look Greg," I said, "why don't you let me up? There's a little too much tension here."

"Hey man, wait—"

"You and your friends talk it out, Greg," I said, moving out from behind the table. "Let me know the next time we meet what you've decided."

"All right, Miles," Foster said. "This is Sunday. We'll see you at the institute Tuesday night?"

"Fine." I turned to the table and said, "It was nice meeting you all."

Brown grumbled to himself, but the others all said good night and Ginger and Fallon both gave me extra wide smiles. Given my looks, I guessed it was just the novelty of having a new male face around.

When I got back to Bogie's Billy offered me a light beer in exchange for information on what was happening with Wood. "Let me make some calls in the office. I'll be right with you," I told him.

I called Lee first, because I felt guilty about not having called at all since leaving her at Bogie's. When she came on the line I filled her in on what Heck and I had found out.

"I'll have to get the rest from Heck," I said, and then, when I checked my watch and saw how late it was, added, "probably in the morning."

"What are you doing now?"

"I just finished working," I said, knowing that it would sound like I was already at work on Wood's case. I felt guilty about that, too.

"Will you call me when you talk to Mr. Delgado?"

"Sure," I said, reacting to the anxiety in her voice. "How are you holding up?"

"Okay, I guess."

"Would you like me to come over, Lee?"

"That's all right, Jack. I've got a lot to do, keeping things going while Wood's . . . away."

"Things couldn't be in better hands, Lee," I said. "Wood knows that."

"I know," she said. "Jack, thanks for—"

"Thank me when I get him out, honey," I said, interrupting her. "I'll keep in touch."

I hung up and, in spite of the lateness of the hour, tried to get Heck at home. When he didn't answer I went out to take Billy up on that beer.

# — seven

I was waiting with Missy early the next morning when Heck arrived at his office.

Eddie Waters had been my best friend and mentor in the business and Missy had been his secretary, gal Friday and gal every other day, as well. After we found Eddie's killer, Missy got a job with a temporary secretarial outfit, working wherever they sent her from day to day, until I recommended that she and Heck get together. They agreed to try it out on a temporary basis, but the job seemed to have become permanent all by itself.

Missy was a beautiful twenty-nine-year-old redhead and, since Eddie's death, we had eased into a comfortable relationship as friends. We both knew we'd never be any more than that, because Eddie would always be there between us. Besides, if we became lovers, who would we talk over our troubles with?

"How's the job?" I asked.

"It's fine, Jack," she said with a smile. "You know, Heck's really not all that different from Eddie."

"You mean that Heck Delgado is disorganized, too?" I asked, feigning wide-eyed disbelief.

She nodded impishly and said, "He's just neater about it."

"Keeping my secretary from her work, Jack?" Heck asked from behind as he entered.

"It would take more than one man to do that, Heck."

"Save that stuff," he said, good-naturedly. "We haven't made a formal announcement, but I guess her job's pretty permanent."

"I want to wish you both the best of luck."

"Jesus, Jack," Missy said, "we didn't get married."

"Give me time."

"You've got ten minutes," Heck said, walking into his office, "and then I'm due in court."

"Ten minutes?" I asked, following him in with a wave to

30

Missy. "Is that enough time for you to tell me about your talk with Detective Vadala?"

"It should be," he said, seating himself behind his desk. "Why don't you sit down?"

"Is that a 'be comfortable' sit down," I asked warily, "or a 'bad news' sit down?"

"Contrary to popular opinion, Jack, it is no easier to take bad news sitting down than it is standing up."

"Bad news, then," I said, sitting down.

"I spoke with Vadala at length, and then I spoke to the D.A. They both seem to believe they have a pretty good case against your friend."

"What do you believe?"

He hesitated a moment, then said, "He was found in the apartment with the body, and he certainly has the skills necessary to have administered a fatal beating."

"Is it that open and shut?"

"It is when there are no other suspects."

"None at all?"

He shook his head and said, "None."

"What about the call the cops received? Was it anonymous?"

"No."

"What then?"

"It was from Alan Cross."

"The dead man?"

"Supposedly. According to Vadala, Cross called and said that he feared for his life. He said that Knock Wood Lee had threatened to kill him and was coming over to his apartment."

"And when they got there, there was Wood . . ."

". . . and there was the body," Heck said, finishing for me. "Hence, their case."

"Come on, Heck, that's flimsy. Anybody could have called and said he was Cross."

"That's true, but I've told you about the cop intellect. Your friend is standing right there in front of them—why should they go looking elsewhere?"

"All cops aren't like that. Hocus isn't like that."

"It's not Hocus's case."

"Vadala's a good cop, Heck, in spite of what he may think of me."

"I don't doubt that, but he really thinks he's got his man, Jack, and the D.A. agrees. They'll arraign him today."

"Well, they're wrong," I said, standing up, "and we've got to prove it."

"Then get me the proof."

"What about Walker Blue?"

"He's away on a case," Heck said. "He left last week. Uh, are you telling me that you cannot work on this case?"

"No, no," I said, quickly. "Wood's my friend, not yours. Of course I'll work on it. I do have another case, however, but I'm trying to wrap it up quickly."

"All right," he said after a one-beat pause. He opened his drawer and took out a brown business-size envelope. "I had Missy type up the particulars last night, including Alan Cross's address. Everything you need should be in there."

"Okay," I said, taking it from him. "I'll go over it."

"I'll try for bail on Wood," Heck said, "but my guess is he'll end up a guest in the refurbished Tombs."

"Yeah."

"What's this other case you're working on, if I may ask?"

"A missing girl. I've been on it for a week."

"Any leads?"

"Some. I've made contact with some people who might be able to lead me to her. I'm hoping to wrap it up soon, don't worry."

"Don't push it, Jack. I can get somebody—"

"No," I said, cutting him off. "I told Wood I'd do it, and I wouldn't charge him. I'll take care of it."

"Well, if you are sure you can. This *is* a little more important than a runaway girl."

I couldn't very well have argued that point with him even if I wanted to.

"I know, I know it is. If I don't come up with something in the next day or so, I'll get some help looking for her."

"I think that would be a good idea," Heck said, checking his watch. "I have to be in court. Keep me informed, Jack, will you?"

"Of course."

We left together and while Heck hailed a cab I started to walk uptown, thinking not about Knock Wood Lee's case, but about Melanie Saberhagen.

That was a situation I was going to have to try my damnedest to resolve.

Seated behind my desk with a late breakfast of scrambled eggs, ham, home fries, toast, and coffee, I was trying to read the material Missy had prepared for me on Alan Cross, but I was unable to concentrate because I couldn't stop thinking about Melanie Saberhagen. She had a father who seemed to have little time for her, whom she blamed for the death of her mother, and an aunt who took her in simply so she could collect checks from her father. I was being paid to find her and bring her back to those people.

Wood's case was, of course, the more serious, but I still owed my client my best efforts in locating his daughter, no matter what I thought of him. I could see where juggling two cases at one time could be a problem. And it was a problem I wasn't all that experienced at handling.

My predicament had an obvious solution. Find the girl quickly, collect the remainder of my fee, and then work on Wood's case.

Clearing my desk of the remains of my breakfast, I decided to apply myself to Wood's case for the day, and then go to the institute that evening. Maybe one or two of the group would show up before their regular Tuesday class, and if they didn't, then I'd talk to Bayard about getting some addresses.

With that settled, I was finally able to concentrate on the material about Cross. Alan Cross had been twenty-nine years old, a bachelor with no family, who lived alone, and worked for an advertising firm on—where else?—Madison Avenue. His home and business addresses were included. I decided to check them both out, after I made a couple of phone calls.

The first one was to Tiger Lee, to give her a not so encouraging update, as well as something else to do.

"Thanks for giving it to me straight, Jack," she said, after I'd relayed everything to her that Heck had told me.

I muttered, "It wouldn't be right to do it any other way. Not with you, Lee."

Now she was awkwardly silent before asking, "Is there anything I can do?"

"That's why I called," I said. "I want you to tell me everything you know about the debt Cross owed Wood."

"Well, all I know is that Alan Cross was always a big player, but he always paid on time. All of a sudden he wants to play on credit—"

"—and since he's always been a good customer, Wood gives it to him."

"Right, and gives it to him again—"

"Okay, we don't need to go any further," I said, cutting her off. "The guy got in over his head."

"And he kept putting Wood off, until Wood had to go and see him."

"Which is where we stand now. All right, here's what I want you to do. Check on some of Wood's competitors and see if anyone else was holding Alan Cross's markers."

"Why?"

"The best way to get Wood off this hook is to put somebody on it."

"You mean pin it on somebody else?" she asked in disbelief.

"No, I'm not suggesting that," I said. "We've just got to show the cops that there were others with as much cause, or more, than they think Wood had."

"Will that get him off?"

"It'll be a start."

"All right, I'll make some calls. What are you going to be doing?"

"I'm going to look over Cross's apartment, and then check out the place he worked for."

"For what?"

"I don't know," I said. "I'm going to look in some drawers, ask some questions, and see what pops up. That's what a private investigator does, Lee."

I could have sworn she was smiling when she said, "Thanks for filling me in on that, Jack."

"I'll talk to you later."

My next call was to Hocus.

"You want me to what?"

"I want you to arrange it so I can get into Alan Cross's apartment for a look-see."

"You're out of the ring what, a year?"

"Just about."

"And you're still punchy."

"Hocus—"

"This is Vadala's case, Jacoby. You want me to get in between you and him? I'm not that good at bobbing and weaving."

"All I'm asking for is a favor, and a small one at that."

"Letting you into a sealed crime scene on a case that isn't even my own, you call that a small favor?"

"Not when you put it *that* way."

"Well, how would you put it?"

"I'd uh . . . yeah, I guess I'd put it that way."

"Fine, we agree on something."

"Will you do it?"

"No."

"Hocus—"

"I don't have to," Hocus said before I could go on.

"What do you mean?"

"Find something to keep you busy until about three o'clock, and you should be able to walk right into the place all by yourself."

"Why?"

"The seal will be lifted by then."

"That's kind of quick, isn't it?"

Hocus paused a beat, then said, "Vadala figures he's got his man, Jack. He's dead sure of it."

"Has he got the D.A. convinced?"

"I've seen the paperwork, Jack, and Wood looks real good for it. I think maybe Vadala's got him this time."

"Maybe," I said, "but don't turn the key in the cell door just yet."

## — eight

Alan Cross had worked for Paul Bishop Associates on Madison Avenue and East Forty-fifth Street. According to the directory in the lobby the company occupied two floors in the twenty-story building, the sixteenth and seventeenth. I took the elevator to the seventeenth floor and presented myself to a porcelain-faced receptionist who probably hadn't aged in ten years. I told her I'd like to see Mr. Bishop.

"Mr. Bishop?"

"Yes."

"What business do you have here, sir?"

"It concerns Alan Cross."

Her face remained expressionless as she said, "Mr. Cross is no longer with this company."

"I know, sweetheart," I said, "he went out the hard way. I'm trying to find out who gave him his pink slip."

She blinked her eyes, which was her way of running a gamut of emotions, said, "One moment, please," and then reached for her phone. She spoke briefly into the phone, and it was obvious that she had perfected the art of talking about someone who is barely three feet away and not letting them hear a word.

When she hung up she looked at me and said, "Someone will be right out."

"Fine," I said. "I appreciate your courtesy."

She went back to doing whatever she'd been doing and I took a seat and picked up a copy of *Sports Illustrated*. That was a mistake, because it was a boxing issue and in spite of everything I'd been telling myself and people around me, boxing was still in my blood. I was replacing the magazine on the table, face down, when a door opened and "someone" stepped out.

"Mr. Jacoby?" the woman said.

I stood up and said, "I'm Jacoby."

"Please, come to my office," she said. She turned and went back through the door, and I followed. She was a handsome, dark-haired woman, obviously the executive type.

I followed her down a corridor to her office, which was small but expensively furnished.

"Please sit down," she said, sitting in her own chair behind a large oak desk that made the room seem even smaller.

"My name is Paula Bishop, Mr. Jacoby."

"Paula Bishop?" I said. "I thought the company was called—"

"Yes, it is called Paul Bishop, but I did that years ago when I first started out, just as a front. It's one of those little tricks a woman has to pull to get anywhere in the business world."

"I see. Well, you seem to have gotten somewhere."

"Yes, I have. May I ask what your interest is in Alan Cross?"

"I'm investigating his death."

"His murder, you mean."

"Yes," I said in direct response to her no-nonsense attitude, "that's exactly what I mean."

"Well, are you a policeman? Do you have some sort of identification?"

"I have identification," I said, taking out the photostat of my P.I. license, "but I'm not a policeman. I'm a private investigator."

She looked over my photostat and handed it back.

"Then you must have been hired by someone."

"That's right."

"By whom, may I ask?"

"I'm not at liberty to say," I said, "but I hope you'll cooperate with me."

"In what way?"

"I'd just like to ask a few questions of you and anyone else in your company who knew Alan Cross. I'm sure you'd like to see his murderer brought to justice."

"That sounds as if it came straight out of 'Barnaby Jones,' Mr. Jacoby," she said, scolding me, "but of course I'll cooperate. I've no reason not to."

"I appreciate that, Miss—uh, Ms.—"

"Miss is fine," she said shortly.

"How well did you know Alan Cross, Miss Bishop?"

"I hired him, four years ago," she said. "I've seen him at work every day since then, had lunch with him when business warranted it."

"A purely business relationship?"

"Of course," she said, and then added, "I was hardly his type, in any case."

"What type was that?"

"Oh," she said, touching the back of her hair, which was cut short, "the type most handsome young men prefer. Empty heads and large chests."

Well, Paula Bishop hardly had an empty head. As for her chest, her suit was mannishly cut, but she did not seem to be too badly off in that department either. Was there a trace of regret—or anger—there?

"Did he have any close friends among your employees?"

"I really wouldn't know that, Mr. Jacoby," she said. "I don't keep track of my employees' personal lives."

"I see. Would you mind, then, if I questioned some of your people?"

She paused a moment with a slight frown making small furrows in her smooth brow, then said, "As long as you don't disrupt my business, I don't see why you shouldn't. It won't take very long, I trust?"

"Oh, not long at all. Just tell me what department Cross worked in and I'll start with his immediate coworkers. Maybe I won't even have to go any further."

"I hope not," she said. "Mr. Cross worked on the sixteenth floor. He wrote copy and was very good at it. Just ask for his office. I'll call down and let them know you're coming."

"That's very kind of you."

"Not at all," she said. "Good day, Mr. Jacoby."

As I left her office I was thinking that Paula Bishop was a very businesslike lady, but I couldn't help wondering what she did for fun . . . and with whom?

I questioned several people who had worked closely with Alan Cross, and it all added up the same way. He was good at work, but he was better when he played, and he played hard. He especially liked gambling, and women.

Sam Griese was the only person I could find who described himself as a friend of the dead man's. Griese seemed a lot like Cross, good-looking and relatively young.

"Did you socialize outside of work?"

"Not a lot," Griese said, "but when we did we had a ball. I tell you, there was one night when we had these girls—" He stopped abruptly, as if catching himself talking out of turn.

I let it pass and asked, "Do you know of anyone who might have had reason to kill Cross?"

"Well, you have to realize how much Alan loved women," Griese said. "You know that Burt Reynolds movie that's out now, about the guy who can't resist women? That was Al Cross."

"You're telling me that he couldn't resist women, even if they were someone else's?"

Griese grinned and shrugged, showing me his palms.

"Was there any special type of woman he liked?"

"Yeah," Griese said, widening his eyes, "young."

"How young?"

"Oh, I'm not saying he robbed the cradle, or was a child molester, or anything like that, but I'm sure there was a girl or two who missed her senior prom because of him."

"How'd you feel about that?"

"Me? Hey, whatever the traffic allows is all right with

me, friend," Griese said. Suddenly he looked sad—or contrived to look sad—and said, "I'm gonna miss old Al. We had some good times."

"I'm sure."

"Hey, look," he said suddenly, jabbing me with his elbow. I turned to see what he was talking about and saw a shapely blond girl walking down the hall away from us. She was wearing skintight jeans and her behind looked as if it had a mind of its own.

"She could tell you a few things about Al Cross."

"Who is she?"

"Her name's Phyllis something or other," he said. "She works in the mail room."

"And she had a relationship with Cross?"

"No girl had a 'relationship' with Al Cross. He was the original pussyhound, you know? But according to Al, he got her one afternoon during lunch—right in the mail room! Anybody could have walked in on them! What a guy!" he said, shaking his head with admiration.

"Yeah," I said, "what a guy."

I watched the girl walk the length of the hallway—no great hardship on my part—and then walk through a door at the end. Was this the truth, I wondered, or simply one cocksman trying to one-up another?

"She was just his type, too," Griese said, breaking into my reverie.

"Empty head and big chest?"

"Oh, yeah," he said, and the dreamy look crept back onto his face again.

I decided to let the girl in the mail room slide for a while. A fast fuck on the Pitney-Bowes did not make her an authority on Alan Cross and besides, it was getting near three o'clock and I wanted to check out Cross's apartment before going up to the institute.

Cross had lived in an apartment building in the East Fifties. While I was getting past the doorman with a story about being sent by Detective Hocus to pick up something from the dead man's apartment—well, I didn't actually *say* I was a cop—I wondered just how much Cross had been getting paid by Paul Bishop Associates. An apartment in a building like that cost a fortune. He must have been damn good at what he did.

The doorman was kind enough to give me the key the "other" policemen had returned to him when they left. I promised to bring it back before I left.

When I'd let myself into Cross's apartment, I decided that he must have been *very* damn good at what he did to be able to afford furnishings like the ones he had in that place. It didn't look like any bachelor pad I'd ever had, or been in.

First of all, it was neat and clean—probably the work of a cleaning woman—and the furniture was straight from Bloomingdale's. Against one wall, shelves held an expensive-looking stereo set, a large TV, and a top-of-the-line video recorder, which was surrounded by tapes. There was a fine coat of powder in some places, left over from the cops.

It certainly was not the type of place I'd expect a bachelor who was a gambler to live in—no, sir.

Eddie Waters had often told me that an "investigation" was looking for something when you didn't know what you were looking for, but knowing it when you found it. That's what I was doing in Alan Cross's apartment, looking for I-didn't-know-what, and the chances were pretty good that whatever it was, the cops had already found it. Still, it wasn't unheard of for the police to leave a clue or two behind, especially when they thought they already had their killer.

The rest of the apartment was furnished as expensively as the living room, and I started to get a bad feeling about that.

Where had the money come from? A fast score? If that were the case, Tiger Lee could probably find out for me.

The bedroom was not as neat as the living room; the signs of struggle and of the police search were still there. There was a bureau and a chest of drawers, and I carefully went through both looking for anything the cops might have missed. Cross's taste in clothes was as expensive as his taste in furniture, but aside from monogrammed shorts and silk shirts, there wasn't much to be found in the drawers.

*Under* the drawers, however, was a different matter.

Another of Eddie's sayings was that movies often dictated where people hid their valuables. I wondered what movie had taught people to tape things to the undersides of dresser drawers.

What Alan Cross had taped to the underside of his bottom drawer was a small phone and address book. It was one of those little, soft-cover books you can fit in the palm of your hand, and each page had been filled with a small, cramped handwriting. It could simply have been Alan Cross's "little black book," but I pocketed it anyway. As it turned out, it was the only thing I took out of the apartment, and I still didn't know what I had been looking for.

## — nine

I stopped at Bogie's long enough to shower and collect my gi and gear, and then left for the institute. I still hadn't had time to look through Cross's address book.

During the subway ride uptown I shifted gears in my mind, adjusting to work on the Saberhagen case instead of Wood's. It was an adjustment I was hoping not to have to make for very much longer.

I arrived at the institute early, changed quickly, and went out onto the floor to warm up. I had originally started studying with Billy Palmer simply as a way to get back in shape, but the longer I studied, the more interested I became in actually becoming as good at it as I could. It wasn't quite like being back in the ring, but at least I was feeling like an athlete again.

While warming up I kept my eyes open for any of the group who might show up that night as well as Tuesday night. I knew Greg Foster wouldn't show, but maybe one of the others would—preferably one of the girls. I hoped at least one would, just to keep me from revealing myself to the director as a fraud. Once I did that, I might as well forget about returning to the institute. I'd miss working out there.

It wasn't until after the "killer class" was over that I conceded defeat. There had been no sign of any of the workout group. I showered, changed, stuffed all of my gear into my tote bag, and went to the office of the director.

"Mr. Bayard?"

His bullet-shaped head moved as he looked up from his desk and he said, "Yes?"

"I'd like to talk to you if I may," I said, "in private?"

His expression didn't change, except for a slight frown, and he said, "Come in and close the door."

I did so and he said, "What is this about?"

"It's about my real reason for coming to the institute."

"Which is?"

I hesitated a moment. I hadn't realized how important karate had become to me.

"Would you like me to tell you?" Bayard asked.

"What?" I said in surprise.

"I said, would you like me to tell you the real reason you are here?"

"You know?"

"Of course I know," he said, staring at me. "Sensei Olden is a close friend of mine."

"He told you?"

He nodded.

"And I agreed to allow you to conduct your investigation—although I do wish you had confided in me."

"I didn't know you—"

"Understandable," he said, holding up one calloused hand. "Tell me, why have you chosen to confide in me now?"

"I don't have as much time as I thought I had to conduct this investigation."

"Why?"

"Because of another case."

"More important than this missing girl?"

"A man's life."

He nodded, and suddenly he seemed less distant to me, and more . . . human.

"How can I help?"

"I need some addresses on some of your students," I said. "I had hoped to be able to talk to them just as another student, on the off chance that they might know something about the girl I'm looking for."

"Melanie Saberhagen."

"Yes." He really *was* well informed.

"Which students?"

"I'm not sure of their last names," I said. "I met a couple of girls named Ginger and Fallon."

"Ah, Greg Foster's friends."

"Yes."

"I believe I can supply you with their addresses," he said. "Just the girls, or the whole group?"

"If it's no problem, I guess I could use the addresses on the entire group."

"Give me a few moments."

I waited while he went to a file cabinet, extracted their files, and wrote down five addresses for me.

"Thank you," I said, accepting them from him.

"Is there any other way I can help?" he asked, seating himself behind his desk again.

"Well, if you remembered Melanie Saberhagen it might be a big help for me to get your impressions of her."

He thought a moment, his shining bare skull furrowing.

"We have so many students," he said. "Do you have a photograph?"

"Yes, I do." I took out the smaller one and handed it to him, watching his face as he studied it.

"Her skill must not have been extraordinary, or I would surely remember her."

"Wouldn't she have had to be extraordinary to some degree to be enrolled here?"

"Of course," he said, "but still, it is the very special ones who attract my attention. The other instructors handle the rest."

"I see," I said, and I couldn't help wondering at what level I fit in. No, that was silly . . . I'd gotten in because strings had been pulled, favors repaid. Don't get carried away with yourself, Jacoby.

"May I hold on to this and show it to some of the others instructors? Someone might remember her."

"Of course, hold on to it . . . and take one of my cards," I said, handing one across to him. I had supplied the phone number at Bogie's when I enrolled in the institute, but now he'd have my office number as well. "Call me if any of them remember anything."

"I will."

Standing up, I said, "Mr. Bayard, I'm sorry about trying to enroll under false pretenses."

"I understand that deception is sometimes a tool of your profession, Mr. Jacoby."

"Yes, I suppose it is."

I thanked him again for the addresses and started for the door.

"Mr. Jacoby."

"Yes?"

"When all of this is over and you have the time, come back."

"To the institute? As a student?"

He shook his head.

"No. Come and see me . . . personally."

I left his office on a cloud and rode it to the nearest phone booth. If there was even a ghost of a chance that he might want me as a student, I'd leap at it!

Fallon's last name was DeWitt, and Ginger was Ginger McKay. They shared the same address and phone number; apparently neither was home, because the phone went unanswered. I debated calling one of the men, but decided against it. I wanted to approach the girls first. There really wasn't much of a chance of my charming even an ounce of information out of one of the guys.

I decided to go back to Bogie's, have some dinner, and make an early night of it. At least one of the girls must have a job to pay the rent, and that meant going home in the morning to change for work. I wanted to be able to get up nice and early and buy them breakfast.

## — ten

The next morning at 7:00 A.M. I was on the girls' doorstep with a bag of doughnuts and three coffees.

Ginger was the one who opened the door and peered out, blinking one sleepy, bleary eye at me.

"Huh?" she said.

"Ginger," I said. "I'd recognize that beautiful blue eye anywhere."

"Yuh—" she said, then stopped, cleared her throat and tried again. "What—"

"Miles Jacoby, remember?" I said. "From the institute?"

"Oh," she said, "yeah, sure. Whataya want?"

"What do I want? I want to buy you breakfast," I said. Holding up the bag I said, "See. Coffee and doughnuts."

"Gee," she said, blinking her eye again, "okay. Wait a sec."

She closed the door, slid the safety chain off, and then opened it wide.

"Come on in."

"Thanks."

"It's kind of early," she said, patting her tousled hair. All she was wearing was a New York Knicks T-shirt, and her chunky breasts and thighs were very much in evidence.

"You did say doughnuts, didn't you?"

"Right here," I said, holding the bag up so she could see it.

"Jelly?"

Glad that I had guessed right I said, "There may be a couple in here." Actually, there were two jellies, two custards, and two plain. Ginger had struck me as a jelly type.

There was a small kitchenette off the equally small living room, and I suspected that the only other rooms in the apartment were the bedroom and bath.

"Is Fallon around?"

"She had to go to work early," Ginger said. "Something about doing an inventory."

"Where does she work?"

"In a small department store called Meyers. She's a management trainee." The way Ginger said it, I knew you'd never catch *her* being something as distasteful as a "management trainee." In fact, I doubted that you'd find Ginger doing something as distasteful as "working" for a living.

"Let's sit," she said, eyeing the bag in my hand.

We sat across from each other at the small, Formica-top table and I took out the doughnuts and coffee.

"How do you take your coffee?" I asked her.

"Light and sweet."

"Right here," I said, putting one of the containers in front of her.

"How did you know?"

"I watched you the other night," I lied. Actually, I hadn't noticed; but she did look like the light and sweet type. I had gotten lucky, and she was simple enough to be impressed.

She took a big bite out of a doughnut, leaving a smear of jelly at the corner of her mouth, and frowned at me.

"Say, how did you know where I live?" she asked. "I didn't mention that the other night."

"I asked."

"Who?"

I was hoping she wouldn't ask that.

"The director."

"Bayard? He gave you our address?" Her face mirrored the disbelief she was feeling. "That's hard to believe."

47

"It was kind of a special case."

"Why?"

She flicked her tongue out to capture the smear of jelly, and then took another healthy bite. It was easy to see where most of the meat on her healthy frame came from.

"What made it so special?" she pressed, when I didn't immediately answer her first question.

I decided to tell the truth while still holding back a little, and see what happened.

"I told Bayard that I was looking for someone, and he agreed to help me. I hope you'll do the same."

She polished off the first doughnut and reached for the second. "Help you with what?" She was still exhibiting more curiosity than suspicion, and I hoped I could sustain that situation. Now that I was alone with her, the fact that she was not very bright was manifesting itself, and I wasn't above trying to use that to my advantage.

"I'm trying to find someone."

"Who?"

"My cousin," I said. "She ran away from home and I'm worried about her. I came to New York to make sure she's all right."

"Your cousin? What's her name?"

"Melanie," I said, "Melanie Saberhagen. She was a student at the institute for a while, but she stopped going there and dropped out of sight. Her family—we lost contact with her, so I came to try and find her."

"Melanie?" Ginger asked, frowning while she chewed the last piece of doughnut.

"Yes. Did you know her, Ginger?"

She slurped some coffee and then said, "Sure, I knew Mel. She was a sweet kid. Funny, she was friendly enough in class, but nobody could really get to know her outside of the institute. A couple of the guys even offered to pick her up at home and drive her, but no dice."

"Did you know the guys?"

"You know one of them," she said. "Greg Foster."

"Who was the other one?"

"I don't know," she said, shrugging. "Maybe it wasn't a couple of guys. Maybe it was just Greg."

That was a start, anyway. Greg knew Melanie, and now all I had to do was get Greg to talk to me the way Ginger had.

She finished her coffee and then stood up, smiling at me.

"I've got to get dressed now. Fallon expects me to do the shopping while she's at work. She'll be sorry she missed you, Miles."

"I'm sorry I missed her," I said, "but your company more than made up for it."

"Really?" she asked, pulling down on the bottom of her T-shirt. The move flattened her large breasts and made the large nipples look like puppy dogs' noses pushing against it. "That's sweet." She stepped forward and kissed me on the cheek, pressing her breasts against my chest. I could feel the heat of her body right through the thin shirt.

"I told Fallon you were a doll."

"Really? Fallon didn't agree?"

She laughed and said, "Fallon's taste in men is . . . strange." She didn't elaborate.

"Did Fallon know Melanie, too?"

"Yeah, but they didn't get along."

"Would either of you know where she is now?"

Ginger shrugged and said, "I don't have any idea, and I doubt that Fallon does, either. Like I said, nobody got to know her too well outside the institute."

"Yeah," I said. "Well, I'd better let you get ready."

She walked me to the door and said, "Come around again, when I've got more time."

"I'll do that," I said. She had started to close the door behind me when I said, "Hey, one more thing."

"What?" she asked, holding the door open halfway and leaning on it. She made quite a sight early in the morning, all that solid, young flesh combined with the innocent, freckled face. I found myself wondering just how far the freckles went. . . .

"Why didn't Fallon and Melanie get along?"

She frowned as if she couldn't understand it herself and said, "They had the same taste in men . . . strange."

"Any man in particular?"

Ginger shrugged and said, "Not that I know of. Fallon just made a comment one day."

"What kind of comment?"

"She said that Melanie better stay away from her man.

"Did Fallon say who the man was?"

"No," Ginger said, but then her face took on a coy look and she added, "but even if she did, I don't think I should be telling you . . . not just for coffee and doughnuts, anyway."

I studied her face for any sign of suspicion, but aside from contriving to look coy, she appeared completely guileless.

"How about just telling me if it could have been Greg Foster?" I asked. "If it wasn't, you don't have to tell me who it was."

She put a fingernail in her mouth while she considered by suggestion, and then said, "I don't think it would be Greg. Fallon wasn't serious about him."

"Was he serious about her?"

"Greg is only serious about karate."

I smiled at her then and said, "Next time instead of coffee and doughnuts, Ginger, we'll make it dinner and. . . ."

She grinned, her face looking totally innocent again and said, "Ooh, it's the 'and' part that interests me."

My next stop was Knock Wood Lee's apartment on Mott and Hester streets, where Little Italy and Chinatown meet. Wood owned the building, which was a block from Umberto's Clam House, as well as the restaurant underneath his apartment—an Italian restaurant.

Wood had purchased the building, assumed the lease on the restaurant, and then broken down the walls of the three apartments above to form one large apartment for himself and Tiger Lee.

I was dropping in on Lee unexpectedly, but I didn't think she'd mind. In fact, I knew damn well she wouldn't.

She was an early riser, a holdover from her Brooklyn days, when you had to get out early to make a buck.

She answered the door wearing a poncho with Oriental characters on it, over a pair of jeans.

"Jack."

"Not too early, I hope."

"Not at all," she said, backing up to allow me to enter. "Come on in."

She closed the door and then padded barefoot ahead of me into the living room.

She looked as serenely lovely as ever, but I knew her and could see the strain on her face.

"Are you all right?"

"Yes, it's just . . . running things. I never realized what a . . . chore it would be. Wood has to be a juggler to keep everything going . . . and I'm no juggler."

I moved closer to her and the tension in her face, beneath the expertly applied makeup, was even more evident.

"Have you been sleeping?"

She smiled grimly and admitted, "Not much."

I took her by the shoulders gently and said, "If I can help, Lee . . ."

She backed up, breaking the contact just as gently, and said, "You already are, Jack. Coffee?"

"If it's made."

"It's made. I'll bring it in."

I dropped my hands to my sides and watched her leave the room. Lee was a smart lady who had worked her way out of the Brooklyn gutters with her brain as well as her body. I'd always liked her, but I'd always stayed at arm's distance because of my friendship with Wood. She was his lady, and had been for some time. That didn't appear to be in danger of imminent change, but there were times when I wondered what would happen if it did.

Hell, my luck with women was too bad to think about. Julie Jacoby, my sister-in-law, was gone and not yet forgotten—not for want of trying, either—Tracy Dean was in Hollywood, trying to get into movies that were not one color—

blue—and Erica Steinway had gone back to Europe "to look for some space." I had two women who were friends, Missy and Tiger Lee, and didn't want to risk either friendship by turning it into something it wasn't meant to be.

"Coffee," Tiger Lee said, walking in with a tray, "black, right?"

"Right."

When she set the tray down on a small table we sat on separate chairs with it between us, and I could see that her cup also held coffee.

"What, no tea?"

"So solly," she said, and grinned. "I can't stand the taste of tea, Chinese or otherwise."

"Have you got anything for me?"

"Not much," she said. "Cross was into a few other bookies, but their markers didn't even add up to what he owed Wood."

"Which was how much?" I asked. "I don't think we ever established that."

"Close to a hundred grand."

I shook my head and said, "I don't understand how Wood could let the man get in that deep."

"He'd always paid off before, Jack," she said. "Wood likes to keep his regulars happy."

"Sure, now all we've got to do is get the cops to believe that."

"Can we, Jack?" she asked, anxiously. "Can we do that?"

"We're giving it our best shot, Lee," I said, finishing my coffee. "I need a list of names, honey."

"The other books?"

I nodded.

She frowned and said, "They won't know where you got their names? Wood's name would be mud if they find out, Jack."

"I know that, Lee, but it's the only way. I've got to check them out."

"I wouldn't give this to anyone else," she said, rising and walking to her small writing table against one wall. Wood's much larger kidney-shaped desk was in another room.

She wrote three names on a three-by-five index card and handed it to me.

"I don't have to tell you where to find them, do I?"

I looked at the names and recognized all three.

"No," I said, standing up. "I'll be able to find them, all right."

Before tucking the card away I noticed that she had also written down the amounts that Cross had owed each man. The total came to about thirty grand, which made Alan Cross's aggregate debt almost one hundred thirty thousand dollars.

"How did a copywriter for an advertising firm get that kind of credit?" I wondered aloud.

"He's a gambler," Lee said.

"That's not a good enough answer, Lee. You've got to have some big money to start with to get that kind of credit from bookies. Did he ever score big off Wood?"

"Not that big."

"Then the question stands," I said. "If I find out where Cross was getting the money to command that much credit, then I might have something to hang my hat on."

"What else can I do?"

She walked me to the door and I said, "You're doing enough right now, Lee. I'll poke around some more and keep in touch." At the door I said, "If the load gets to be too much, give me a call, okay?"

"All right," she said. There was an awkward moment between us and then she moved forward hesitantly and planted a gentle kiss on the corner of my mouth, as if she had been undecided about whether to kiss my cheek or my mouth. "Thank you, Jack."

It became awkward again, and I simply touched her face and left.

# — eleven

I went to Packy's for lunch, since I hadn't been there in some time.

"Jack!" Packy shouted as I entered.

"'Lo, Packy," I said, seating myself at the bar.

"We don't see you around here much, anymore," Packy said, complaining.

Packy was an old pug, something he says I was too smart to become. I got out, he said, before the label fit, and he never did. Still, he had no regrets, and his favorite fight story was how he stood in the ring with Marciano, and would have beaten him if somebody had thrown him a crowbar.

He was a mountain of a man who looked like the prime choice to play the lead in the Primo Carnera story, but inside he was a pussycat, which was probably the main reason he had never made it big in the ring.

"Don't see you around much anymore, Jack," Packy repeated.

I frowned and said, "Well, I guess I've just been kind of busy, Packy."

"Sure," he said, "since you moved uptown."

"Chelsea's not exactly what I'd call 'uptown,' Packy."

"If you spent all your time down here, you would. What can I get you?"

"One of your sandwiches, and a light beer."

"Comin' up."

While waiting I took out the list of bookies Lee had given me: Arnie Court, Mort Snow, and Leo Piper. I knew Snow personally, and the other two by name. None of them would be very willing to talk to me, and I couldn't use Wood's name to open them up. I was going to have to come up with something else.

When Packy came back with the sandwich and beer I showed him the list and asked, "Do you know any of these guys?"

He frowned at the list, as if he had a hard time reading it, then said, "Sure, I know Arnie Court. We go back a long way. Why?"

"How well do you know him?"

"Real well."

"Will he do you a favor?"

"I think so. He made a few bucks on me years ago. He took bets from the suckers who thought I had a shot with Marciano."

A dubious reason for a bookie to do an ex-fighter a favor, but maybe Packy had more going for him than that with Arnie Court.

"You need a favor?" Packy asked.

I nodded.

"I'm going to need some information from him that he may not want to give me. Think you could give him a call and pave the way a little?"

"I can try. Eat your sandwich."

Packy often kept a roast beef going in the back for regular customers—or old friends—and he'd given me a thick sandwich with the slices rare, just the way I liked them, on French bread. I was halfway finished when he came back.

"Arnie says for you to come on over, Jack," he said. "He'll listen to what you have to say, and see if it's worth a favor to me. That good enough?"

"It'll have to be. Thanks, Packy."

"Sure, but now *you* owe *me*."

"What do I have to do?"

"Just come around more."

"You got it."

I gave my large friend a critical once-over and asked, "Are you losing weight?"

"Some."

"You look too thin."

"I'm not even down to my fighting weight," he said. "You're just used to seeing me with more meat on my bones."

"You're not thinking of making a comeback, are you?" The thought struck me as frightening.

"It's tempting, what with all that money floating around out there," he said. "A white hope could make himself a real bundle, you know?"

"I know." Purses had gone up considerably just in the time since I'd retired, and Packy had been retired ten times as long.

"Does that mean—"

"No," he said, "it doesn't."

"Good." I wiped my fingers on a napkin and washed down the last of the sandwich with the last of my beer. "You and me, Pack, we're out for good."

"Yeah," he said as I climbed off the barstool.

"How much?"

"Forget it," he said, but when I insisted on paying he said, "Pay me what it was worth."

"Pal," I said, putting a ten down on the bar, "I ain't got that much money. See ya."

Arnie Court turned out to be as little as Packy was big, and about ten years older. Actually, he could have passed for seventy-five instead of sixty-five if he wanted to, but that didn't strike me as something he'd want to take advantage of.

"You and Packy friends?" the old man asked.

"Yeah, a few years now."

Court wheezed for a few moments, and it took me a couple of seconds to realize that he was laughing.

"Sonny, me and the Pack go back over thirty-five years, when he was just starting out."

"So I understand."

Arnie Court's apartment was in a rundown building on the corner of Eight Avenue and Eleventh Street, over a laundry. The place was literally filled with stacks of newspapers, some of which were neatly tied, while others simply spilled over onto the floors. Court had an odd habit of walking around his small living room while he talked, touching things as if to assure himself that they were still there. He shuffled when he walked, which could have been the result of an injury or simply a by-product of his age.

"Packy said you had some questions you wanted to ask me," he said.

"One or two."

"Well," he said, touching a stack of newspapers piled up on top of a small black and white television, "fire away and I'll see if I feel like answerin' them." The newspapers fell over when he removed his hand, but he seemed unconcerned.

"I need some information on a man named Alan Cross."

"He's dead."

"I know. I believe he was a customer of yours?"

"That the first question?"

"It is."

He thought about it for a moment, then said, "Okay, yeah, he was a customer."

"A good one?"

"Until lately, yeah," he said, touching a lamp. His hands were black from dusk and ink, but he didn't seem to mind. I hadn't shaken hands with him when I arrived, and made a mental note not to do it when I left.

"What happened lately?"

"This the question we been leading up to?" he asked, closing his right eye and glaring at me with the watery left one.

"That's the one, Mr. Court."

"Call me Arnie," he said, opening the right eye. He wiped at the left one with his thumb, leaving a smear of dirt on his face. "Knock Wood Lee is up for this rap, ain't he?"

"He is."

"You tryin' to get him off?"

"I am."

"Finding somebody else Cross was into heavy would help, wouldn't it?"

"Wouldn't hurt."

"You're honest about it, anyway," Arnie said. "Packy said you'd be honest."

"I'm not trying to pin anything on you, Arnie."

"No, I guess you ain't," the old man said. "All right, yeah, Cross was into me for about seven grand. That ain't enough for me to kill him. Hell, that ain't even worth a phone call to me. He was always good for it in the past, I was willing to go with him for a while."

"Seven thousand."

Arnie Court looked closely at my face and said, "Not enough, huh? How much was he into Wood for? As much as I heard?"

"A lot."

"Well, if it's any consolation to him, it could have been any of us," Arnie said. "Like I say, Cross was usually good for it. Guess he got in over his head this time."

"In more ways than one."

"Yeah."

"Thanks for talking to me, Arnie," I said, heading for the door.

"Hey, you know I seen you fight."

"You did?"

He nodded.

"Took some money in on you once or twice. You had the same problem Packy did, you know."

"What was that?"

"You wasn't mean enough. Packy, as big as he was, didn't belong in the ring, especially not with Marciano."

"He was given a pretty good chance, I heard."

"Sure, his size fooled a lot of people for a lot of years," Arnie said. "You were smart to get out when you did, son."

"So I've been told before," I said, "by Packy, too, as a matter of fact."

"He should know."

"I appreciate you talking to me, Arnie."

"I did it as a favor to Packy."

"Thanks, anyway."

As I left his phone started ringing, and he was rummaging about among his old newspapers muttering, "Now where the fuck did I put that phone?"

58

# — twelve

I spent the rest of the day trying to track down Mort Snow and Leo Piper. Bookies do not tend to sign long-term leases.

Snow I knew, but Leo Piper was sort of a new one on me. I'd been hearing his name around, but knew nothing about him. I had to assume that he didn't know much about me, either, so I simply passed the word on the street that I wanted to talk to him and let it go at that for a while.

When I couldn't locate either man I decided to stop by Greg Foster's apartment, which was in the West Eighties, but he wasn't there. I had the addresses of his two friends, J.C. Smith and Dan McCoy, but they were too far away to make the trips that evening. Smith lived on the East Side, and McCoy lived in Queens.

Winter was close enough to spit at and I was starting to feel the chill from being on the move all day. I decided to head back to Bogie's for some French onion soup and maybe some veal.

When I got down to Twenty-sixth Street, Bogie's was filling up for dinner, but Billy had kept my table open.

"The Gumshoe," he said as I walked in. He's started calling me that after he had me over to his apartment to watch a tape of a movie of the same name, and I'd loved it.

"Right now 'Flatfoot' would fit me better," I said.

"Been pounding the pavement?"

"Working on two cases at once is a bitch."

"How are they going?"

"Slowly. I might have to give up on the girl if I'm going to do Wood any good."

"That'd be too bad for her."

"Yeah," I said, "maybe. I'm going to go in the back and catch a shower. Could I get some French onion soup and veal parmigiana?"

"A crock."

"What?"

"You want a bowl or a crock?"

"The bigger the better."

"You got it."

"I'll be back in about fifteen minutes." I waved my thanks and went up the steps to the kitchen. Exchanging greetings with the cook, I walked through and went out the back door. It was already getting dark out, but in that enclosed space behind Bogie's, it was already pitch black, so I didn't see or hear him coming. I had started up the steps to the office when somebody hit me with a good kidney punch from behind. Paralyzed, I fell to the steps on my left side, reaching for my right kidney. My stomach was exposed and I was struck a second blow there, just as good as the first.

My nose was pushed into one of the steps as I fought for breath.

"Get up," a man's voice said. His tone of voice was flat, without emotion, and he spoke barely above a whisper.

I opened my mouth to answer, but hadn't yet recovered enough breath to do so.

"Come on," the man said, his tone changing to one of impatience. "I didn't hit you that hard." I felt his hand on my shoulder, and he turned me over so that I was lying on my back. All I could see was the silhouette of what appeared to be a fairly big man. I couldn't see any part of his face at all.

"I said up," he said, reaching down to grab me by the front of my coat. As he pulled me to my feet I was able to take my first decent breath, and it was like ambrosia, but I had the feeling that he didn't intend to give me much time to enjoy it.

"Wait—" I croaked.

"What for?" he asked. He spun me around and propelled me toward a brick wall with enough force to bounce me back off it. He was waiting for me and hit me with a well-executed roundhouse kick. I went flying back toward the wall, hit it, and slid down onto the cold ground. My lip was split and I could feel the blood running down my chin.

Bells were ringing in my head and for a moment I

thought I was back in the ring, with the referee counting over me.

The Ricardi fight, I thought. My last fight. The ref could have counted over me all day in that one.

Putting my hands behind me, against the wall, I pushed myself to my feet.

"Why—" I started to say, but he cut me off, planting his foot on the other side of my face. I slid along the wall until I fell on my left side, spitting blood. That time he'd hit me harder, and if that trend continued I figured he just might end up beating me to death.

I had to do something. If I didn't fight back, then I had to make enough noise to attract some help.

If I could get up again.

Come on, Jacoby, I told myself, planting my hands on the wall again, beat the count . . . seven . . . eight . . . nine . . .

I was up, leaning against the wall, and the silhouette of my attacker was coming closer. Behind him were the lights of Bogie's kitchen, shining on the bank of garbage pails.

As he moved toward me I marshaled whatever reserve strength I had for a final round flurry. Pushing off the wall I shouted at the top of my lungs and lunged for him. He was faster, as I knew he would be, and stepped aside, tripping me up. I was losing my balance, but I pumped my legs as hard as I could, desperately trying to stay on my feet until I could reach the trash pails.

I hit the pails like a bowling ball mowing down ten pins, only I made ten times as much noise. There was some shouting from inside the kitchen—in Korean, from the cook—but by the time the back door opened, bathing the area in light, the silhouetted figure had gone.

That made the time right for me to close my eyes and take a little nap. . . .

When I woke up I was in the office lying on the bed, and one of the waitresses was bathing my face with a damp, warm cloth.

"He's awake," she said to someone behind her.

Over her shoulder I saw Billy come into view, a look of concern on his face.

"You okay?" he asked.

"I don't know yet," I said, sitting up. The waitress stood up and went into the bathroom to dampen the cloth again. When she came back I said, "Thanks," and took it from her.

"That's okay, Alison," Billy said. "Thanks."

"Sure."

She left and I got to my feet, dabbing my mouth with the damp washcloth.

"What happened?" Billy asked.

"Somebody was mad at me," I said, walking into the bathroom. I ran the cold water over the cloth and applied it to the back of my neck.

"Did you see who it was?"

"It was too dark," I said, "but I know one thing."

"What?"

"He had more than a working knowledge of karate. I don't know who he was, but at least that narrows it down."

"Somebody from the institute?"

"Maybe," I said, pulling the chair out from behind the desk and sitting down.

"Why?"

I shrugged, fanning the cloth out to wipe my face. I smelled pretty ripe from the garbage pails, and had several ugly smears on my pants. My coat was on the floor and bore similar splotches.

"I don't know, unless—" I started to say, but we were interrupted by the telephone.

"I'll get it," Billy said, and picked up the receiver before it could ring again. He spoke briefly and then held it out to me.

"It's for you. A woman."

I took the phone and said, "Hello?"

"You creep!" a woman's voice said.

"Who is this?"

"Pig!" she said. "You may have fooled Ginger, but you can't fool me."

"Fallon? Is that you?"

"You bet it is, cop."

"Fallon, I'm no cop—"

"If you're not, you're something worse. You're a spy."

"Fallon, listen to me—"

"I don't know what you were trying to pull with that story you told Ginger—"

"What I told Ginger was true," I said, interupting her. "I am looking for Melanie Saberhagen."

"I didn't like the little bitch," she said, "but it's still her right not to be found, if she doesn't want to be. You won't get any help from us."

"Fallon, look, let's meet somewhere and talk about this. Maybe I can make you see—"

"Forget it. I don't like cops, spies, or whatever the hell it is you are."

"Fal—"

"And don't come around the institute," she said, plowing right on. "Greg and the others wouldn't mind giving you a lesson in full contact karate."

I started to reply, but abruptly she hung up and I was left with a dead line.

"That was one of the girls from the institute?" Billy asked.

"Yeah," I said, hanging up. "Damn it, Billy, I blew it. I pushed too hard. Ginger must have told Fallon I was there this morning, and Fallon's smarter than her roommate." I threw the washcloth down on the desk in disgust and said, "None of them will talk to me now, that's for damn sure."

"Well, look at the bright side," Billy said. "You can work on Wood's case now."

"Yeah, I guess."

I took the washcloth back into the bathroom with me and began to strip for a shower.

"You still want that soup?" Billy called to me.

"You bet," I said, realizing that I was chilled to the bone from rolling around on the ground and in the garbage.

"Hey, Jack."

"Yeah?"

"Do you think what happened out here tonight has anything to do with that phone call?"

"It had occured to me, but there's another question I'd like answered, too."

"What's that?"

"How did she know to call me here at Bogie's? And how did my friend know to wait for me out back?"

"Somebody's following you?"

"Looks like it, which brings up questions I'm just too beat to think about right now. All I want is a hot shower, some hot food, and then I'll roll all those questions up, stick them underneath my mattress, and sleep on them."

I took a long, leisurely shower, secure in the thought that Billy would keep my food hot. My face ached on both sides, and as I stood beneath the hot spray, I hoped my jaw wouldn't swell up too badly. A few other aches and bruises were slowly manifesting themselves, but there was nothing that seemed too major.

When I finally made it to the restaurant, Detective Hocus was already seated at my table, enjoying a plate of linguine with clam sauce. I looked at Billy, who simply shrugged and then looked away guiltily.

"On duty or off?" I asked Hocus, seating myself across from him.

"What's the difference?" he asked. "Either way a man's got to eat."

"Billy call you?"

He looked up at me over a forkful of linguine and said, "Yeah, he did. He said somebody had bounced your head off a wall a few times, and he didn't think you were going to call me."

"Why should I call you? If I wanted to make a complaint I'd go down to the local precinct."

At that point Alison came over, a pretty, dark-haired girl who had only been working at Bogie's for about a month, and asked me if I was ready to eat. I said I was, and she went off to get my long-awaited crock of soup.

"Where's your partner?"

"Wright can't eat this stuff, you know that," Hocus said. "Not with his ulcer."

Alison brought my soup over and told me to let her know when I was ready for my veal.

"Your face looks like shit," Hocus said.

"Thanks. It feels like it, too."

"What happened?"

I ran it down for him while trying not to let my soup get cold, and then he asked, "You never got a clear look at his face?"

"Not once."

"Any ideas?"

"One or two . . . maybe."

"What are you working on?"

"You know that. A missing girl, and the Knock Wood Lee case."

"You think this had anything to do with Wood's case?"

"I don't see how, or why. I haven't really come up with anything, or stepped on anyone's toes."

"What have you done?"

"I've put out a few feelers," I said, waving to Alison that I was ready. "I'm looking for a couple of guys."

"Who?"

"Mort Snow and Leo Piper."

"Bookies."

"Yeah, so?"

"You want a drink?"

"A beer."

Alison brought my dinner over, and Hocus asked her to bring us two beers. He watched her walk to the bar, then looked back at me.

"Leo Piper's nobody to play with," he said.

"Piper? Why is he any different from Snow, or Arnie Court?"

"Arnie Court?" Hocus said, laughing. "Is that old geezer still making book?"

"When he can find his phone."

"You looking for him, too?"

"I already found him."

"Was Cross into him?"

"For seven grand."

"And you're looking to find out if he was into Snow or Piper, too?"

"Sure. It's the logical move, isn't it?"

"Oh, it's logical, all right," Hocus said. "And maybe one of them decided it was logical to have someone come over and bounce you around a little."

"Maybe."

"You've been in the ring with men who were trying to hurt you," Hocus said. "Was this guy trying to kill you?"

"I don't think so," I said, then added, "well, not at first, anyway, but he might have been working his way up to it."

He finished up his linguine just as Alison came with the drinks, and she took his plate.

"Did you find out anything about the guy?" he said, lifting his bottle of St. Pauli Girl.

"Yeah," I said, touching my jaw, "he hits hard, and he knows karate."

"Karate?"

"Yeah, he threw a couple of roundhouse kicks that were things of beauty."

"Wood knows karate."

"That's a coincidence," I said, and then added, "hell, so does Billy."

"What about this missing girl thing?"

"Didn't I tell you about that?"

"No, you didn't."

"Just a missing girl," I said. "Her old man sent her to New York to go to school, and she split."

"That's it?"

66

"What more could there be? It's a simple case, but it's time-consuming. I think I'm going to turn it over to someone else so I can work exclusively on Wood's case."

"That makes sense," he said, draining his beer bottle and setting it down on the table.

"Another?"

"No, I've got to get back," he said, standing up. "Sorry I can't stay and watch you eat. Are you going to make a complaint?"

"There's no point," I said. "I can't give a good description of the guy."

"Be careful, then," Hocus said, "especially around Leo Piper. He is not a nice man."

"I'll remember."

"You, uh, want me to run that girl's description downtown for you?"

"I already did," I said, smiling. "I've got a contact in the MPU."

"I don't want to hear about your stoolies in Missing Persons," he said. "Just remember what I said. Be careful, and watch your tail."

"It's not my tail that got beat up on," I said, wiggling my jaw and rubbing my sore kidney, "but thanks for the warning."

After Hocus left I stared at my veal morosely, acutely aware that I hadn't given Robert Saberhagen his money's worth. I was halfheartedly buttering a piece of bread from the bread basket when Billy came over and sat down.

"Mad?"

"At you? For what?"

"Why are you looking so down, then?"

"Guilt, I guess."

"About what?"

I put the bread and knife down and said, "I blew it, Billy. I was so concerned with Wood's case that I pushed too hard and didn't give my other client a fair shake."

"There's still time."

"Wood can't wait."

"What are you going to do, then?"

"Call him, explain it to him."

"Give him his money back?"

I made a face and said, "I don't know if I feel that guilty."

"You could get someone else to work on it for you."

I picked up the bread and said, "I'll call him first, let him decide what he wants to do. He should know that I fucked up."

"Why?"

"I don't know."

"Well, I know one thing."

"What?"

"You'd better eat that veal before it gets cold," he said, standing up, "or you'll have my cook to answer to, and he's mad enough at you for upsetting his garbage pails."

"Yeah," I said, "when it rains it pours."

I had just slid between the sheets when the phone rang. That late at night it just had to be for me. I also had the feeling that it had to be bad news.

"Jacoby," I said.

"Jack, it's Heck."

"What's wrong?"

"I just thought I'd let you know . . . Knock Wood Lee was arraigned today, without bail."

"What charge?"

"Murder one."

"I thought they only said that on television." Heck recognized that for the feeble attempt at humor that it was and ignored it.

"When's his trial?" I asked.

"Three weeks."

"That's kind of soon, isn't it?"

"There was an opening on the calendar, and Judge Willis doesn't like bookies, Chinamen, . . . or murderers."

"Yeah, okay. Thanks for the call, Heck."

"You're welcome. Goodnight."

"Not so far," I said, and hung up.

## — *thirteen* —————————————

In the morning I left through a small alley between buildings that lead to Eighth Avenue—which was probably how my attacker had gotten in and out the night before—and crossed the street to have breakfast at McDonald's. I lingered over it long enough so that when I did call Saberhagen in Detroit I was fairly sure he'd be in his office. It was bad enough that I didn't have good news for him, without waking him up to tell him so.

Saberhagen listened patiently while I explained that I hadn't yet found his daughter, and that another matter concerning murder had come up. I didn't bother going into detail.

"I see," he said, finally.

"I'm sorry, Mr. Saberhagen. I think if I had more time—"

"Couldn't you have another operative work on finding my daughter?"

"It would cost more," I said, feeling just a hint of guilt about bringing it up.

"That doesn't matter. You must be close after all this time. Another man might be able to pick up where you left off."

"All right," I said. "I'll be in touch as soon as we find out anything."

"Remember," he said, "just let me know where she is when you find her. Don't approach her, or she might disappear again."

"I'll remember, Mr. Saberhagen."

"Thank you for staying on the case, Mr. Jacoby."

"Thank you for understanding my situation. I'll be talking to you soon." And thanks for keeping me among the gainfully employed, I added mentally.

"I hope very soon," he said, and hung up.

I hung up, hoping the same thing.

I already knew who I wanted to use to find Melanie Saberhagen, and I made that my next call.

Henry Po was a friend of mine, a licensed P.I. who worked almost exclusively in the world of horse racing. He was employed as an investigator for the New York State Racing Club, but on occasion he had been willing to help me out.

I called his apartment, hoping that I'd find him in and not have to try and track him down, and I got lucky.

"Hank, it's Jacoby."

"Jack, hi. What's up? I was just on the way out."

"Are you busy?"

"I was just going to get some breakfast—"

"No, I don't just mean now," I said, "I mean, are you really busy?"

"Oh. Well, no, I'm not *really* busy. I mean, I don't think I'm in any danger of being sent out of town in the near future. Why, you got a tough one?"

"I've got two, which is why I need you."

"Which one do I get?"

"The one I'm getting paid for," I said. "This way I can pay you, too."

"Well, it sounds encouraging already."

"Why don't we get together for lunch and I'll fill you in on the details."

"Fine. Where?"

"What's easy for you?" I asked, and then at the same time we both said, "Debbie's."

"Okay. I'll see you there around twelve."

"Sounds good."

"All right, Hank, and thanks."

"See you later."

When I hung up I felt a little better. Hank would continue to search for Melanie, while I worked on clearing Wood. There was no reason for me to feel guilty about either case any more.

I took out the photo of Melanie and looked at it for a moment, but when I thought I started to detect a reproachful look on her face I put it away and left for my office.

Debbie's was a special hangout of Hank Po's. It was a little no-name tavern on Tenth Avenue, just off Eighteenth Street, two blocks from his loft apartment. Debbie was a gorgeous blond who ran the place with her cousin Rosellen, an equally beautiful strawberry blond. Both of them had blue eyes you wouldn't believe, and the food in the place was the same way. I'd often wondered about Hank's relationship with the two girls, but I'd never asked.

I had stopped by my office first to pick up my file on Melanie, and to let my fingers do a little legwork on finding the other two bookies, Mort Snow and Leo Piper, over the phone.

Before leaving for my appointment with Hank Po I ran through my mail. I put aside the bills for later and was surprised to find a postcard from Hollywood, from Tracy Dean.

Before she went to California, Tracy and I had had a relationship that was hard to define. She had been a model and soft-porn movie actress, but some time back she had gotten an offer to go to Hollywood to appear in a legit motion picture. It had been a small part, but it had led to another, and I felt that she was now firmly entrenched in California. She'd probably never return to live in New York.

Her postcard merely said that she had gotten a part in a third movie, and that things were really going well for her. She hoped that they were going well for me, too.

I missed Tracy, I'd admitted that to myself not too long ago. I had taken her for granted for a long time, and just when it had seemed that things might progress between us past the physical stage, she'd received that offer from Hollywood. Now she was gone.

I had put aside the postcard, picked up the file, and left to meet Hank. He was already at Debbie's when I arrived, seated at the bar talking to the owner herself.

"Hello, Jack," she said, favoring me with one of her sunny smiles.

"We don't see enough of you around here," she said.

"Didn't he tell you?" I asked. "Your friend Po here threatened me if he ever saw me around you."

"Don't I wish," she said, smiling at both of us. "You fellas plan on having lunch?"

"You bet," I said.

"Well, grab a table then and I'll send Rosellen over to take your orders."

"That alone will be worth the trip," I said.

Hank Po laughed and said, "Come on, Jack. We'll have a couple of beers while we're waiting, Deb."

I walked to a table by the front and Hank came after me with two bottles of Bud.

"Here's the file," I said, putting the brown envelope down in front of him. "You can read it later, but I'll run it down for you now, briefly."

I gave him everything I had on Melanie and the people at the institute, then told him about the attack on me, and the phone call from Fallon.

"You fucked up," he said.

"Tell me about it."

"It's understandable, though. I probably would have gone the same way, Jack."

"No, I don't think you would have, but thanks for saying so, anyway."

At that point Rosellen came over and asked us what we'd like. Hank and I exchanged glances, then decided to play it straight and gave her our orders. She was taller and not as full-bodied as Debbie, but she didn't give away much to her gorgeous cousin.

"Ginger might be the easiest to talk to," I continued, "or she might not. It depends on what her relationship is with Fallon, who is the smarter of the two."

"What about the fellas, Foster and the others?"

"I don't know, I haven't observed them all together long enough to see if she's hooked up with any one of them. The older one, Brown, seems a bit possessive about the women, but that doesn't necessarily mean there's anything going on outside of his imagination."

"You haven't got an address on him," he said, looking over the file which was, at best, skimpy. Keeping records is not my strong suit.

"He's not an institute student anymore."

"They might have something on him, though, even if it's an old address. I'll check it out."

Henry Po had been in the business longer than I had, and his experience was showing.

"Here," I said, taking out the photo of Melanie and handing it to him. "Bayard, the director of the institute, has the other one. I'll call him and let him know about you."

"Okay," he said, looking the picture over. "Pretty girl."

"Yeah."

## — fourteen

Before taking up my search for Mort Snow and Leo Piper I stopped in to see Heck. As I entered I caught Missy with her right leg up on the desk. She was removing one of her skintight legwarmers and the hem of her brown skirt had ridden up her thigh. I didn't know why I had never noticed it before, but she had absolutely perfect legs.

She looked up when I walked in and when she saw who it was she went back to doing what she was doing. If a stranger had walked in I felt sure she would have taken her leg off the desk top and stood up. I didn't know whether to feel complimented or insulted.

"Hello, Jack."

"Hi, Missy."

While removing her other legwarmer she told me that Heck was in court on another of his cases and probably wouldn't be back until late. I told her to let him know that I was no longer working on the missing girl case, and was therefore devoting all of my time to Wood's.

"How are you doing on that?" she asked, dropping her left foot to the floor and smoothing her skirt over her thighs. Her outfit was held at her waist by a wide belt and it hugged her like a long-lost lover.

"I have a few leads that I'm following up, but nothing concrete yet."

"Did you find the girl you were looking for?" she asked, seating herself behind her desk.

"No, but I've got someone else working on it for me. Remember Henry Po?"

"Of course. He's a good man."

"Yeah, he is. If anyone can find her, he can. God knows he won't mess it up the way I did."

She frowned and said, "Is there a problem, Jack?"

"Not anymore, love," I said, "and don't tell Heck I said that, all right? I'm just a little down about some things."

"Anything I can help with?"

"Not really, but if I come across something I think you can help with, you know I'll tell you."

"You'd better," she said, and then changed the subject. "I was trying not to ask, but what happened to your face?"

"Oh, this? I've been working out with Billy Palmer, using karate to get back into shape. I think we may have gotten into it a little heavier than we intended the other night. It's not as bad as it looks."

"It looks terrible."

Actually, I didn't think it looked all that bad. I had some discoloration on each side of my mouth, and a split lip. It was what she couldn't see that hurt most of all, and that was my sore kidney.

"It's not that bad," I said, again. "What time do you expect Heck, anyway?"

"He should be back later this afternoon, before he goes home. He's got some papers to sign and pick up and . . . and we're going out to dinner."

"Oh, really?"

"Don't get smart, Jack. We're just having dinner. We've done that before."

"Oh, really?"

She gave me a stern look and I said, "All right. Tell Heck I'll check in with him from time to time, okay?"

"Sure."

I started for the door, but turned when she called my name.

"Jack?"

"Yes?"

"Be careful, huh? I mean, at karate practice?"

I touched my bruised mouth and said, "Oh, sure, Missy. I'll be careful."

I left the office, knowing full well that I hadn't fooled her, and wondering why I'd even tried.

When I returned to my office I found a message on my answer phone. It was from what the newspapers call an "unimpeachable" source, and it was telling me where I could find Mort Snow at 3:00 P.M. A check of my watch told me that I had an hour and a half before I'd find him there. Since finding Snow would take me in the direction of Bogie's, I decided to stop in there to talk to Billy about something that had been bothering me.

"Are you all right?" Karen Palmer asked me as soon as I entered.

"I'm fine, Karen."

"Your face doesn't look fine."

"But then that's what comes from having been a fighter, right?"

"Oh, shut up."

Karen was a bubbly, energetic woman with soft brown eyes and brown hair who never seemed to run down, and she and Billy complemented each other perfectly.

"Billy around?"

"He's in the back in your—I mean his—ohh, he's in *the* office," she said, laughing.

"Good," I said, because that was what I wanted to talk

to him about. "I'll go and talk to him and see you on the way out."

"I won't be here," she said. "I've got to run, but I'm glad I got the chance to see you." She gave me a hug, then and said, "Be more careful, huh? We like having you around."

"Don't worry," I said, "I like being around."

We said good-bye and she went her way, and I mine, to see Billy.

When I walked in on him he was seated behind *his* desk in *his* office—struggling with his bookkeeping.

"Sometimes," he said, looking up at me, "I wish you were an accountant instead of a detective."

"Sure," I said, "and my mother always wanted me to be a doctor."

He laughed and said, "How do you feel?"

"Fine, physically."

He put down his pencil and said, "That means you've got something on your mind."

"Yes."

"What is it?"

"This place," I said, indicating his office.

"What about it?"

"I've used it long enough," I said. "In fact, it's getting to the point where I'm abusing your hospitality."

"That's ridiculous," he said, "but go ahead and have your say."

"Remember, when we made this arrangement it was supposed to be temporary."

"That may be so, but don't move out now because you're feeling guilty. If you want your own place, that's another thing, but you're still welcome here as long as you like."

"I appreciate it, Billy—"

"Just don't make a big thing out of it," he said. "Next thing I know you'll want to pay me for karate lessons."

"That's another thing—"

"Forget it!"

"No, not that," I said. "It's about the institute. You'd better tell your friend Olden that Bayard and I had a talk."

"He told Bayard about you, didn't he?"

"You knew?"

He shook his head.

"I figured, from the way he was talking . . . did it hurt your case?"

"No, I managed to do that all by myself."

"Boy, we've got some case of the guilts today, haven't we?" he said with mock severity.

"Yeah," I said, grinning sheepishly, "I guess I do."

I checked my watch and it was time to go and have my talk with my old friend, Mort Snow.

"I've got to get going."

"We'll talk again," he said. "Where are you off to now?"

"I've got to see a bookie about some old bets."

## — fifteen

My informant had told me that Mort Snow would be at an address on Tenth Avenue and Twenty-eighth Street at 3:00 P.M., which was perfectly reasonable. Snow always liked to be set up within spitting distance of Madison Square Garden.

I had Mort Snow down in my book as the one bookie— that I knew of—who had never taken a bet *on* me. He wasn't one of my staunchest supporters during my ring days, which stemmed from the time I had laid him out during an argument. The way he told the story he hadn't blinked when I hit him with a right, but what he never told anyone was that he was unconscious, and few people blink when they're in that condition.

The doorway was unmarked, but judging from the addresses on either side it was the right place. I walked up a flight of steps, careful to avoid the urine puddles but unable to avoid the stench. When I reached the top the door was locked and I knocked. At best, the light bulb in the hall was twenty watts, and had probably been there for years. It was one of those bulbs that would probably always seem to be on the verge of winking out. It did more to hurt the eyes than help them.

When the door opened a crack and a gray eye appeared I said, "I want to see Snow."

"Who are you?"

"Jacoby."

"Wait."

The door closed and I waited in that dank, dark, smelly hall to see a man I didn't like.

When the door finally opened again the same eye appeared and the same voice said, "He ain't here."

"You tell Mort that I want to place a bet."

"He ain't—"

"Tell him."

"Uh, what kind of a bet?"

"Tell him I want to bet that he doesn't make it through the day without not blinking."

"What?"

"Tell him."

There was a moment's hesitation and then he said, "Wait."

Finally the door opened again, this time all the way.

The owner of the eye was a man of medium height who looked as if he'd once been a fighter during Packy's era. Squat, going to fat, with lumps on his face where many a fist had landed, I wondered if I'd remember him if I heard his name.

"I know you," he said.

"Do you?"

He closed the door, then turned to peer at me intently.

"I know the name."

I couldn't wait for him to figure it out and I didn't have the inclination to help him, so I simply said, "Snow."

78

"Right. Follow me."

The apartment wasn't much better than the stairway and hall had been, but then I expected as much from Mort Snow. He was never one to operate above his station.

The ex-pug led me to a closed door, opened it, and said, "Here he is, Mr. Snow."

"All right, Mickey," Snow said. "Get lost."

As Mickey closed the door behind me Snow's phone rang, but he ignored it.

Mort Snow was an offensive man. His personality was offensive, his appearance was offensive, and even his odor was offensive. He'd always smelled as if he'd had onions for lunch, and this occasion was no different.

"Christ, Snow, you stink."

"That's precisely what you did in the ring, Jacoby," he said, unruffled. "What do you want?"

Snow was in his mid-forties, a small man who wore elevated shoes because he thought adding two inches to his five-foot-two-inch frame made a big difference. I had almost felt bad about laying him out five years before, but the feeling had passed as soon as he woke up and opened his mouth again.

It struck me then how much he would look like Arnie Court in about twenty years.

"I've been looking for you."

"Don't I know it," he said with a look of disgust, "I've been avoiding you. How'd you find me?"

"I have my sources."

"Bullshit. I doubt that you're any better a detective than you were a fighter." He peered at me then and added, "And judging from your face, you haven't improved much in that area, either."

"Look, Snow, I didn't come here to lay you out again, but the temptation is getting more powerful by the minute. Can we get to what I did come here for?"

"I wish you would," he said, and when his phone rang again he added, "You're putting a crimp in my business. What do you want?"

"I want to talk about Alan Cross."

"Cross? The guy they collared that Chink for killing?"

"His name's Knock Wood Lee."

"Typical Chink name. What's that got to do with me?"

"I understand Cross was into you for a tidy sum."

"Who told you that?"

"Those sources that you don't respect."

"They lied."

"No, they didn't. Look, it's just me now, Snow, but I could come back with a cop."

"I wouldn't be here."

"I'd find you again."

He frowned and said, "Yeah, you probably would. One thing you always were was stubborn."

"Careful, Snow. That sounded awfully close to being a compliment."

"Bite your tongue."

"What about it, Snow? Cross?"

"Yeah, yeah, he owed me some money."

"How much?"

"Fifteen thousand, give or take a hundred bucks. Not much, really."

"Really?"

"Cross was a good customer . . ."

"Until recently?"

"Yeah, how'd you know?"

"I'm a detective, remember."

He made a rude noise with his mouth and went on.

"He was getting in over his head and I had to cut him off. He had the same problem with a few others."

"Yeah, I know."

"That Chink, he let him in too deep, though. That shows his lack of experience."

I had never thought of Wood as inexperienced, but I guess that's what he was, compared to Arnie Court and Mort Snow. What about Piper?

"What do you know about Leo Piper, Snow?"

"Piper?" He made the same rude noise and said, "He gives my profession a bad name. He's ambitious, but he's just a punk."

"Would you tell him that to his face?"

"Shit, no!"

"What's he like, exactly?"

"You'll find out," Snow said. "At the very least I don't think you'll be able to make him *not* blink."

"I'll let you know," I said. "You wouldn't be able to tell me where to find him, would you?"

"Why don't you ask your sources? They helped you find me, didn't they?"

"Yeah, but that wasn't hard, Snow," I said. "All they had to do was follow the smell."

I started for the door, but he called out before I could reach it, in a funny tone of voice, as if he had just thought of something.

"Hey, Jacoby, wait a minute!"

"What?"

"Listen, you ain't gonna give my name to the cops are you?" he asked, nervously.

"Not if I don't have to, Mort."

"What's that mean? What would make you do that?"

"I could do it just because I don't like you."

"Hey—"

"Or I could do it if I find out you had anything to do with killing Alan Cross."

"Hey, the guy owed me money, why would I want to punch his ticket?"

"You know, that line of reasoning isn't doing much for the police, Mort, so why should it do anything for me?"

I started for the door again and he grabbed my arm.

"Hey, look, so we're not friends, so what? That doesn't mean you have to throw me to the wolves just to get that Chink—I mean, your friend—off the hook, does it?"

"Nobody said anything about throwing you to the wolves, Morty," I said, getting a perverse sort of enjoyment out of his obvious discomfort.

"I didn't have anything to do with killing Cross, Jacoby. That's the truth."

"Then you've got nothing to worry about, Snow. The truth shall set you free."

"Jacoby, you gotta believe me!"

"No, Mort," I said, turning toward the door again, "I don't."

I walked into the next room and found his man, Mickey, waiting.

"Show me the door, Mickey."

"Sure thing."

He lumbered ahead of me and when he opened the door for me he said, "I remember now. Wasn't Benny Jacoby your brother?"

"Yeah, he was."

"I fought him once, late in my career. He knocked me out, and retired me. How's he doing?"

"He's dead."

"Too bad. How did he die?"

I started down the stairs and said over my shoulder, "I guess you could say somebody retired him, too."

## — *sixteen*

I spent the rest of the day trying to scare up Leo Piper, with no luck. I went back to Bogie's and called Hocus to see if he had anything on Piper to give me.

"Even the boys in vice can't put their finger on him, Jack," Hocus said.

"I don't get it. What makes him so much harder to find than the others?"

"You haven't exactly been quiet about looking for him, you know. Maybe he's just gone underground."

"That would indicate that he was either nervous about

me, or afraid of me. That doesn't sound like the Leo Piper I've been hearing about."

"You're right. He has no reason in the world to be afraid of you."

"Thanks a lot."

"I mean, you're no immediate danger to him."

"So why doesn't he want to talk to me?"

"I've got an idea."

"What?"

"When you find him, ask him. Can I get back to work now?"

"Yeah, why don't you?"

When I hung up I sat at the desk for a while, wishing I had Eddie Waters to talk to. I'd never know how good a detective I could have been if I'd had the opportunity to work full time with him for a while—and that was the least of the reasons I missed him. Eddie had always said that your next step was usually right in front of you, all you had to do was take a step toward it.

Just for something to do I opened the top drawer of the desk and there it was, right in front of my nose. The little notebook I had taken out of Alan Cross's apartment. I hadn't yet had time to really go through it, so I sat back and put my feet up on the desk and began flipping pages.

If it was meant to be his "little black book," then Alan Cross must have swung both ways, because he had men's names and numbers in there as well as women's. There were no addresses, just names and numbers, and some kind of letter code following them: "Mindy, 265-8152 (L)," or, "Terry, 677-9743 (L, GS)." There was even one that read: "Joe, 765-8764, (H, B, G, A)."

What the letters meant I couldn't even begin to guess. Maybe the thing to do would be to call somebody up and ask.

I picked a girl's name at random and dialed the number, without having any idea what I was going to say if someone picked up.

"Hello?" a woman's voice said.

"Hi, Mindy?"

"Yes. Who's this?"

"Hi, I'm a friend of Alan Cross's. He gave me your number and I was wondering—"

"Alan's dead," she said, cutting me off shrilly. "Who is this?" Then, just like a woman, she hung up after asking me a question without giving me a chance to answer it.

I debated whether or not to dial another number, then decided to wait until I knew exactly what I was going to say.

The book was just another piece of the puzzle, but you can't start fitting them together until you've got a couple of them in place, and I hadn't even gotten that far yet. I stuck it in my pocket where I could get to it quick if the need arose.

Taking my feet off the desk, I picked up the phone and dialed Tiger Lee's number on an impulse.

"Lee, it's Jack."

"Oh, hello, Jack. Is anything wrong?"

"I was just wondering if you'd had any dinner yet."

"Dinner? No, I haven't, but then I haven't been eating much, lately."

"Why don't you come out with me tonight and get something? Maybe if we put our heads together we can come up with something that might help Wood."

"Like what?"

"I don't know, Lee. Maybe there was something Wood said or did that you don't remember right now, something that might help us set up his defense."

"I don't know what I could—well, all right. I still have some work to do, though, so I'll have to get back early."

"That suits me, Lee. I'll pick you up at eight."

"Fine. See you then, Jack."

"I don't know what else I can do for you, Jack," Lee said.

We were at a small restaurant not far from the apartment she shared with Wood. Neither of us had suggested eating in the Italian restuarant right beneath them, because neither of

84

them ever went there. For Wood, that would have been mixing business with pleasure.

"That's all right, Lee," I said. "I just thought maybe talking would bring something to mind."

"Wood doesn't really discuss business with me. Oh, he talks to me more than anyone else, but he never really gets into it too deeply, you know?"

"Yeah, he's a close-mouthed person, all right. Maybe if he talked a little more. . . .Lee, can you see what you can dig up on Leo Piper for me? He's the only one I'm having trouble locating."

"I'll make some calls, but I don't know if I can come up with anything."

"Give it a try, anyway."

"Of course I will."

I looked at her plate, which was half full.

"Are you finished?"

"Yes," she said, also looking at the plate. "I told you I haven't had much of an appetite lately."

"I understand. Come on, I'll walk you back."

During the walk I asked her, "Lee, have you and Wood ever met Piper?"

She hesitated a moment, then said, "Once."

"When?"

"He came to see us—to see Wood when he first came to New York."

"What did he do, propose a partnership?"

"Hardly. He wanted Wood to work for him."

"Wood said no, of course."

"Of course."

"What was Piper's reaction?"

"He threatened Wood."

"What?" I asked, stopping abruptly and grabbing her by the shoulders.

"He made a threat—"

"You see? This is what I meant by jogging something loose. Was he specific in his threat?"

"No, not that I remember," she said, thinking back. "He just said that Wood would be sorry, and left."

Realizing that we were standing stock still on a darkened New York street—not the healthiest thing to do in that part of town—I said, "Let's go upstairs."

When we reached the door to the apartment she said, "Are you coming in?"

I shook my head.

"Just give me a description of Piper."

"Same age as you and Wood, tall, well built, dark hair, neat but long. New breed." She recited it very clinically, almost coldly.

"Like Wood?"

"In a lot of ways, I'd say. Cool and calm, in control."

"Attractive?"

She stared at me a moment, then said, "Yes."

"All right," I said, "thanks, Lee. Make those calls, huh?"

"Tonight, and I'll call you in the morning."

"Good enough."

I started down the hall and she called, "Jack?"

"Yeah?"

"Thanks for dinner."

"My pleasure, princess. Get some rest."

"I will."

When I got down to the street I started walking towards Canal Street to get a cab.

Lee hadn't fooled me with that business about Wood not confiding in her. I was willing to bet that she knew almost as much about his business as he did. Otherwise, how could she run it while he was away?

There was something else, too. When the subject had been steered to Piper, I had gotten some bad vibes from her. She hadn't reacted. Her answers had been cool and unemotional, even when talking about how he had threatened Wood. I'd chosen not to pursue it right then. I was much more interested in the fact that Leo Piper had threatened Wood. Could Piper have killed Cross and pinned it on Wood?

That was a distinct possibility, the kind a good lawyer like Heck Delgado could get some mileage out of.

I hoped.

## — seventeen

As promised, Lee called me the next morning, but she didn't have anything to give me.

"I made some calls, Jack, but apparently Piper keeps a very tight lid on where he is at any given time. He seems to stay put for about as long as it would take to get a cup of coffee. I'm sorry, Jack."

"Don't worry, Lee. That little bit of information you gave me last night might make up for it."

"Do you really think so?"

"I'm going to see Heck today and find out. I'll let you know what happens."

When I had returned home—to Bogie's—the night before, I had called Heck and asked if I could see him early the next morning.

I got to the office before Heck, but Missy was there behind her desk, as she always seemed to be.

"Isn't this a little early for you?" I asked.

"I get started early from time to time," she said. "Besides, somebody had to be here to let you in."

"Why not Heck?"

"Because he's the boss, remember?"

"Oh, right."

At that moment the boss walked in and said, "Come on inside, Jack."

"Got time for a cup of coffee?" Missy asked him.

"One."

"Jack?"

"Yeah, thanks."

In his office Heck said, "What have you got, Jack?"

I told him about the conversation I'd had the night before with Lee about Leo Piper, and how Piper had threatened Wood.

"How long ago was that?"

As soon as he asked I realized what a dunce I had been. When Lee mentioned the threat I'd been so excited I'd forgotten to ask how long ago it had occurred.

"It was . . . back when Piper first came to New York," I said, but I couldn't let it go at that. "I just got so excited when she told me that I . . . forgot to ask exactly when it happened."

"That's all right, it doesn't really matter, anyway."

"Why not? We've got a threat against Wood—"

"Only Wood wasn't the one who was killed," Heck said, interrupting me, "Alan Cross was. To suggest to a judge or jury that Leo Piper threatened Knock Wood Lee, then killed Alan Cross and pinned it on Wood is—well, Jack, it's a bit fanciful."

"Fanciful?"

"To take into a court of law, yes."

"Heck—"

"We need facts, Jack, not suggestions."

Missy came in carrying two cups of coffee and immediately sensed my discomfort. She put the two cups down on Heck's desk and left without a word.

"Look, Jack," Heck said, leaning forward with his hands clasped atop his desk, "it's something, I admit, but it's something for us to pursue further in the hope of coming up with some facts. Just keep at it, Jack."

"Yeah, sure."

"Missy told me what happened at Bogie's," he said, changing the subject. "Is that connected with Wood's case?"

"I can't be sure."

"Well, just be careful, then. Who did you turn that missing girl case over to?"

"Henry Po. Didn't Missy tell you?"

"That's right, she did," he said, shaking his head. "I've been so busy of late . . . I don't think I know him."

"He's a good man, a better detective than I am."

I stood up and Heck said, "Jack—"

"That's just a statement of fact, Heck," I said. "I'll get out of your hair now and check in when I have something more concrete."

"All right."

When I left his office Missy said, "Jack, everything all right?"

"Sure. I just made a fool of myself, that's all."

"Eddie did that a time or two."

I looked at her and the concern was so evident on her lovely face that I smiled.

"Yeah, he did, didn't he? Thanks, kid. I'll be talking to you."

"Sure, Jack. Why don't we have lunch or dinner together?"

"I'll call you."

I left, consoling myself that I'd learned a valuable lesson about clutching at straws, which made it a profitable morning.

Sure.

I was closer to Bogie's than to my office on Fifth Avenue and Forty-ninth Street, but I wanted to be alone, so I walked all the way uptown despite the cold weather.

When I got to my office I sat behind my desk and rubbed my face with my hands. I sat staring at the ceiling, waiting for the ghost of Eddie Waters to come down and tell me what my next move should be—but that wasn't about to happen. Besides, I knew what my next move was: Piper. The only problem was I was either too dumb to find him, or he was too smart to let me.

I called Lee and asked her the question I should have asked her last night.

"When was it that Piper came to see you and Wood?"

"Oh, months ago, when he was just setting up in New York."

"How many months ago?" I sounded impatient, but my impatience was with myself.

"Five, six months." The tone of voice I'd noticed the night before was creeping in again, and I was so frustrated that I decided to ask.

"That's a little vague, isn't it, Lee?"

"Well, I can't remember exactly."

"Why not?"

"Jack—"

"What's going on, Lee?" I asked. "What is it that you're not telling me . . . and why?"

"Nothing, Jack. I just—"

"Lee, I don't have to tell you how important this is to Wood, do I?"

"Of course not."

"Did you see Piper again after that time with Wood?"

There was a pause and then she said, "You won't tell Wood?"

"Not if there's no reason to."

"I did . . . see Piper one time after that."

"Where?"

"He came to the apartment."

"Wood wasn't there, of course."

"No, he wasn't, and Piper knew it."

"What did he want?"

"Me," she said. "He wanted me to leave Wood and go with him."

"To work?"

"No, just to be with him. He said he'd pay me a lot of money to leave Wood and be his lady."

"When was that?"

"A week after he spoke to Wood."

"I don't understand, Lee," I said, puzzled. "Why didn't you tell me last night?"

"I don't want Wood to find out."

"What would he do if he found out?"

"Jack, if Wood found out . . ." she began, but she let it trail off and she took a long, shuddering breath.

"Lee?"

"I . . . don't . . . know exactly what Wood would do," she said, haltingly.

"You're afraid he'd go after Piper?"

"Yes."

"And kill him?"

"I don't know."

"Lee, do you think Wood killed Cross?"

"No, of course not!"

"But you are afraid he would have killed Piper if you had told him what happened?"

"I told you, I don't know!"

"All right, Lee, all right. Have you seen or spoken to Piper since then?"

"No."

"Did he leave you a number or something so you could get in touch with him if you changed your mind?"

"Yes, but I threw it away."

"And you don't remember it?"

She hesitated, then said, "No."

"Do you think you could? If he's a bookie, he'd want his customers to be able to remember his phone number, and it would probably be an easy number to remember."

"I'll try."

"Okay. If it comes to you, give me a call."

"I will."

There was a long silence, and then she broke it.

"Jack, I'm sorry."

"It's all right, Lee. Just don't . . . hold anything back from now on, okay?"

"Sure. Did you talk to Mr. Delgado about Piper?"

"Yeah. He's of the opinion that we need a little more, so my next step is still to find him."

She didn't reply.

"Lee, I won't tell Wood. There's no reason to."

"All right."

"I'll talk to you tomorrow."

"'Bye."

I hung up, feeling more confused than ever.

On one hand, Lee was insistent that Wood couldn't have killed Alan Cross, yet on the other hand she was worried that Wood would kill Piper—or at least do something violent—if he ever found out that Piper had approached her with an offer when he wasn't around.

In addition to that, she'd muddied the waters even more by coming up with a perfectly good motive for Wood to kill Piper.

Now all I had to do was hope that Piper didn't turn up dead.

Somebody turned up dead, all right, but it wasn't Leo Piper.

When I returned to Bogie's, Billy was working behind the bar, but when he saw me he dropped everything and came rushing out to meet me.

"Where've you been?"

"I was in my office for a while, and then I went walking, to do some think—"

"Hocus has been trying to get in touch with you for hours," he said, interrupting me.

"What for?"

"I don't know. All he'd tell me was that it was urgent, and that you should call him at Bellevue."

"Bellevue? What the hell is at Bellevue?"

"The emergency room."

"And the morgue."

"No, he said for you to call him in the emergency room, or his office if he wasn't there anymore."

"And he didn't say what it was about?" I asked, starting for the pay phone in the back of the room.

"No, not a word," he said. Hurrying behind the bar, he palmed the bar phone and said, "Here."

I altered my course, took a bar stool, and accepted the phone from him.

"Uh, Bellevue's number—"

"Here," he said, pushing a napkin over. I read the

number written on it and dialed it. When the voice answering the phone said, "Bellevue emergency," I asked for Detective Hocus.

"Jacoby?" Hocus said, almost shouting into the phone. "Where the hell have you been?"

"Never mind. What's happened?"

"Your friend Po—"

"Is he dead?"

"No, not dead, but he's in pretty bad shape."

"What happened to him?"

"Somebody beat him up pretty bad, Jack."

"Did he say who?"

"I told you he was in pretty bad shape," he reminded me. "He hasn't regained consciousness yet."

"You mean he could die?"

"The doctor says it could go either way, Jack," Hocus said. "I'm sorry."

"I'm on my way."

"There's one more thing."

"What now?"

"You had Po looking for that girl for you, didn't you?"

"That's right. Why?"

"He found her."

"He found her? Where?"

"She's here, too," Hocus said, gravely. "In the morgue."


# — eighteen

I was still in shock when I got out of my cab and met Hocus in front of the hospital.

"You want to see the girl?" he asked as we entered side by side.

"If she's dead," I snarled, "she's not going anywhere."

"Up then," he said as we reached the elevator bank. "They finally got a room for him."

"Shit," I said as we entered the elevator and Hocus pressed the button.

I was angry, more angry than I could remember having been in some time. I was angry because Hank had gotten hurt, because Melanie Saberhagen was dead—and I was still hoping that was a mistake—but most of all I was angry at myself for bringing Po into it.

"This way," Hocus said, leading the way as we got off the elevator on the second floor.

"Yeah."

I followed him to a door that he opened to let me go through first.

It was a semiprivate room, but only one bed was occupied, and that by Henry Po. I became even angrier that it had taken them so long to put him in an otherwise empty room.

"They kept him in emergency so long because they couldn't find any insurance info on him, or any next of kin."

"How'd they get to you?"

"They found my name and number on him and finally called."

Hank was hooked up to an intravenous feed, and his head was swathed in bandages. His face was the same color as everything else in the place, hospital white.

"How bad?"

"He's got a concussion and some broken ribs. They did a CAT scan and took all kinds of X- rays. They're still checking him out. I told them someone would take care of the bill, and they took me at my word."

I looked at him and he added, "I said it real loud."

"Don't worry, someone will," I said. "Either me or his boss."

"He wasn't working for his boss when he got trashed."

"They're friends," I said, the remark fueling my anger.

I walked closer to the bed to get a better look, but it didn't get any better.

"What happened?"

"Somebody did a number on him, Jack—maybe like somebody tried to do on you the other night?"

I looked at Hocus and then said, "Let's talk in the hall."

We went outside and Hocus said, "What do you think?"

"If she was just missing, I'd say I don't know."

"She's dead, though."

"Let me go down and see for myself."

He nodded, and led the way.

We took the elevator down to the morgue, where Dr. Mahbee was waiting for us. Mahbee was the medical examiner Hocus took perverse pleasure in calling "Dr. Maybe." Mahbee was an East Indian gent, tall, handsome, in his forties.

"This way," he said. He took us into a cool room filled with body drawers and opened one for us. A filing system for bodies, I thought sardonically.

"That her?" Hocus asked.

"Jesus," I said, "how can I tell?"

The face resembled a lump of clay, the features all flowing into one another. Sure she was blond, probably young, and about the same size. . . .

"Looks like the same girl to me, Jack," Hocus said, "but we'll have to wait on her old man for a positive i.d."

He took out the two pictures Saberhagen had given me and returned them to me. Her father had said she'd changed since the pictures, but he didn't know the half of it. . . . and I was the one who was going to have to tell him.

"Close it up," Hocus told Mahbee.

We followed Mahbee to his office and I asked, "What did she have on her?"

"Nothing."

"Nothing at all?"

"She was found floating naked in the Hudson a couple of days ago," Mahbee said.

"You should have kept checking in with the morgue," Hocus told me. "Po did, and he found her. He called me and we were supposed to meet, but he didn't show up. Some cabbie found him underneath the West Side Highway and brought him."

"West Side Highway?" I asked. I'd been in a fight once beneath the highway and had been stabbed. I knew how frightening it must have been for Hank.

"Yeah, in the upper fifties."

I looked at Mahbee and said, "How long?"

"How long has she been dead? Hard to tell. She was in the water a long time, maybe over a week. Dead at least that long. She was weighted down, but sloppily."

"What do you mean?"

"Whatever the killer weighed her down with, he only tied it around one foot."

"So?"

"That foot is . . . gone. When it was eaten away, or torn loose, she floated to the surface."

I felt sick, for the young girl, and for my friend, who had been badly beaten while doing my job.

"Did the hospital call Po's boss?" I asked Hocus. "He must have been carrying his i.d."

"His wallet was gone."

"How'd they get your number?"

"He had a small spiral notebook in his back pocket."

Hank's experience again. I made my notes on napkins and on matchbook covers.

"I'll call his boss, then."

"And the girl's father?"

"Yes."

"Before you leave I could use some information on the girl," Mahbee said.

"Sure."

"I'm going upstairs to arrange for a blue suit to stand by Po's door. I want somebody there if—when he wakes up. After that I'll go back to the precinct."

"Okay."

"Are you all right?"

"Fine."

"Call me later and we'll have a drink, huh?"

96

"Sure." I was being short, and Hocus deserved better than that. I looked at him and said, "Thanks." It was all I had to offer at the moment.

"See you later," he said, and left.

I stayed long enough to fill Mahbee in on the particulars concerning Melanie Saberhagen and assure him that her father would be in to claim the body as soon as he could get there from Detroit.

Before leaving the hospital I went upstairs to Hank's room. The cop was already on the door, but I showed him my i.d. and he let me in.

"The detective told me you'd be up," he said, and I nodded.

Hank looked as if he was sleeping, but I knew that people died in their sleep all the time.

"You sonofabitch," I said, "you die on me and you can kiss your fucking fee goodbye!"

I left my business phone and my number at Bogie's with the hospital desk, and then left. I also told the cop on the door to make sure I was called the moment Po regained consciousness.

I called Robert Saberhagen's home as soon as I returned to Bogie's, but there was no answer. At that time of night it made no sense to call his business phone.

Your daughter's dead, I thought angrily, and where are you?

I got some ice from the bar and took it back to the office with me, then helped myself to a bottle of bourbon from Bogie's stock. Billy had told me a long time ago that I was welcome to whatever I wanted, but this was the first time I'd taken him up on it.

When half the bottle was gone I dialed Saberhagen's number again, although negotiating the rotary dial through eleven digits in my condition was no easy task. When there was still no answer I cursed him out again, and poured myself another drink.

Later I tried to dial again, but I kept getting lost after seven digits, and finally got tired of starting over. The last thing I remember about that night was getting up to get another bottle from the shelves.

I don't think I ever made it.

## — *nineteen* —

The ringing of the telephone jarred me awake from an alcohol-induced slumber the next morning. I found myself lying on top of the bedcovers, fully dressed, and rolled off the bed in the direction of the phone. The noise I made into the receiver was unintelligible, even to me, but that didn't seem to bother the caller.

"Jacoby!" Hocus said harshly into the phone. "How many rings does it take to get you to answer the goddamned phone?"

"I don't know, how many does it take to penetrate a whole bottle of bourbon?"

"Oh fine," Hocus said, sounding disgusted. "Is that what you did when you got home last night?"

"Seemed like a good idea at the time," I said, then put one hand to my pounding head and said, "but now that I think about it—"

"Never mind. You wanted to know when Po woke up. Well, he's awake."

"How is he?"

"Out of danger, and he says he wants to talk to you."

"Okay," I said, running one hand over my face. "Let me take a quick shower and I'll be right over."

"I won't be there, but the man on the door has instructions to let you in."

"Did you talk to Hank already?"

"Yeah, and I don't need to hear it again. What I do

need, however, is you in my office after you've spoken to him. Okay?"

"Yeah, sure."

"Did you call the girl's father yet?"

"Tried to last night but there was no answer. I'll try again this morning before I leave for the hospital."

"I'll see you later, then."

"Right."

I hung up and staggered into the bathroom to take a much needed shower. That done, I felt less dirty and my eyes felt less gritty, but it hadn't done very much for the ringing in my ears. It would take time for that to fade.

After dressing I sat at the desk and once again dialed Robert Saberhagen's phone number. When he answered, he spoke in a bleary, sleepy voice, but several moments later he was wide awake.

I identified myself to the cop on Po's door, and he allowed me to enter.

"Hey, Hank."

He had been staring out the window, and at the sound of my voice turned his head slowly in my direction.

"Hello, Jack."

I approached the bed, feeling at a loss for what to say. "Sorry" seemed so inadequate.

"I guess you must have heard me last night?"

"I wasn't hearing much of anything last night," he said. He straightened up in bed some and grimaced. Rubbing his ribs he asked, "What did you say?"

"I told you that if you died I wouldn't pay your fee."

"Oh, was that you?" He laughed lightly.

"Feel like telling me what happened?"

"Might as well give you your money's worth."

Hank's first stop had been to see Bayard at the institute.

"It took some convincing, but I guess I've got an honest face. He gave me Brown's address, which he had in a back file, and he also gave me the other picture of Melanie."

After that, Po had gone to see each of the men from the

institute, including Brown and the three whose names I had given him. He played it straight, never mentioning my name, only that he'd been hired to find Melanie Saberhagen.

"Surprisingly, Smith and McCoy were very helpful. Foster, on the other hand, wasn't, and Brown was downright rude. Poor fellow's got a terrible personality."

"Tell me about it."

"He had a girl in his apartment at the time, and she was pretty well banged up."

"He beat her up?"

"That's what it looked like. In fact, I think I might have interrupted him at it."

"Any idea who she was?"

"From your description, I'd say she was Fallon DeWitt."

I pulled a chair over and sat down next to the bed while I digested that bit of information.

"That must be what Ginger meant about Fallon having strange taste in men."

"If Brown's an example, I agree," Hank said. "He started to get tough and I backed out only when the girl told me to leave, too. She might also have strange taste in getting her jollies."

I was thinking back to my conversation with Ginger.

"Ginger also said that Fallon and Melanie didn't get along because they had the same strange taste in men."

"Melanie and Brown?"

"Maybe."

"How was she killed?"

"Don't you know?"

"I was on my way to see Hocus when I got hit. I called the morgue and found out that they had a Jane Doe fitting her description. I was supposed to meet Hocus on Eighth Avenue and Fifty-fifth Street, where he was doing some business. I never got there. Next thing I knew I was under the West Side Highway getting the shit kicked out of me."

"By whom?"

"It was dark, but he kicked a lot, which makes me think it was your friend from behind Bogie's."

"You didn't see him, either?"

"No."

"Could it have been Brown, or one of the others?"

"Sure, it could have been. Did you see the girl?"

"Yeah, but I didn't find out what killed her. I was still a little shocked."

"That's understandable."

"I'm seeing Hocus later. I hope he'll show me an autopsy report."

"If she was beaten to death—"

"I'm with you there," I said, cutting him off. "We already know that Brown likes to beat on women."

"It might do you some good to talk to Fallon DeWitt."

"Yeah, or for Hocus to."

"You're not going to work on this?"

"On the girl's murder? I don't know, Hank. I've still got Knock Wood Lee's case to worry about, and we found the girl."

"I hope you don't mind if I poke around some."

"In your condition?"

"It may be few days, but I sure don't intend to take a beating like this and let it go. Next time I want an even chance, without being hit from behind first."

"Well, I can't blame you for feeling that way. I do blame myself, though, for what happened."

"Why would you do that?"

"You got hurt while doing my job."

"Hey, you're paying me—you are paying me, aren't you?—which made it my job."

"All right," I said, standing up, "we'll talk about it. Take it easy for a while and don't look to get out of here too soon."

"It can't be too soon."

"Want me to call your boss?"

"I already did."

"Hank, just add the medical expenses to my bill, all right?"

"The N.Y.S.R.C. will take care of it, Jack. Thanks for the offer."

"Need anything?"

"Yeah, get me a nurse who looks like Debbie, will you?"

"Hell, if I find one like that I'll keep her for myself. Take care. I'll be back to see you."

"Thanks, Jack . . . and don't take the blame for this, okay?"

"Sure. See you."

On the way to see Hocus I stopped at a coffee shop and bought several containers of coffee. I kept two and left the rest with the cop on the front desk.

"Here," I said, holding one out to Hocus. He looked up from his desk and didn't smile. He didn't frown, but he didn't smile, either.

"Thanks. Sit down."

He took the coffee, and I took a seat and opened my own container.

"Is that the autopsy report on the girl?"

"Yeah."

"You know, I was thinking on the way over here."

"About what?"

"Well, that dead girl's been in the water a long time, and all we have to go on are a couple of photos. What if it isn't Melanie Saberhagen?"

He looked up at me and said, "Did you call her father?"

"This morning. He's catching the first plane."

"Then he'll make the final i.d. on her."

"What's wrong with you today?"

"I don't like murder," he said, "and I don't like P.I.'s who hold out on me."

"What are you talking about?"

He pointed at me with a blunt index finger and said, "You shrugged me off this missing girl thing, had me thinking that you'd been beaten up because of the Knock Wood Lee case."

"That's what I thought."

"And now she turns up dead . . . maybe."

"How was I supposed to know that? I didn't know who she was running with in New York."

"What about this Brown guy?" he asked. He opened his notebook and added, "And Greg Foster, and—"

"Those are just students at the same school where she was studying martial arts."

"Martial arts, like karate, right? Like the guy that worked you and Po over, right? The guy neither one of you seems to be able to identify."

"You think we're covering up for the guy?"

He jabbed the air with his finger and said, "If your client identifies his daughter, I'm putting out a wanted alarm on this guy Brown, who seems to like to beat up women."

"She was beaten to death?"

"Yeah. We couldn't see any bruises because she'd been in the water too long, but somebody did a number on her."

"And you think it was Brown?"

"I'll want to talk to him about it, yeah, but I don't want to find that you and your friend Po have been there first."

"What are you talking about?" I asked, moving to the edge of my chair. "Hocus, what the fuck do you think I am, some comic book private eye out for revenge?"

"No, of course not," he said, feigning a look of surprise. "You wouldn't pull something like that, would you?"

"Of course not."

"Sure, that Max the Axe thing, that was different."

"Of course it was different," I said, defending my actions when it came to the man who had killed Eddie Waters.

"And all this guy did was kill a young girl and beat up you and your friend Po."

"We don't know that—"

"Look, all I'm saying is don't get in my way on this, Jack."

"So all I've got to do is conduct my investigations without getting in your way or Vadala's way."

"I have nothing to do with Vadala's case. I'm talking about *this* case," he said, tapping the autopsy folder.

"Okay," I said. "Besides, I don't have any intention of looking for Melanie Saberhagen's killer . . . if that's her. That's your job."

"You'd better get out of here before the shit gets over my head," Hocus said, "and take your shovel with you."

I stood up, left my unfinished coffee on his desk, and headed for the door.

"Oh, listen," I said, turning back to face him.

"What?"

"I'll be bringing my client to the morgue when he gets here—"

"Bring him here and I'll take him over."

"Okay, sure, but you don't mind if I tag along, do you?" He glared at me because I'd just said I wasn't interested in the case, and I added, "I just wanted to make sure it's her because if it is, my job's finished."

"You know," he said, pointing at me with the pen in his hand, "you're getting real good at this P.I. shit. You must be watching a lot of TV lately."

Hocus protested a lot when we worked together, because he never wanted me to think I was getting my way too easily.

"My client should be in sometime today. I'll see you in a while."

"Ah, get out of here," he said, pointing toward the door, fighting back a grin. I didn't let him know that I'd seen it.

I turned to leave and walked headlong into Detective Vadala.

"Jacoby," he said, managing to get a yard of distaste into my name. "What are you doing here?"

"Leaving."

"Good."

I thought I was going to make it, but I should have known better. When I reached the head of the stairs he called my name out again.

"Jacoby!"

"Yes?" I said, turning resignedly.

"I've got your friend in a box, Jacoby. I know you've

been poking around, trying to find some way of getting him out, so I just want you to know something."

"What's that?" I asked, knowing that he wasn't about to wish me luck.

"There's plenty of room in that box for you, too."

"I'll remember that, Vadala."

## — twenty

I had told Saberhagen to check into a hotel when he arrived, and gave him Bogie's number to call. I'd check in with Billy Palmer from time to time during the day. I was anxious to find out if the girl in the morgue really was Melanie. All that was really evident was that she was blond and young. For the rest, we'd have to wait for her father.

From the precinct I went back to my office and arrived in time to pick up the phone before my answer machine did.

"Jacoby," I said.

"This is Piper. I understand you've been looking for me."

"Leo Piper?"

"Have you been looking for another Piper?"

"No, I haven't."

"What do you want?"

"I want to talk to you."

"So talk."

"Not on the phone."

Silence.

"Piper?"

"I'm here," he said, but that was all and I decided to wait him out.

It took several moments for him to come to his decision, during which time I listened very closely to his breathing. I could have been getting paranoid, but just before he spoke I switched my answer machine on to "record."

"All right, Mr. Jacoby," Piper said. "I will send a car to get you. Be in front of your building in a half an hour."

"Listen, something might come up—"

"I hope not," he said, interrupting me, "because if it does, I may not make this offer again. It's for a limited time only, as they say on television."

Before I had a chance to answer, he hung up, leaving me with a dead line. I hung up, hoping that Robert Saberhagen wouldn't call during the next half hour.

I had been standing out in front of my office building only five minutes when a black limo pulled up. As I approached, the power window opened.

"Are you Mr. Jacoby?" the driver asked. I had the impression that he was nothing more than he seemed to be, a professional chauffeur, and not one of Piper's men.

"Yes, I am."

"Shall we go?"

"Yes, of course."

I opened the back door and got in, and he pulled away from the curb.

"Do you know Mr. Piper?" I asked after we'd gone a few blocks in silence.

"Sir?"

"Piper? Do you work for him?"

"I work for the limo agency, sir. I'm just following my dispatcher's instructions."

I believed him, and sat back to await our arrival at whatever our destination was.

He turned off Fifth onto Forty-ninth, took that to Eighth where he made a right, and then made another right on Fifty-sixth. We crossed Seventh Avenue and stopped halfway down the block in front of a bookstore.

"Here?" I asked, looking out the window.

"You're to wait in front of this bookshop, sir. That's what I was told."

I shrugged and got out of the limo, wondering idly if one tips a limo driver. I decided that this one didn't.

The bookstore was called the Mysterious Bookshop, and specialized in mystery fiction and nonfiction, judging by the material that was in the window. A sign in the window said that an author named Mallory was going to be there later in the week to autograph books.

I became aware that a man had left the bookshop and walked up the few steps to the street.

"Do you read mysteries?" he asked.

"No," I said, turning to face him. "No, Mr. Piper, I don't read mysteries. There are enough mysteries in real life to keep me occupied."

"I read them voraciously," he said, showing me that the bag he carried was full of books. "I've spent more money in this store than anywhere else since my arrival in New York."

"Real mysteries," I repeated, "like who killed Alan Cross."

The name appeared not to faze him, but he stopped talking about books.

"Would you come with me, Mr. Jacoby?"

"Where?"

"Just next door, where we can talk."

Next door—actually, a couple of doors away—was one of New York's newest hotels, the Parker-Meridien. Piper didn't speak again until we were in the elevator.

He was everything Lee had said he was. He was about my age, taller, well built, attractive. He was also very cool as he explained that he didn't live here, but was simply using a friend's apartment for this "little meeting."

We rode the elevator to one of the top floors, which he said housed permanent apartments, and I followed him to a door with the number 2102 on it.

"Would you like a drink?" he asked me as he tossed his sack of books onto an expensive-looking couch. I could probably have bought a car for a lot less than that couch cost.

"No drink, thanks," I said. "I'd just like to talk to you. I've been looking for you long enough."

"Yes, I know you have," he said, pouring himself a drink from behind what appeared to be a well-stocked bar. He straightened up with his drink in hand and said, "Why is that, Mr. Jacoby?"

"Alan Cross."

"Yes, you mentioned his name earlier. He's dead, isn't he?"

"That's right."

"I guess that means I won't be paid the money he owes me."

"That's right, too."

"Is that what you wanted to know? Whether or not he owed me money?"

"That and how much."

"How much?" he said, and then laughed. "Certainly not enough for me to kill him. No one owes me that much money, Mr. Jacoby. I wouldn't allow myself to be put in such a postion. That is the difference between Mr. Knock Wood Lee and myself."

"I see. Is that the way you put it to his lady?"

"His lady? The lovely Miss Tiger Lee, you mean?" He laughed again, this time at something he really thought was funny, and I had the uncomfortable feeling that I'd never know what the joke was.

"She certainly is a lady, I'll grant you that," he said. "What she and I talked about is none of your business, however. In fact, all of my business is none of your business, Mr. Jacoby, but I will tell you this. Cross owed me, oh, close to ten grand, which is top limit with me. I get some real good regular customers, I may let them go higher, but right now that's it, and that isn't near enough to kill a man for, even if I was in the habit." He sipped his drink and added, "And that's all I'm going to tell you. I trust you won't get lost on the way out."

"Not so fast. Why'd you decide to see me after ducking me for so long?"

"That's curiosity, Jacoby. It's bad business to let your curiosity get the better of you."

"I guess that means that you didn't see me just out of curiosity."

"Hardly." He freshened his drink and then seemed to study a spot on the ceiling. "I simply wanted to stop hearing my name being bandied about the streets, Jacoby. You see, I grew up on the streets. Now I try to stay as far above them as I can, like in this apartment." He spread his arms wide without spilling a drop of his new drink.

"That's it, huh?"

He looked at me then and said, "That's it—except for one more thing."

"What's that?"

He was holding his drink in his right hand and he uncurled his index finger from around the glass and used it to point at me.

"Don't ever think that I was ducking you. If I was ducking you that would mean I was afraid of you, and if I was afraid of you I'd have some muscle on hand." He spread his arms again and asked, "Do you see any muscle?"

As cool as he was, ego had succeeded in creeping into the conversation. I was grateful for that. It gave me some ammunition I might otherwise not have had.

I looked directly at him so there would be no mistake and said, "No, Piper, I surely don't."

It was nice of him to be concerned but no, I did not get lost on the way out.

The first thing I did when I hit the streets was to call Bogie's and check to see if Saberhagen had arrived yet. He had, and was staying at the Waldorf, which figured.

The remainder of the day was occupied with meeting my client, bringing him to Hocus—who took a statement that included everything Saberhagen had told me and vice versa since I'd been hired—and then taking him down to the morgue to identify "the remains."

He stared at the corpse without expression, and when

we all went into Mahbee's office he said, "How in the name of God am I to identify that for sure?"

Hocus and I looked at each other, but it was Mahbee who answered him.

"If you could give us some sort of medical information on your daughter, sir, that we could use to make a positive identification."

"What do you suggest?" Saberhagen demanded. "I didn't exactly bring her dental records with me."

That remark got me a dirty look from Hocus, which I tried to ignore. I didn't need to be told that there was something else I had forgotten to do that week.

"I think we can find something, sir," Mahbee said.

Saberhagen and Mahbee put their heads together and came up with an appendix scar and a bone Melanie had broken when she was a child.

"Can we wait?" Hocus asked.

"If you like," Mahbee said.

We waited in silence. Hocus was still too angry with me to talk to me, and I was feeling an odd sort of anger myself. Saberhagen seemed to be in another world. I wondered if there might be an important business meeting he was missing for this.

Mahbee came out what seemed like hours later and gave us the confirmation. The dead girl was definitely Melanie Saberhagen.

Robert Saberhagen took it without expression. To my way of thinking, I took it harder than he did—hell, even Hocus seemed to take it harder.

"Detective, could you have someone drive me to the airport?" he asked. "I have a plane to catch."

"Of course," Hocus said, frowning, "but what about—"

"I've made arrangements, if that's your concern. The body will be picked up."

"I'll arrange for transportation to the airport," Hocus said.

"Thank you."

Saberhagen turned to me then and I tried to keep my face as expressionless as his was.

"Mr. Jacoby—"

"I'll send you a bill, Mr. Saberhagen."

He simply nodded and then left with Hocus, who took the time to throw me a frown.

As I left Mahbee said, "That was kind of cold, wasn't it?"

"Doc," I said, "that man wrote the book on cold."

From the morgue there was only one place to go and that was to the nearest bar. With a bourbon in front of me I decided that in order to be able to work effectively for Knock Wood Lee, I was going to have to consider the Melanie Saberhagen thing closed. Leave it to Hocus to find the killer, I told myself. That was his job. I only hoped that he'd have the man—or woman—before Henry Po came out of the hospital. That would keep Po from going after him, in which case I would feel obliged to help him. I couldn't afford that and neither could Wood.

I finished the drink and debated the merits of ordering another one. Remembering the night before—and the morning after—I decided instead to go over to Bogie's and have something to eat, after which I'd turn in. Come morning I'd think of nothing but getting Heck the evidence he needed to build a solid defense for Wood—right after I made out Robert Saberhagen's bill and mailed it off to him.

As a good businessman, he'd appreciate my promptness.

## twenty-one

Over breakfast the next morning I thought about Leo Piper. The man interested me, probably because I didn't know anything about him. What I needed to know was where he came from, so I could run a background check on him. I only had his word that he wouldn't kill a man for ten thousand dollars.

From my office I called the Seventeenth Precinct and asked for Hocus.

"What do you want?" he asked when he came on the line. He wasn't any happier with me today than he had been yesterday.

"Will you lighten up?" I said, scolding him. If I couldn't chide him out of his black mood, it might get in our way for days. "I need some information and you're not going to give it to me in the mood you're in."

"Is that a fact?"

"I need some information on Piper."

"I still don't know where he is."

"I spoke to him already."

"Is *that* a fact?" he said in a different tone.

"Yes, it is."

I explained how the meeting had come about, and then told him what I wanted to know.

"I don't think even Vice knows where he came from, Jack. He just showed up and set up shop."

"What's he into besides making book and girls?"

"Anything that has to do with them."

"Drugs?"

"Not that I know of, why?"

"If he was into drugs somebody would know something about him. Narcotics, the feds, maybe even Caggiano."

"And you'd go to Don Carlo and ask him?"

"Either him or Carl Jr."

Don Carlo Caggiano was the head of the biggest of New York's "families" and his son, Cagey Carl, had broken off and started his own line of business. I had crossed both their paths while looking for a stolen pulp magazine collection months ago.

"Stay away from the Caggianos, Jack," Hocus warned me. "I don't think Carl Jr. likes you, and to Don Carlo you're just insignificant."

"Can you check with Narcotics for me?"

He sighed heavily and said, "Yeah, okay, I'll check, but I doubt anything will come out of it."

"Thanks, Hocus."

"Yeah," he said, and hung up.

I made out Saberhagen's bill then, although I couldn't quite bring myself to gouge him the way I thought he deserved. I simply charged him for Henry Po's services—and medical expenses—and then added double my usual fee.

I had started to seal the envelope when I remembered the two photographs of Melanie that Saberhagen had given me. I took them out of my jacket pocket and made the mistake of looking at them. I could have sworn there was a disappointed look in her eyes, but I couldn't help her anymore. I folded the larger of the two photos and then stuffed both of them into the envelope with my bill.

I didn't think Robert Saberhagen would mind the creases.

I went out into the hall to drop the envelope down the mail chute, then returned to my office and dialed Heck's office number, just to check in.

"He's in, Jack," Missy said. "Hold on."

After a few moments Heck came on the line.

"Jack, how are you doing?"

"All right, I guess. I'm off that missing girl case for good, now."

"Really? Did you find her?"

"Somebody killed her, Heck. It's Hocus's job now to find out who."

"I see. I'm sorry, Jack."

"Yeah, so am I. I just thought I'd let you know that the matter has been . . . resolved. I'll keep in touch."

"Have a good weekend, Jack," he said, with heavy emphasis on the word "good."

I knew what he meant without being told. I still had two weeks and a bit to find something that he could bring into that trial with him.

"I'll do my best, Heck," I said, and hung up.

I sat back in my chair and took out Eddie Waters's phone book, which had come in handy on more than one occasion.

Eddie had known a lot of P.I.'s in his time, and he had them all listed in that book by city and state, so that whenever he needed work done outside New York all he had to do was take out his book. That was what I had done in order to check on Saberhagen in Detroit. If I knew where Piper was from, I could do it again, check Piper out and see what his claim to fame was.

Leafing through the book I could see that Eddie had a name and number from almost every major city in the United States, but calling them all would be a hell of an expensive proposition, and not only in phone bills. Each of these P.I.'s would command a fee, and what if Piper was from the one city I missed?

I put the book down and reminded myself that I had to send Amos Walker a check. I scanned my mail for the first time in a couple of days. There were plenty of bills, but none from Amos. I opened a side drawer and dropped them all in it to be handled later. I picked up the phone book to put in the top drawer, and suddenly it hit me. I had the means to find out where Piper was from; all I had to do was play it right.

I was on my way out when the phone rang, and retraced my steps to answer it.

"Jacoby, Hocus."

"So soon?"

"It doesn't take long to come up empty, Jack, and that's what I came up."

"Thanks for trying anyway, but I may have come up with another angle."

"Like what? What have you got in mind?"

"Shopping," I said, "for books—mystery novels."

"What are you talking about?"

"You ought to read more, Hocus," I said. "It would broaden your horizons."

"I don't need my horizons broadened," he said, "but I think you need your head examined. Let me know if you come up with anything on Piper. We wouldn't mind knowing about it."

"You got it, pal."

"Yeah, I know, and you gave it to me."

There were two ways I could have played it. One was to go right to that bookstore I'd seen Piper come out of and try to find out if they knew where he was from. The other way was to go and see Billy, who had a leg up in that world, and see if he could help me.

I chose to go and see Billy.

"In for lunch?" he asked me when I walked into Bogie's.

"Lunch and . . ."

"And what?"

"And a word with my assistant detective."

His eyebrows shot up and he said, "Shall we sit at your table?"

"Let's."

No sooner had we sat than Alison came over to see what we would have.

"Cheese sandwich," I said, "and coffee."

"American cheese," Billy said, "and make it two, Allie."

She smiled at me and left.

"Why is it lately every time I look up she's my waitress?" I asked, watching the sway of her slim hips as she walked to the kitchen.

"Karen. She's playing matchmaker again."

"Great."

"What's up?"

"Do you know of a bookstore that sells only mysteries?"

"Of course," he said. "Murder Ink, on Eighty-seventh Street."

I frowned and said, "That's not the one."

"The Mysterious Bookshop on Fifty-sixth?"

"That's the one. Do you know anyone who works there?"

"Sure. I know the owners of both places, why?"

"I'm interested in a regular customer of the one on Fifty-sixth."

"What's his name?"

"Leo Piper."

"The bookie?"

"What do you know about him?"

He waited before answering while Alison brought our coffee, mine black and in a cup, his with milk—in a glass.

"Sandwiches on the way."

"Fine," Billy said.

When she left he said, "I know the name, but that's about all."

"I want to know where he came from."

"And you think the people at the bookstore would know?"

"He told me he shops there all the time. Maybe the first time he went he used a check or a charge card with his old address on it. Maybe he let something slip to one of the employees about where he lived before he came to New York. I need to run a background check on the guy, Billy, but before I can do that I have to know where he was before he came to New York."

"Why not ask yourself?"

"It's easier if you know somebody," I said. "I know you."

The cheese sandwiches came and we fell silent again until Alison left.

"All right," Billy said, "I'll see what I can find out, but I'll ask in both places."

"Why?"

"If he's a serious mystery reader, he'll patronize both stores, not just one."

"Okay."

"When do you want this information?"

"Yesterday."

He stopped with his sandwich halfway to his mouth.

"Can I eat this first?"

"I wish you would," I said, and then added, "because then I'll know mine is safe to eat."

## — twenty-two

While I was waiting for Billy to come up with the info I needed, I figured I'd go and see how Hank Po was doing. When I walked into his room Debbie was there sitting next to the bed and they both looked up. She had been holding his hand, but dropped it abruptly as if I'd caught them at something.

"Am I interrupting?"

"I wish you were, but my ribs won't allow it," Hank said. "Come on in. You don't happen to have a hamburger or a slice of pizza on you, do you?"

I snapped my fingers and said, "Ah, I ate them in the elevator."

"I have to get going," Debbie said, standing up.

"Not on my account, I hope," I said.

"No, on Rosellen's," she said. "She'll scream that she had to do all the work today, and besides, she wants to come up and see Hank, too."

"I should be so lucky," I said.

She kissed Hank on the cheek, then touched my arm on the way out.

"Take care, Jack," she said, "of both of you."

"I'll do my best."

We both watched her walk out, and then I looked at Hank and said, "This place doesn't look so bad, anymore."

"It's the pits."

"Yeah," I said, sitting in the chair that Debbie had warmed up for me.

"How are you making out?"

I told him about Saberhagen coming in to view his

daughter's remains and then flying right out again after making "arrangements."

"He was all broken up, huh?"

"I don't get it, Hank. Why'd he even hire me to find her if he didn't care that much?"

"Maybe simply because she was his. People get that rich they tend to get very jealous of their possessions."

"So that's all she was, huh?" I asked. "Just another possession?"

"I've been through that," he said, and then explained to me about a girl named Penny who'd been treated the same way by the two men she loved.

"She died young, too," he said, and we sat there and thought about dying young. It was such a waste of the time they'd never know, the good times they'd never know, and even the bad ones. Everybody had a right to their own good and bad times.

After that we started talking about Leo Piper, and Hank knew about as much about him as I did.

"I wonder," he said.

"What?"

"Who's the best P.I. in the business, Jack?"

"The best, or the most expensive? It doesn't matter really," I said, before he could answer, "they're both Walker Blue."

Then I saw what he was getting at.

"I see," I said. "If anybody would know about Piper, he would."

"You've got to admit he's got an uncanny knack for knowing things other people—including the cops—don't know. All you've got to do is to ask him."

"You think so?"

"You know him, don't you?"

"Some."

I had a grudging respect for Walker Blue, but I always felt . . . inferior when I was in the same room with him. Still, it *was* a possibility that I couldn't afford to pass up.

"Maybe I should have let Heck bring Blue in right at the

beginning," I said. "If it turns out that he had the information all the time that could have cracked this thing . . ."

"Don't be beating yourself over the head so much, Jack. You're a good detective, with a knack for it, but you've got to give yourself time."

"Thanks."

"Just don't start trying to compare yourself—or compete with—Walker Blue."

"Good advice," I said, standing up.

"You'll go see him?"

"Might as well. Do you know when you'll be getting out?"

"Probably not until after the weekend."

"Well, let me know and I'll come and get you."

"You don't have to—"

I was halfway through the door when he called out, "See if Blue will give you a professional discount!"

Fat chance.

## — twenty-three

I had never been to Walker Blue's office. In fact, the first two times I had spoken to him were at funerals, Eddie's and my brother Benny's. Since then I'd run across him a time or two in Heck's office.

When I called Blue's office from a pay phone his secretary told me he was back from out-of-town and asked me if I had an appointment.

"I would just like to see if he could spare me a few moments."

"Hold, please." She put me on hold and I listed to Muzak for a few moments until the line opened up again and Blue himself came on.

"What can I do for you, Mr. Jacoby?"

"I'd like to come up and talk to you for a few moments, if I may."

"About what?"

"Leo Piper."

There was a moment's hesitation, and then he said, "Very well. Do you know where my office is?"

"Yes."

"Come on up, then."

I started to say thanks, but he had already hung up.

Blue's office was on the mezzanine of the Pan Am building and when I got there his secretary—a handsome, mature lady in her early forties—told me to go right in.

Blue stood up and offered me his hand as I entered, then sat back down behind his desk and offered me a seat.

"What's this about Leo Piper?" he asked.

"I'm involved in a case that he seems to have become a part of."

"Has this to do with Nok Woo Lee?"

"Yes, it does. How did you know?"

"I know that you and he are friends, and that Heck Delgado is his lawyer. I also know that Hector did not retain me to investigate for him." He shrugged and spread his hands, as if to say that the rest was obvious.

Blue had a long-jawed face and neatly clipped gray hair. He was tall and slim, in extremely good shape for a man in his early fifties. He wore the kind of suits that come with a warranty.

"How has Piper become involved?"

"The dead man owed him some money."

"I'm sure the dead man owed money to quite a few bookies in town."

"He did, and I know about the others, but I know very little about Piper."

"And you thought I might know more?"

"The thought had occurred to me, yes."

He stared at me impassively for a few moments and I felt like a military student sitting in the headmaster's office.

"I do have a file on Piper," he admitted finally.

120

"May I see it?"

"It's not very comprehensive," he said. "In fact, I've seen no need to attempt to make it so."

"What *do* you have on him?"

"What do you need?"

Apparently he wanted to play it close to the vest, not giving me any more than I needed, if that.

"All I really need is where he was before he came to New York."

"Actually, I don't have much more than that. He came here from Ohio."

"Ohio?"

"Cincinnati, to be exact."

"What the hell was he doing in Cincinnati?"

"I haven't found any need to check into that further."

"Why do you have anything on him at all?"

"I simply like to keep myself up to date on names I hear on the street."

Walker Blue didn't strike me as the "street" type.

"I do go into the street occasionally."

"I see," I said, standing up. "I appreciate your taking the time to talk to me."

"Not at all," he said, also standing. "I don't mind extending a little reciprocal professional courtesy from time to time."

I actually found myself feeling flattered by his use of the word "reciprocal." That indicated that he felt that I might be able to help him sometime in the future.

We shook hands and I started for the door.

"Oh, there is one other thing I can tell you," he said.

"What's that?"

"Where he grew up."

I frowned at him and said, "You know that?"

"It was something I came across quite by accident."

I'll bet.

"He was born and grew up in Brooklyn."

"Brooklyn?"

"People do grow up there."

"I know," I said, "I know. Thanks again."

"Not at all," he said, again. "Good luck with your case."

As I left his office, wished a cheery "good day" by his handsome secretary, it struck me that I personally knew at least one other person who had been born and grown up in Brooklyn.

Tiger Lee.

Before going back to Bogie's to tell Billy that I already had the information I was looking for, I stopped by my office to make use of Eddie's phone book. I looked up Cincinnati in the book and found the number of a P.I. named Harry Stoner. I had never met Stoner, but had heard Eddie speak of him once or twice.

I called Stoner and introduced myself and found out that Eddie had mentioned me to him once or twice, as well. He told me how sorry he was about Eddie's death and then asked me what he could do for me.

"Leo Piper," I said.

"I know that name," he said, "although I haven't heard from him in a few months."

"He's here in New York, Harry, and I need any information on him that you can get me, as fast as you can get it."

"I'll do what I can," he promised, "and call you back."

I gave him the number at Bogie's in case he couldn't get me in my office.

"Thanks, Harry. Send me a bill."

"Sure," he said, "hold your breath."

Billy could barely contain his excitement when I arrived at Bogie's, but the dinner rush was in full swing and he was stuck behind the bar. Alison showed me to my table and took my order, and then brought me a beer.

"Billy says he'll be over as soon as he can," she said, putting the beer down in front of me.

"That's all right, there's no hurry."

She smiled and started away.

"Alison."

"Yes?"

I studied her then, for the first time, as a person and not simply as a waitress. She had long brown hair, brown eyes, a wide, full-lipped mouth that was quick to smile. She was wearing a Bogie's T-shirt, which showed off her small but well-formed breasts.

"I don't remember thanking you properly for helping me the other night."

She smiled and said, "That's all right. You have a lot of other things on your mind."

"Yeah, you're right about that," I said, "but that won't always be the case."

"No?"

"No."

"I'll see about your dinner."

I watched her walk to the steps that led to the kitchen and then Billy was sitting across from me.

"What are you so excited about?" I asked, watching her walk up the steps.

"Let me tell it my way or it won't be any fun."

I didn't have the heart to tell him that I already knew what I needed to know.

"I tried the Mysterious Bookshop first because it was the closest, and being as clever and sneaky as I could I tried to find what they knew about Leo Piper."

"And?"

"And they don't know anything. From the first day he walked in there he's paid cash for everything, and said very little."

"And?"

"So then I went to Murder Ink, where I have a firmer foothold—I used to work there, you know—and I asked straight out what they knew about Leo Piper."

"Which was?"

"The same. He pays cash. He's never used a check, and they don't take plastic even if he had wanted to use it."

"I can see now why you're so excited."

"I'm not finished!"

"I'm sorry."

"I stayed a while to talk—and I bought some books—and the girl who works there remembered something."

"What?"

"Apparently Piper let it slip one day that he had been born in Brooklyn!"

"Really?"

"Isn't that great? That's even more than you asked for."

"About what I asked for, Billy—"

"Wait, wait," he said, waving his hands in front of my face. "I found out what you wanted to know—" he began, but Alison came over at that moment and he stopped short to see what she wanted.

"There's a call for Jack."

"Thanks, Alison," I said, standing up. "I'll be right back, Billy."

I walked to the bar and took the phone.

She put her hand on my shoulder and said, "Your dinner is ready, but I'll keep it warm for you."

I winked and said into the phone, "Jacoby."

"I've got what you wanted, Jack," Harry Stoner said.

"Jesus, Harry, that was fast."

"All it took was a few phone calls," he said. "Leo Piper came to Cincinnati eight years ago and fell in with the wrong crowd—or right crowd, if you look at it from his point of view—right away. He started working for some known criminal figures as a runner, and worked his way up the ladder fairly quickly. About six months ago he left Cincinnati without saying where he was headed."

"New York."

"So you say."

"What's the word on him, Harry?"

"He's ambitious, smart, cool. A few people here figured that he left when he finally got his confidence built up to the point where he could handle a bigger town. He was a fairly big fish here, Jack, but apparently he considered this too small a pond."

"What about his tactics?"

"He had some muscle on his payroll, but he didn't use them very much. Mostly for show. Nobody crossed him, Jack. He had big friends."

"Anybody pave the way for him to come here?"

"Like I said, nobody really knew where he was headed. Sounds to me like he decided to take on the Big Apple by himself. How's he doing?"

"Not bad, but then he is a native New Yorker."

"One other thing."

"What?"

"I don't think his name was Leo Piper when he got here, but I haven't been able to scare up a confirmation. Want me to keep digging?"

"No, I think I can cover that here. Harry, I'm looking at Piper for a possible homicide. Was he ever involved in anything like that there?"

"He was never arrested, but there were some accidental deaths that the cops talked to him about once or twice."

"All right. Harry, thanks for the quick work. Send me a bill."

"You owe me one," he said, and hung up before I could argue.

I stood at the bar for a few seconds and suddenly Alison said into my ear, "Ready?"

I turned my head and her face was inches from mine.

"I'm ready."

"I'll bring it over."

I went back to my table where Billy was waiting impatiently.

"Important?" he asked.

"That was a P.I. from Cincinnati with some information—" I started to answer automatically but then stopped short when I realized what I'd said.

"Cincinnati?" he asked, looking alarmed.

"Billy—"

"You already knew."

"Well—"

"Here I was all excited about getting the information—how'd you find out?"

"It was sort of by accident," I said, but I hurried to add, "it helps to have confirmation, though."

"Don't pull my chain, Jacoby."

"Look, you did a good job," I said. "I just happened to come across the information during the course of the day."

He tried to look angry, but couldn't pull it off.

"Brooklyn, too?" he asked.

I looked sheepish and nodded my head.

"Damn."

Alison came over with my dinner then and said to Billy, "You're needed in the kitchen, Billy."

"It's nice to be needed," he said wistfully, standing up.

"Billy," I said.

"What?"

"You're not mad at me, are you? Pal?"

"Me, mad?" he asked, looking surprised. "Of course not."

"Good."

He stopped Alison before she could walk away, grabbed my beer bottle, and put it on her tray.

"This man is in training, Alison," he said. "Bring him a Perrier with lime."

"Wait a minute—" I started, but she'd already walked away.

Billy gave me an exaggerated grin that was barely visible beneath his bushy mustache and said, "Enjoy your dinner . . . pal."

## twenty-four

Over dinner I realized what my next stop had to be, and it wasn't one I relished. I grabbed a taxi on Seventh Avenue and gave the cabbie the address of Wood's apartment. I didn't call ahead, but I was fairly sure that Lee would be there.

When she answered my knock she appeared surprised, but then smiled and said, "Hello, Jack."

"Can I come in?"

"Of course."

She allowed me to slip in past her and then shut the door behind us.

"Can I get you something? Coffee?"

"No thanks, Lee. I came to talk."

"About what?"

"About something you might not want to talk about."

"Like what?"

"Leo Piper."

I got the same impression I'd had the other times I had mentioned his name, like a curtain falling across her eyes.

"What about him?"

"Can we sit?"

She shrugged, but walked into the living room and sat on the couch. I sat in an armchair across from her and leaned forward.

"You knew Piper before, didn't you, Lee?"

"Before what?"

"Before he came to see Wood that day," I said, and then, watching her eyes, added, "before he was Leo Piper."

Her eyes, which had been studying the floor, flicked up for a quick look at me, and then fell to the floor again.

"Want to tell me about it?"

She took a deep, shuddering breath and said, "Jesus, no . . . but I will." Then she looked at me again pleadingly and said, "Jack, Wood must never know what I'm going to tell you."

"Lee, maybe we should worry about getting Wood out of jail first and then worry about what he should or shouldn't know."

She put her hand over her mouth, then took it away and said, "You're right, of course."

"Just relax, honey, and tell me what you know about Leo Piper."

"He was born Leopold Piperneski and he always hated that name," she said.

"You knew him when his name was Leopold Piperneski?"

"Yeah," she said, nodding her head. "We were kids together in Brooklyn, Jack. We grew up together."

I let that sink in for a moment and then said, "Lee, that's very interesting and it brings up a few questions, but before we get to that . . . why does admitting this to Wood frighten you?"

She looked at her hands, which were wrestling with each other in her lap, and said, "He's also the man who turned me out, Jack."

"Oh," I said, trying not to appear as stunned as I felt.

So that's what she was afraid of, that the man who had taken her off the street would meet the man who had turned her out.

"Lee, Wood has to know that someone started you out in the business."

"Sure, but he certainly wouldn't want to meet the man who did, Jack—especially if the man was trying to get me back into the business."

"Yeah, but Wood himself has some girls out there too, Lee. To think that he would react violently to meeting the man who . . ." I let myself trail off, because thinking about it more and more, I believed that Knock Wood Lee probably would react . . . adversely.

"You see?" she said.

"Lee, why didn't you tell me this before? I asked you not to hold anything back."

"I know, but I was frightened."

"I'm sure Wood is frightened, too."

Maybe I shouldn't have said that, but her silence *could* have jeopardized Wood's case.

"I know," she said, studying something at her feet.

I leaned forward and put my hand over hers before she yanked off a finger or two.

"Lee, just tell me about Piper."

"There isn't much to tell. I thought I was in love with him. I was seventeen and for two years I was convinced that I was hooking because I loved him . . . and then he left."

"For Cincinnati?"

"I didn't know where he was going, I only knew that he was gone and I was still out on the street. I still thought I loved him, too, but I wised up pretty quick, and then I met Lee."

"Did you hear from Piper at all?"

"One letter, just before I met Wood."

"What did it say?"

"I don't know. I tore it up without reading it, but I did notice that the postmark was Ohio."

I thought about the letter that I had received from Julie, which I had kept in my office for months before finally tearing it up without reading it.

"When he showed up at the door six months ago, I was shocked," she said. "All I could think of was that he was going to tell Wood and that Wood would—" She stopped short and actually started to laugh. "That sounds funny, you know? That Wood would?"

"That he'd what, Lee? Kill him? Or vice versa?"

"I just didn't want anything to happen, that's all. And then he had the gall to come back and tell me he wanted me back!"

"Lee, is Piper violent?"

"Eight years ago he had a bad temper, Jack, but now he seems too cool and controlled. He's changed."

"Has he spoken to you again since then? At all?"

"No, but he sent me a dozen roses when Wood was arrested."

"What happened to them?" I asked, looking around.

"I threw them out."

"Oh," I said, realizing that it had been a dumb question to ask.

"There was a card that said 'You've still got a place with me.' And you know what surprised me the most?"

"What?"

"That I didn't hate him. I always thought that if I ever saw him again, I'd hate him . . . but I didn't."

"What did he call himself back then?"

"He was always Leo, but he used to use his mother's maiden name, DeGuere. He said it sounded classy. I didn't know he was calling himself Leo Piper until he showed up here that first day and introduced himself."

"Do you think he might have framed Wood to get you back?"

She gestured helplessly and said, "I don't know what to think, Jack. I wouldn't think that any woman would be that important to Leo."

"Lee, you're not just any woman."

"Thanks, but still . . . for Leo to go that far . . . I just can't see it."

"Okay, Lee. Is that all of it?"

"That's it. I know I was foolish to hold back as long as I did." She looked at me and said, "You're a good detective, Jack."

"Sure," I said, "I'm Sam Spade and Sherlock Holmes all rolled into one."

We rose together and she walked me to the door, holding my arm.

"You know something?" she asked.

"What?"

"I feel better. I feel like I can breathe again."

"Is everything else going all right?"

"Yes, I'm handling it."

She opened the door for me and I said, "Lee . . ."

"Yes?"

"I'll get him out."

"I know you're trying, Jack. We both appreciate it."

"Take it easy, kid," I said, stepping into the hall, "and call me if you need me."

"I hear you. Thanks, Jack."

It was dark when I hit the street, but the moon was reflecting off the icy patches in the streets and that seemed to brighten the night up a bit. There's no love lost between ice and snow and me, but if it wasn't for the ice I might have ended up having my head handed to me.

As I started toward Canal Street, a man with a neck like a turkey stepped out of a doorway with intentions of laying a jack against the back of my head, but his foot hit a patch of ice and went out from under him. The jack glanced off the point of my left shoulder as he went down. I saw the second man come from around the corner, where he had probably been waiting in case I went that way.

My arm had gone all but dead and useless, and if I stuck around there was still a good chance of getting badly hurt, since they obviously were not there to play games. I stepped in and kicked the man who had gone down while he was trying to get back to his feet. He grunted as the point of my shoe dug into his ribs, and then I turned and ran, hoping that I wouldn't encounter a treacherous patch of ice before I reached Canal Street.

I heard the second man stop briefly by his fallen comrade, which gave me the head start I needed to reach Canal without being caught—and then, miracle of miracles, I saw a cab that had probably come off the bridge from Brooklyn and was looking for an uptown fare.

"Go," I said, jumping into the back seat.

"Where?" the driver asked lazily.

"Just move. I'm being chased by a couple of muggers."

He peered out the window in the direction I had come and said, "I got a piece, mac. You wanna take them out?"

"I want you to get moving, dammit!"

"Okay, okay," he said, pulling away from the curb. "Geez," he muttered, "try an' help some people."

Once we were underway I gave him the address of Bogie's and sat back, trying to massage some feeling back into my left arm.

"They get anything?"

"Just keep driving," I said, testily. What I didn't need was a talkative cabbie.

What the hell was that about, I wondered. *Was* it simply an attempted robbery, or something else? Another try at bouncing me off a couple of walls?

I didn't think it was connected with that had happened to Hank Po and myself—that guy didn't need a jack, or help—so I was left with two possibilities. A mugging, or an attempt to get me off Knock Wood Lee's case.

By Leo Piperneski? Asking him wouldn't be the easiest thing in the world to do, but I was going to give it a shot.

## — *twenty-five*

"Pipersneski?" Hocus asked.

"No," I said, correcting him, "neski, Piperneski. It's a Polish name."

"No shit?"

I had presented myself at the Seventeenth Precinct early that morning and offered to take Hocus out for breakfast.

"What did you have in mind?"

"Ham and eggs and . . . information."

"For me or *from* me?"

"For you, of course."

"Let's go."

He took me to a small coffee shop on Third Avenue where an elderly waitress greeted him by name.

"Why haven't you ever taken me here before?" I asked, running my finger over the booth seat before sitting.

"You never offered to pay before. It's not the cleanest place in the world, but the food's good."

He was right, the food was very good, and came in large portions. The money they saved on appearances obviously went into the food.

Over breakfast I told him what I had found out about Leo Piper.

"Where did you get this information?"

"Sources," I said, "well-informed sources."

"And what do you want in return?"

"In return?"

"Jacoby, stop pulling my prick, I'm trying to eat breakfast."

"All right. I'd like to know what the police in Brooklyn have on the name Piperneski, or Leo DeGuere."

"From eight years ago?"

"Or more."

"And what if there is something?"

This was dicey.

"I don't want you to tell them that you know where he is."

"Oh?"

"I need something I can use on him, Hocus. When I'm through with him you can have him."

He finished chewing what was in his mouth and washed it down with a sip of coffee.

"You're crazy."

"Why?"

"You want me to make an official request for information and then not act on it?"

I shrugged and said, "So make it an unofficial request."

"And what if there are no outstanding warrants on him?"

"I'll have to try something else."

"What are you up to, Jack?"

"I can't tell you the whole story, Hocus. You'll have to ask Heck Delgado . . . after we've cleared Knock Wood Lee."

"Are you that sure of his innocence?"

"Yes," I said. "I'm as sure of his innocence as I was of

my brother's when you arrested him for killing Eddie Waters."

Hocus frowned, looking uncomfortable, and waved the waitress over. She freshened his coffee and then did the same for mine when I nodded.

"Well?" I asked when she left.

"I don't know why I should—" he started, then stopped and sipped his coffee. "All right, I'll see what I can do. If there's nothing on paper I might know someone with . . . a long memory."

"I appreciate it."

"You're going to owe me a big one for this, Jack."

"What?" I asked, pretending to be surprised. "Breakfast doesn't cover it?"

"Not hardly!"

I paid the check and walked him back to the precinct.

"What's happening with the Saberhagen case?"

He looked uncomfortable again.

"It's not going too well. We haven't been able to come up with anything."

"Did you question her . . . friends . . . at the institute?"

"Yeah, we questioned everybody, and now we're going to question them again."

"Before you mark it inactive."

He shrugged.

"If I had the time . . ."

"Forget it," he said when he saw that I wasn't going to continue. "You've got enough on your hands."

"Yeah."

He started inside and then turned back.

"What was that other name again?"

"DeGuere."

"Right, and Pipersneski?"

"Neski," I said, "Piperneski."

I had awakened that morning with a gorgeous bruise on the point of my left shoulder, and a problem raising the arm above shoulder level. I took a hot shower and four aspirin, and called the precinct to make sure that Hocus was going to be in that morning. After that I made some calls and started the word going around that I was looking for a man named Piperneski. If that didn't draw Leo Piper out, nothing would.

I admit that my spur of the moment decision may not have been a good one, especially when I thought about Tiger Lee. It wouldn't take Leo Piper two seconds to figure out how I found out his real name.

Ray Carbone was a friend of mine who had just retired from the ring himself at age thirty-five. Actually, much as in my case, he was "retired" during his last fight. Never a top ten fighter, Ray was always the man that managers put their boys in with when they wanted them to have a "tough" fight. He was also ducked by a lot of fighters whose connections felt they weren't ready to get in with a banger like him. He was the most respected unranked middleweight—or fighter, for that matter—I ever knew.

And right now he was looking for work, so I decided to give him some.

"Ray, it's Miles Jacoby."

"Hey, Jack. How goes it?"

"I should ask you that."

"Ah, I just got to get used to it. You know how it is."

"Yeah, don't I. Need some work?"

"Doing what?"

"Looking after somebody."

"I ain't a headbuster, you know. I ain't looking for that kind of work."

"I know that. I'm not looking for a headbuster. I'm looking for somebody I can trust to look after someone who's a friend of mine."

"Like who?"

"You know Knock Wood Lee?"

"Sure. He's in the slammer, ain't he?"

"He is, but his lady isn't."

"The tiger lady?"

"Right."

"Somebody gonna bother her?"

"Somebody might try, Ray. I want you to make sure that they don't."

"Who's picking up the tab?"

"My client."

"Okay, Jack, you got yourself a boy. When do I start?"

"You know where they live?"

"Yeah, down on Mott."

"Well, get on over there and check in with me from time to time by phone."

"How long is this job gonna be for?"

"I'm not sure, Ray, but hopefully not very long. My client will go for fifty a day."

"Who's the client? The man in the can?"

"Can't say."

"Well, I'll take good care of her, Jack. She's a dish."

"Just make sure nobody breaks that dish."

"I hear ya."

With Lee covered, and Hocus doing some digging on Leo Piper, I went to my office to indulge in what Eddie used to call "a good think." He used to do it with bourbon, but I'm a new breed and I do it with coffee.

Most of my work on Wood's case so far had been with the other bookies that Alan Cross owed money. Out of that, an interest in Piper had been born. I still had not, however, delved into Cross's private life beyond his place of business. That made me think of his book, and I brought it out and put it on the desk next to my coffee container.

Leafing through it idly I wondered how I could get it to do me any good, since all it had were first names and phone numbers, and no addresses. I could have asked Hocus to check the numbers out for me through the phone company—and through official channels, of course—but he couldn't check them all, and how would I know which ones to have him check?"

The book was arranged alphabetically, and I glanced idly at names until I came to the page with names starting with

"F." I stopped short when I recognized one of the names, and then turned to the "G's." Both names were there, and the phone numbers were the same.

Fallon Dewitt and Ginger McKay were both in Alan Cross's book!

That revelation started a whirlwind of thoughts flashing through my mind. First, I had come into contact with both Fallon and Ginger during my search for Melanie Saberhagen. Now their names had shown up during my investigation in Knock Wood Lee's case. How could such a coincidence have occurred?

Also, now that their names had popped up, each had the skills to have beaten Cross to death, given the proper circumstances.

*Was* this a coincidence, or was it a legitimate connection between two seemingly unconnected murders?

I picked up the book and started to go through it page by page. I didn't have to go any farther than the "B's," though, before I came across another name I knew.

Brown.

Granted, it's not an uncommon name, but that's all it said, "Brown," with the phone number and those odd letter abbreviations after it.

I flipped through the rest of the book but I didn't find Greg, Dan, or J.C. I didn't find Melanie either, although I did find the name "Mel." There was no indication as to whether it was a male or a female, though.

I put the book down and picked up the phone. There was one other thing I wanted to check, which would blow the word "coincidence" right out of the water.

"The institute," a voice said, answering the phone.

"I'd like to speak to the director, please," I said to the woman.

"Who may I say is calling, please?"

"Tell him it's Miles Jacoby."

"Hold, please."

He came on the line a few moments later.

"I read about Melanie Saberhagen, Mr. Jacoby," he said, "if that is what you're calling to tell me."

Did I detect a hint of disapproval in his tone? I didn't have time to stop and wonder.

"I'm calling to ask you one question, sir, and the answer may be important both to the Melanie Saberhagen murder and another case I'm working on."

"I see. One question."

"Yes, sir."

"Very well, then. Ask it."

"I'm sure you've read about the murder of a man named Alan Cross over the past week."

"Yes," he said, thoughtfully, "but I believe they've made an arrest. It involved gambling, didn't it? They arrested a bookie, I believe."

"Yes, they did. Sir, my question is this. Was Alan Cross at any time a student at the institute?"

"Yes," he said, and I was surprised at how quickly he answered.

"Yes?"

"That is what I said, Mr. Jacoby. He was a student here at the institute."

"How long was he a student?"

"Three years. He was quite promising, too."

"I see. Up until what time was he a student?"

I knew I had gone past my one question limit, but it didn't seem to concern him, so I just steamrolled along.

"Up until the day he was killed, Mr. Jacoby," he said, stopping my steamroller right in its track.

So much for coincidence.

I thanked Bayard, hung up, and discovered that I was holding my breath. I let it out slowly and picked up Alan Cross's book.

What did it all mean now? At least three of the people I had met while looking for Melanie Saberhagen knew Alan Cross well enough to have their names and phone numbers in his book—whatever kind of book it was. Had Melanie been at the institute long enough to get to know Cross? Was she the "Mel" in his book?

I turned the pages of his book again to the "M's" and looked at the phone number next to the name "Mel." I didn't recognize it, but nobody was going to call *me* and tell me whose it was, so I picked up the phone and dialed it.

She said "Hello," and all of her bitterness managed to come out in that one word.

It was Ida Saberhagen's telephone number.

## — *twenty-six* —

I was unsure of what to make of—or do with—all the new information I had in my hands now, so I decided to go over to the hospital and bounce it off Hank Po to see what he thought of it.

He listened patiently, thankful for the reprieve from boredom, and then said, "It sounds confusing enough but I think all you really need is to go over it again, step by step."

"Are you volunteering to listen?"

"Am I in a position to do anything else?"

"Okay, then," I said, standing and beginning to pace as I spoke, trying to get matters into the right perspective.

"On the one hand I'm hired to find Melanie Saberhagen and on the other hand, I take on the task of clearing Knock Wood Lee of the charge of murdering a man named Alan Cross." I stopped and scratched my head. "This is silly. I'm making it harder than it should be. The simple fact of the matter is that there was never any reason to believe that these cases were connected, and now certain connections have arisen that can't be denied."

"The connections being that Alan Cross knew some of the people at the institute, was in fact a student at the institute himself, and may have even known Melanie Saberhagen."

"Who is now also dead, killed in a similar fashion."

"Well, there's a connection, all right, you can't deny that."

"The question is, what do I do about it?"

"Give it to the cops."

"I thought you'd say that. Give it to Hocus, huh?"

"Or Vadala. He's got Wood's case."

"Yeah, but he's not *working* on it. At least Hocus is working on the girl's murder . . . if he hasn't marked the case inactive by now."

"Or you could work on it yourself and wait until you have something more concrete to take to Hocus. If you give Hocus something he can sink his teeth into, he'd talk to Vadala and Vadala would have to listen."

"We all know he'd never listen to me."

"Well, you'll have to make up your mind, Jack."

"I think I had it made up already, Hank. Talking to you has just clinched it."

"You're going to work on it?"

"How'd you know?"

"I know you," he said, "and it's what I would have done."

"I'll talk to the girls first," I said, thinking out loud, "especially Fallon. She's the smarter one, and she seems to have a relationship with Brown."

"Watch Brown, Jack," Hank said, warningly.

"I'll watch him. I think my priority might be to find out just what kind of book this is," I said, taking the book from my pocket.

"Can I see that?"

"Sure," I said, handing it him, "maybe you can figure out what it all means."

I watched him while he leafed through the book, waiting for a light bulb to appear over his head, but ultimately he frowned and handed it back to me.

"Beats me."

"Wait a minute, maybe we can dope this out together," I

said, leafing through the book myself. "You ever see abbreviations like this before?"

"They're either abbreviations, or some kind of code," Hank said. "Either way, I've never seen them before."

"Well then, what kinds of people keep a book like this?"

He shrugged and said, "Bachelors?"

"That's got to be out. This is more than just a guy's little black book. He's got guys' names in here."

"So maybe he swung both ways."

"Brown strike you as that type?"

"No."

"Me neither," I said. "So who else?"

"Prostitutes?"

"You trying to tell me Cross was hooking on the side and this was his trick book?"

"No good, huh?"

"I think maybe you're getting a headache."

He touched the bandage on his head and said, "You know, I think you're right."

I put the book away in my pocket and said, "Let me get out of here and let you rest. Thanks for listening."

"I'm sorry I couldn't help more. Maybe when I get out—"

"When you get out of here you'll still have a lot of resting to do." I started for the door and said, "I'll keep you posted."

"Do that . . . and don't forget to watch out for Brown. More and more I'm starting to believe that he's the guy who did a number on us. He's a bad dude, Jack."

"Hey, when I was fighting, I was pretty bad too, you know."

"Yeah," he said as I left, "that's what I heard."

# — twenty-seven

My next move was going to require a lot of patience. In the ring I was the kind of fighter who constantly applied pressure, trying to make something happen. Outside the ring, I had little more patience than I'd had inside, but this time I was going to have to make an effort.

I rented a car and parked it illegally across the street from the apartment shared by Fallon and Ginger. I took up position in a deep doorway and proceeded to keep my eyes on the front door of their apartment building. What I wanted was to catch Fallon when she was alone and see how she stood up under some pressure. There had to be something she could tell me about Alan Cross, otherwise why would her name be in his book?

I had been in position about an hour when Ginger left the building. I waited for her to turn a corner, and when she did I crossed the street, entered the lobby, and rang the apartment bell. There was no answer. Either Fallon wasn't in or she wasn't answering the bell.

I left the lobby and found a pay phone. When I dialed their phone number and no one answered after a dozen rings, I chose to believe that the apartment was empty, and went back to my doorway.

Ginger came back an hour later, stayed for under an hour, and left again, and there was still no sign of Fallon. After four hours I was starting to lose my patience, but I remembered stories Eddie used to tell me about hour-long, day-long, sometimes even week-long stakeouts. Eddie was a very patient man, just one of the attributes that made him an excellent detective. It was the lack of patience that would probably keep me from ever being as good.

I decided I'd give it until the end of the day and then try something else.

Ginger came back again and left in under an hour again, but this time she was dressed to stay out. I was amazed that she had been able to get changed that quickly.

It was about a half an hour after Ginger left that final time that Fallon showed up. A car pulled up in front of the building and I could see the driver's face clearly.

It was Brown.

Fallon's face wasn't clear to me, but I recognized her by

her profile. She got out of the car, kept her back to me, and entered the building. I waited for Brown to pull away and disappear before I left my doorway and crossed the street. Too late I realized I should have gotten his plate, but it was probably too dark.

This time when I rang the bell there was an immediate buzz, which unlocked the door. She must have thought it was Brown coming back.

I rapped the door with my knuckles once and it swung open before I could hit it again.

"Brownie, I knew you wouldn't—" she started, but she stopped short when she saw me.

"Tell me what it is. I probably wouldn't, either."

"You!"

She had a fresh bruise alongside her left eye and I was amazed that her delicate bones were able to stand up so well to Brown's fists. She was wearing tight jeans and a yellow sweatshirt.

"Me," I said, stepping past her and inside before she could try to shut the door in my face.

"What do you want?"

I turned to face her and said, "Well, you could try shutting the door for starters."

She glared at me for a moment, then defiantly slammed the door shut, as if showing me that she wasn't afraid to.

"Brown is going to be here any minute. He'll take you apart."

"I doubt it. He just dropped you off, so I don't think he'll be coming back so soon. As for him taking me apart, that's been tried before by professionals."

"That's right. You were a boxer once, weren't you?"

Without giving me a chance to answer she threw a roundhouse kick at my head. It hit me high on the right side of the head, hard enough to knock me off balance. By the time I regained it she had removed her tight jeans and was bouncing around on the balls of her feet.

"Come on, fighter," she said tauntingly. "Let's see what you've got."

Underneath the sweatshirt she was wearing nothing but a pair of powder blue panties. Her small, firm breasts bobbed up and down as she moved around, waiting for me to come to her.

"Honey, you're out of your weight classification."

"We'll see."

She had a cocky grin on her face, which looked odd against the backdrop of that bruise.

"Honey—"

"Don't call me that."

"You don't like it?"

"I'm not your honey."

"Is that a fact . . . honey?"

She lost her temper, something you should never do when you're in the ring.

She moved toward me and threw another kick, but I anticipated the move and ducked under it. Reaching up I grabbed hold of her ankle and yanked, pulling her other leg out from under her. She fell to the floor with her cute little butt making an audible thud, and I stepped back.

"Come on, honey," I said, taunting her now, "let's see what *you've* got."

She got to her feet and started to rub her behind, but pulled her hands away when she realized what she was doing. Still angry, she charged me again. She threw a front kick instead of a roundhouse, and I blocked it the way Billy had taught me, crossing my forearms in front of me. When her ankle banged into my arms I reversed my right hand, grabbed her ankle again and dumped her back on her ass.

"Ooh," she cried angrily, and leaped back to her feet. She charged at me, throwing two quick roundhouse kicks, both of which I ducked under, but then she surprised me. Kicking low, she knocked my legs out from under me. As I hit the floor on my back she leaped on top of me. Forgetting her karate training she tried to rake my face with her nails, but I succeeded in grabbing her wrists in time to save my skin.

144

"Damn you," she said, bringing her knees up to crush my nuts, but I moved in time to avoid that, too.

Locked together now we rolled over on the floor a few times, knocking over a table and a lamp, and when we came to a stop she was on top again. There was a change in her, though. No longer was she trying to rip my face, now she was trying to rip my clothes.

The coupling was violent, just the way she obviously liked it. I had never experienced anything like it before, and it left me feeling exhausted, exhilarated, . . . and just a little bit dirty.

"Is that the only way you can get off?" I asked, when most of our clothes were back in order. She hadn't put her jeans back on, so I kept alert for another attack—of either sort.

"I didn't notice you complaining," she said, picking up the table and lamp we'd knocked over. That done, she faced me with her hands on her hips and said, "Tell the truth, Jacoby, you never had it so good."

"I've never had anything quite like it," I said, "but I wouldn't say I've never had it so good."

"Bullshit!" she said, dropping her hands and adopting a belligerent pose.

"You start throwing kicks at me again and I'll do more than dump you on your butt."

"What do you want?"

"I want to talk about Alan Cross."

"Cross? Not Miss Melanie Bitch?"

"She's dead."

"What?" she asked, and her shock appeared genuine.

"She was beaten to death, just like Alan Cross."

All the fight seemed to go out of her and she sat down heavily on the couch.

"What do you want from me?"

"I want to know what was going on with Alan Cross, Fallon. What got him and Melanie Saberhagen killed?"

"Who says there's a connection between the two deaths?"

"They knew each other, didn't they? They were both students at the institute."

"They met, sure, but that doesn't mean they knew each other."

"Then what was her name doing in his book?"

"What book?"

"The same book you, Ginger, and your friend Brown have your names in," I said, producing the book.

She frowned at the book in my hand and then her eyes widened as if something had suddenly frightened her.

"What kind of book is this, Fallon? And what do these abbreviations after each name mean?"

"I don't know."

"There's an awful lot of letters after your name, Fallon." I opened the book and started to read them off. "B, 3W—oh, here's and interesting one: LOWG. What does that mean?"

"How do I know?"

"I think you do know," I said, moving closer to the couch so that I was hovering over her. "Wouldn't you like to find out who killed Cross and Melanie?"

"I don't care," she said, sullenly, "Leave me alone."

Things hadn't gone quite the way I'd planned them. I was afraid that if I tried to pressure her further, or even knock it out of her, we'd end up rolling on the floor again. I didn't think my back could take it.

"All right, Fallon," I said, putting the book away. I took out my business card and almost wrote Bogie's number on the back when I remembered that she had called me there once. That was another question I wanted the answer to, strictly to appease my own curiousity.

"Call me," I said, handing it to her, "here or at that other number."

"What other number?"

I stared at her and she said, "Oh, that number."

146

"Would you like to tell me where you got that other number from?"

"I can't," she said, prodding her lower lip with the corner of my card. She looked frightened and said again, "I can't."

"Are you afraid of Brown?"

She didn't respond.

"Did he do that to you?" I asked, pointing to the bruise. Her hand flew up to touch it, and then she nodded.

"For fun? Or does being a punching bag turn you on, too?"

She closed her eyes and said, "Would you please leave?"

"Sure, Fallon, I'll leave, but call me when you feel like talking. Whatever you're into, you're too smart to get into it any deeper."

I walked to the door and opened it, then turned back to look at her.

"Tell your friend Brown I'll be talking to him."

She looked up at me and said, "He'll kill you."

It might have been ego, or it might have been that it was the only decent exit line I could think of.

"You mean, he'll try," I said, and left.

While I was hoping that Fallon would have second thoughts and call me, there was no way I could count on it. That left either Ginger or Brown, and that left tomorrow. It was late and I was still feeling . . . wrung out from my session with Fallon, and on top of that, the scratches on my back were itching the hell out of me. I could feel the shirt sticking to them.

I crossed the street to my rented car and drove it back to Bogie's. It had been something of a wasted expense and it occurred to me then that I could have used it to follow Brown and brace him instead of Fallon.

Did I have the beatings he'd administered to me and Hank Po in the back of my mind when I decided to let him go and talk to Fallon? No, I told myself, that wasn't it. My plan all along had been to talk to Fallon. The car had simply been a precaution. If she had driven off in a cab, I would have been able to follow her, but she had made it easy for me—or so I'd thought.

Business was light at Bogie's that time of night, with only the diehard regulars still around. I unzipped my coat and walked to the bar, where Billy was. The jukebox was playing "Key Largo."

"You look like you had a rough day," he said.

"The day wasn't bad, but the evening was a bitch."

"You want a drink?"

I considered it for a moment and then said, "I guess I could take a bottle of beer into the back with me."

He nodded and produced a bottle of St. Pauli Girl. As I reached for it my shirt gaped open, reminding me that I had lost most of the buttons.

"What happened to your shirt?" Billy asked.

The man on the next stool, a regular named Warren, looked at my shirt and asked, "What happened, couldn't she wait?"

"Pal," I said, taking my beer, "you don't know the half of it."

"Key Largo" was starting up again as I left.

The phone was ringing when I got into the back office, but I ignored it and sipped my beer as I undressed. A few moments later the intercom sounded.

"Yes?"

It was Billy.

"Jack, the call is for you. It's a girl."

"Thanks, Billy."

"You want anything from the kitchen before we shut it down?"

"No—oh, yes, okay. Maybe just a sandwich. Whatever's easy."

"You got it. I'll send it back."

"Thanks."

Was the girl on the phone Fallon? Had she come to her senses already?

"Hello?"

"Miles Jacoby?" It wasn't Fallon, but whoever it was sounded very nervous.

"Yes?"

"This is Ginger. You know, Fallon's friend?"

"Yes, Ginger, I know who you are. What's wrong?"

"I have to talk to you."

"Go ahead."

"Not on the phone."

"I'll come there—"

"Not here, either," she said quickly, "and I can't come there. After what you told Fallon tonight—we have to meet somewhere."

"Are you all right, Ginger?"

"I'm just scared, that's all. Fallon is too, but she's too scared to talk to you. I'm not."

"Where should we meet?"

She thought a moment and then said, "Oh, I don't know. I don't know where it's safe."

"Usually where there's people," I said. "Why don't we meet at the institute?"

"The others will be there."

"Are you afraid of them?"

"Of course not. They're not—"

"They're not what?"

"I—not on the phone."

"All right, Ginger."

"I'll see you tomorrow evening."

"Will you be all—" I started to ask, but she had already hung up.

So, the visit to Fallon hadn't been wasted. It hadn't loosened her tongue, but maybe Ginger would have enough to tell me for both of them.

There was a knock on the door and, thinking it was Billy, I wasn't bothered about being in my underwear. I called out, "Come in."

Alison came in carrying a sandwich and a cup of coffee

on a tray. She stopped short when she saw me, but didn't appear embarrassed.

"I'm starting to get sick of 'Key Largo,'" she said, walking forward and putting the tray down on the desk.

Trying to be cool, I picked up my pants from the bed, but she said, "Oh, don't on my account, I'm just leaving."

She turned and started for the door, but she couldn't hold it in any longer and started laughing just before she left.

What a nice girl.

While eating my sandwich I took out Cross's book and looked at both Fallon's and Ginger's entries. I found myself comparing the letters that accompanied each of their names. Fallon's entry read: "Fallon, C, B, SM, 3W, LOWG." Ginger's read: "C, LOWF." Why were there so many next to Fallon's name, and so few next to Ginger's? And why were the final entries similar, except for the last letter?

I finished the sandwich, beer, and coffee without figuring it out, and tried to go to sleep.

## — *twenty-eight* —

I had a restless night. I kept dreaming that I went to meet Ginger and that she and Fallon beat the shit out of me and left me lying helpless on the floor. At that point in the dream Brown always came walking in. It was one of those half asleep/half awake twilight type dreams that keeps repeating itself, and finally I staggered out of bed and took a cold shower to wake myself up.

Over breakfast in a coffee shop I realized that the dream meant that I was subconsciously aware that Ginger might have been setting me up. Still, if that were the case, she wouldn't have let me name the meeting place, right?

I got to my office early, but there was already a message on my answer machine.

It was from Leo Piper.

150

"You're doing it again," his voice said, "and I don't like it. Call me at this number," and then he rattled off a number and hung up.

I picked up the phone and dialed the number right away. When a man answered I said, "Piper."

"Who wants—"

"Let me talk to Piperneski!"

The phone went dead, and then Piper came on the line, madder than hell.

"Stop using that name!"

"You don't like that name, huh?"

"I don't like the name, and I don't like you."

"Well, you can change your name, pal, but you can't change me. You tried that once, but your muscle failed. You should teach them to watch out for ice spots."

"I see," he said. "I think we should talk."

"Going to have another limo take me to a mystery bookstore?"

"No," Piper said. He had taken control of himself again and now he said, "We'll have lunch."

"How civilized."

"Do you know a restaurant called Goings On?"

"Yes." I certainly did know the place. It was owned by Carl Caggiano, Jr. I'd had lunch with him there once, and the food was very good.

"Meet me there today at one."

At one o'clock the place would be mobbed with the lunch crowd and there wasn't much chance that he'd try something. I wondered if he knew who owned the place, and then decided that he must.

"All right. I'll meet you there."

He hung up.

That made two meetings set for that day, and I hoped that they would both make things much clearer to me.

I took out Cross's book again, which was fast becoming the bane of my existence, and leafed through it for the millionth time. I turned to the "B's" and examined the letters next to Brown's name: S, B, SM, 3W. It looked familiar, and when I checked Fallon's and Ginger's entries I found out why. It was almost identical to Fallon's, except for the last group of hers, the "LOWG." And how did that differ from the "LOWF" next to Ginger's name?

I looked at some of the other female entries, and although there were many with "L" next to their names, none had any with "LOW" in them. The only thing that I could think of was that the "G" in "LOWG" stood for "Ginger" and the "F" in "LOWF" for Fallon, but that didn't help me figure out the rest.

I put the book away in frustration and starting sorting through my mail. Bills weren't all that much easier to figure out, but at least I knew what to do with them.

I left my office at twelve-thirty, but I called Hocus first, to find out if he'd found anything on Leo Piperneski from Brooklyn.

"I've got an old rap sheet, but it's petty stuff, the kind of thing you'd expect from a street kid. The biggest thing they ever got him for was running some girls."

"Anything on the girls he might have been working with?" I was worried that Lee's name might turn up.

"No, nothing. I've got a friend who remembers Piperneski as a tough kid with brains. He said he thought the kid might be able to drag himself off the streets."

"Well, I guess he did."

"There's nothing here you can use, Jack. Sorry."

"Thanks for the shot. I've got to ask you one more thing, though."

He sighed and said, "What now?"

"You still keeping tabs on Caggiano?"

"Which one?"

"Both of them."

"They're not in my department."

"I know that."

Hocus had a relationship with Caggiano Sr. years ago, while working undercover. He had gained the old man's affection and respect, and still held the latter. Also, he didn't get along with Caggiano Jr. very well. Carl Jr. had been jealous of the affection the old man had once had for the detective. Jr. and Sr. had never been on the best of terms.

"Yes, I'm still . . . aware of their business."

"Has Cagey Carl had any dealings with Piper that you know of?"

"Piper eats at Goings On occasionally, but I'm not aware of any business dealings between them. Why? What do you know?"

If I had anything on the Caggianos, Hocus would expect me to give it to him, and I didn't disappoint him.

"I'm meeting Piper at Cagey Carl's restaurant for lunch."

"Who set that up?"

"Piper."

"You want some backup?"

"If you showed up there it would create a lot of tension."

"I know."

"I think there'll be enough of that as it is, but thanks for the offer."

"Just be careful. You're not on Carl's list of top ten friends, either."

"Oh, really?" I asked. "I didn't know he had that many."

As I was about to leave the phone rang, and I grabbed it instead of letting the machine pick it up.

"Jacoby."

"It's me, Ray."

"Is everything all right, Ray?"

"Fine, as far as I can see. She's home and I'm calling from a phone across the street."

"Have you spotted anyone around?"

"No."

"Has she spotted you?"

"I don't know. Maybe."

"All right, Ray. Keep me posted, will you?"

"You're the boss."

At least Lee was all right. After I spoke with Piper, I might be able to pull Ray off.

I turned the answering machine back on and left.

As luck would have it the first person I saw when I entered the restaurant was Cagey Carl himself.

"Jacoby," he said. He had been playing host, talking to some people at a table, and had turned around just as I walked in.

"Hello, Carl," I said. "I heard you got married. Congratulations. My invitation must have been lost in the mail."

"Like hell," he said. "What are you doing here?"

"Having lunch with a . . . business acquaintance. Maybe you know him? Leo Piper?"

"Piper? Yeah, I know him. You a friend of his?"

I shook my head.

"Like I said, a business acquaintance. Is he here yet?"

"He's here," he said, and he didn't look very happy about it. "I'll have a waiter take you to his table. Do me a favor, will you?"

Surprised I said, "What?"

"Since you're here, and I don't make a habit of refusing to serve people, order something expensive."

"Sure, Carl. Anything to help a friend in need."

He waved a waiter over who took me to Piper's table on the second level, which overlooked the first.

"Jacoby," Piper said as I pulled out the chair across from him. "Thanks for coming."

"This is on you, I hope. I don't make a habit of eating here."

"I do," he said, smugly. "I guess it would exceed your means."

"Personally, I'd prefer Nathan's in Coney Island," I said, watching his face, "but as a Brooklyn boy, you'd probably feel the same way."

"Well, I don't," he said, tightly. He made a visible effort to control his emotions and said, "You've been talking to Lee, haven't you?"

154

"Yes."

"I was afraid of that."

"Why? There's nothing on Leo Piperneski but an old rap sheet filled with kid's stuff."

"That's true."

"Is that why you had your two—friends—pay me a visit outside her place the other night?"

He stared at me for a moment and said, "All right, I'll admit that was a mistake. I'll even apologize for it."

"That's big of you."

"But you've got to stop spreading my . . . my real name around. I've had my name changed legally to Piper, and that's all I want to be called."

"Fine with me," I said. "Can we order now? You did invite me to lunch, didn't you?"

"Yes, I did," he said.

I did as Carl had asked and ordered something expensive, partly because I didn't eat that well often, but also to make Piper dig deeper into his pocket than he might have wanted to.

Over coffee he said, "What do you want from me, Jacoby? What do I have to give you to keep you from broadcasting my name all over town?"

I studied him for a few moments, then put my coffee cup down.

"For starters, I don't want anyone to touch Tiger Lee."

"I never had any intention—"

"You never intended to use muscle on me either, remember?"

"All right," he said. "No one will go near her." He shook his head then and started to laugh. "Whoever would have thought that little Anna Lee from Brooklyn would become Tiger Lee."

"She did."

"Yeah, I suppose she did. She was always better than everyone else I knew back then. You won't believe this, but she's the only thing I missed when I left."

"You should have stayed away, then. That would have been the best thing you could do for her."

"I had to come back, Jacoby. You wouldn't understand that. You've never been to Cincinnati, have you?"

"No."

"This is the only place to be," he said, meaning New York. "And if I'm going to be here I want to be in control."

"You can't control Lee."

"I did once," he said, "but I know I can't anymore. Don't worry, I won't bother her."

"Good."

"Is that all?"

"Not quite. I want to know if you had anything to do with killing Alan Cross."

"I told you before, I don't kill for pennies."

"I'll take that as a no, Piper," I said, standing up.

"What about—"

"Leo Piperneski?" I finished for him, and he winced at the mention of the name. "As long as I don't find out you lied to me, Leo, he'll stay dead. Thanks for the lunch."

## — twenty-nine

Goings On was on West Seventy-fifth Street and West End Avenue, while the institute was on East Eighty-third Street and Lexington. Although my meeting with Ginger wasn't for another two and a half hours, I walked up to Eighty-sixth Street and took a crosstown bus.

I killed some time over coffee and the sports pages of the *News* and *Post*, and walked into the institute half an hour early for our meeting. To my surprise, Bayard was expecting me.

"Mr. Jacoby, I'm glad you've come in early," he said, approaching me.

"Really? Why is that?"

"I have a message for you."

"From whom?"

"Ginger McKay. Would you care to step into my office?" he asked, and then went that way without waiting for an answer. I had no choice but to follow.

When we were in his office with the door closed I asked, "Is anything wrong?"

"Not that I know of. Miss McKay called and asked me to tell you that she would not be here tonight."

I didn't like the sound of that.

"We had an appointment," I said, and the dismay was obvious in my voice.

"Has this to do with your work?"

"Yes, it has."

"I suspected as much. The young lady sounded very agitated."

"Do you know who she is?"

"I believe so. Isn't she the young lady who is built a little more, er, pneumatically than is common with our students?"

"Delicately, but correctly put."

"She's actually quite good, considering . . ." he said.

"Sir, do you have any idea why she won't be here tonight?"

"I believe I do, yes. She and her friends will be attending the kick-boxing contests tonight at the Felt Forum. It's also been called full contact karate."

"I read about it. What makes you think she's going there? Did she say so?"

"Now that was odd," he said. "I had the feeling that she wanted to say that, but after she asked me to tell you she wouldn't be here, she hung up rather abruptly."

"Someone might have walked in on her."

"I see. Is this young lady in danger, Mr. Jacoby?"

"That's very possible."

"Well, her friend Mr. Foster was here earlier."

"Why?"

"Actually, he got the tickets for the fights from me," Bayard said, looking a bit sheepish. "I gave him five and assumed he would be accompanied by Mr. McCoy and Mr. Smith, and Miss McKay and Miss Dewitt."

"I see. I hope I can still get a ticket."

"I believe I can help you there," he said, opening one of his desk drawers. He took something out and handed it to me.

"I know some people and usually get tickets for my better students. I'm sorry this one is not in sequence with theirs."

Under other circumstances, I might have been flattered, but in this case I knew better.

"Thank you," I said, tucking the ticket away in my shirt pocket, "now all I've got to do is find them among twenty thousand or so people."

"Then I would suggest you get there early and catch them going in."

"Good point," I said, and it was my turn to look sheepish. "Thank you for your help, Mr. Bayard."

"That's quite all right," he said. "I've never had the opportunity to aid a private eye before."

I was surprised at both his words and the animation that showed on his normally placid face.

"If you have an opportunity," he said, then, "try and pay special attention to the featured bouts tonight."

"Why?"

"Jean-Yves Theriault is really quite amazing," he said, "but in particular I would like you to watch the PKA junior featherweight champion, Yoel Judah."

Having just killed time reading the sports page, I realized what he meant.

"He's the ex-prize fighter who turned to kick-boxing."

"And became a champion," Bayard added. "Keep that in mind, will you?"

"I will," I said, feeling slightly puzzled. Was he trying to tell me what I thought he was?

"Then come and see me," he said, as he had said once before, and I knew that he and I had some serious talking to do when I was done with this case.

The kick-boxing card was scheduled to start at 8:00 P.M. I got to Madison Square Garden early and wandered the lobbies, trying to decide how to play it. When Ginger, Fallon, and the others arrived, would it be better for me to trail them to their seats, or approach them immediately? How would Foster, McCoy, and Smith react to seeing me after what Fallon must have told them . . . or had she told them anything?

As it turned out, all my scheming was for naught. I ran into someone I knew, and after a short conversation I turned and literally walked into Ginger and her group.

"Jack!" she said, or she may have been on the verge of saying "Jacoby," but my reaction to seeing her surprised even me, and that was all she was able to get out before I grabbed her and kissed her on the mouth. She tensed for a moment, but then melted into my arms as if she understood what I was trying to convey to the others.

When we broke the kiss I kept my arm around her waist; her friends' reactions surprised me.

"Hello, Miles," Greg Foster said, putting his hand out to be shaken. "Haven't seen you in a while."

"I've been busy."

The look on his face, and the faces of Smith and McCoy, said that they had some idea who'd been keeping me busy. Fallon, on the other hand, had not reacted at all, aside from tightening her mouth.

"Let's all sit together," J.C. Smith suggested.

"Well, to tell you the truth," I said, "I'm kind of here unexpectedly, and I'd really like to sit with Ginger . . . if you all don't mind, that is."

"Hey," Foster said, "why should we mind, right?"

Smith and McCoy nodded, while Fallon maintained her silence.

"Thanks," I said. "Enjoy the card."

"We will," Foster said. "You two enjoy yourselves, too."

I waved, and propelled Ginger away from them. I turned

back once and found the three men in deep conversation, all of them smiling, while Fallon glared after us, tight-lipped.

"That was quick thinking," Ginger said, and I was actually surprised at how quickly she had reacted. "How did you know I'd be here? I didn't have time to tell the director where I'd be."

"He figured it out."

"Thank God," she said, leaning hard against me in relief. "When Greg told me he had these tickets I didn't want to arouse suspicion."

"Are you afraid of him?"

"Not him, or the others," she said, "but I thought Brown was going to be here!"

"Let's find some seats."

"Are we going to stay?"

"Aren't there enough people around to make you feel safe?"

"I suppose."

A few bucks to an usher got us two seats together, even though our tickets were some numbers apart.

As we sat down I could feel the tension returning to her body, and said, "Ginger, try to relax. You're safe here."

"As long as Brown doesn't show up."

"Actually, Brown isn't really the one I want to talk about."

"I know," she said, looking down at her hands, "you want to talk about Alan Cross."

"That's right."

"Cross and Brown were tight while Brown was at the institute," she said. "Even after Brown left, he worked for Cross."

"Worked for Cross? Doing what?"

"Putting pressure on people, beating people up—"

"Wait a minute," I said, stopping her short. "Alan Cross was in the advertising business."

"That was his regular job."

"He had a sideline?"

"It was more than a sideline," she said, "much more."

160

"Ginger, do you want to tell me what kind of sideline we're talking about?"

"I guess I should."

"If you don't, then there wasn't much point to our meeting, was there?"

"I suppose not."

The initial match was coming to a close as one fighter closed in on his opponent for the kill. The crowd was shouting for blood, and Ginger had to shout so that I could hear her answer.

"Movies!"

"What?"

"Cross was making movies!"

The hurt fighter went down and was counted out, and the crowd sat back to await the next bout.

"You said Cross was making movies?"

"Yes."

"You mean he was financing them?"

"Financing them, and casting them . . . with amateurs."

"Ginger," I said, thinking about Cross's book, "what kind of movies are we talking about here?"

"Porno movies," she said, leaning closer to me, "Cross was making porno movies."

Pornographic films.

Blue movies.

Fuck films.

Was that where Cross had been getting the money to gamble so heavily? Still, even if he was investing heavily in porno, were his returns really that large? He couldn't have been in business alone. He might have been only one of the investors but an investor who was actively involved in auditioning "actresses" for the films.

The book!

"Ginger, was that was Cross's book was all about?"

"Fallon told me that you showed her a book," she said, nodding. "That's what we figured. He must have been putting the names and phone numbers of the people he used in a book."

"That means—"

"Yes," she said, breaking in on me as if she wanted to say it herself, "that means that Fallon and I . . . if that book gets into the wrong hands, Jack . . . we never thought—it started out as . . . as fun—"

I stopped her before she could get so worked up that we attracted attention.

"All right, calm down," I said, taking her hand. "I have the book, so let's not start worrying about it getting into the wrong hands."

"Okay, I'm okay."

"Ginger, was Melanie Saberhagen's name in the book?"

"I don't know."

"There is an entry for someone named Mel," I said. "Could that have been her?" I knew it was, but I wanted to see how much she knew.

"Jack, I really don't know. I never noticed Cross and Melanie getting particularly close."

Then again, Melanie was younger than the others. Maybe Cross didn't want anyone to see them together.

"Ginger, why don't you relax for a while and watch the bouts," I said. "This is all new to me and I've got to think about it for a while."

"Okay."

The only problem was that I found it very difficult to juggle my thoughts with all of the activity that was going on around me, and then while both Theriault and Judah were in the ring I found myself enthralled in spite of myself.

Kick-boxing is a combination of karate and boxing, with rules in common as well as rules of its own. In addition to wearing boxing gloves the fighters wear foot pads covering the tops and sides of their feet, leaving the soles of the feet bare. The fighters are required to execute a minimum of eight above-the-waist kicks in each round. Failure to execute the minimum number of kicks results in a two-point penalty.

162

After the last feature bout, Ginger looked at me and said, "They were terrific."

"Yes, they were. Are you ready to go?"

"There are a couple more bouts."

"I'd like to go somewhere and talk. I can't concentrate here. I'd also like to avoid the crush on the way out."

Crowds tend to work two ways. You can be relatively safe in a crowd, but they also act as good cover for pickpockets and worse, especially when people are pressed together.

She seemed unsure about leaving and I said, "Don't worry about your friends, Ginger. We've got them convinced we don't need them around."

"Except for Fallon."

"You'll have to deal with Fallon later. You've made your decision to talk to me, don't start worrying about how she's going to feel."

She thought that over for a while, then nodded and said, "All right, let's go."

Once we left the Garden, I suggested we go to Bogie's.

"Fallon knows about that place."

"I know. She called me there. Who gave her the number? Brown?"

"Yes. He didn't like you, so he followed you there."

"I still think we should go there. Once we're inside I doubt that anything will happen."

Her look seemed to say, "What do we do until we get inside?" but she agreed and I hailed a cab even though it was an easy walk.

## — *thirty* —

As it turned out, Bogie's was a good place for us to talk. Ginger might have been scared, but that didn't do anything to damage her appetite. Luckily we made it just before the kitchen closed, and by the time Alison brought our food, we were virtually the last ones in the dining area.

"Will you be needing anything else?" Alison asked.

I looked past her to make sure there was still coffee on, and then said, "I don't think so, Alison. Thanks. I'm sorry if we kept you."

"You didn't keep me," she said, and walked away, untying her apron.

"Sorry," Ginger said.

"About what?"

"She's your girl, isn't she?"

"Alison?" I asked, surprised. "Whatever gave you that idea?"

"The way she's been looking at me."

"It's your imagination."

She shrugged and said, "If you say so. The food is really good here."

She had almost decimated her plate of lasagne, so I pushed mine across the table and said, "Help yourself."

"Mmm, thanks."

She polished that off, along with the basket of bread and breadsticks, and then I got up and poured us two cups of coffee, waving away Billy's help. He was behind the bar and busy enough with the late drinkers.

"Can we talk now?" I asked, setting her coffee in front of her. "I didn't want to talk while you ate."

"That would have been okay," she said. "Nothing ever seems to ruin my appetite. If I didn't exercise I'd be as fat as a house."

I took out Cross's book and put it on the table between us, and she stared at it as if it had sprouted spider's legs.

"Ginger, do you have any idea what the letters next to each name stand for?"

"Why, is it important?"

"Actually, I guess not," I said. It was something I was very curious about, but it really wasn't all that important.

She shook her head and said, "No, I don't. I've never

seen the book before today, and I only heard about it from Fallon last night."

"All right," I said. I picked up the book and put it back in my pocket, because it seemed to disconcert her. I wasn't completely convinced that she was telling the truth about it.

"Ginger, I need to find out some things about Cross."

"But he's dead."

"I know, but I'm trying to find out who killed him, and I think if I can do that I'll find out who killed Melanie, as well."

"I don't know that much about him."

"Then why did you want to talk to me?"

"I wanted to talk about Brown!"

"What about him?"

"I'm afraid of him."

"Because he's violent?"

"He's the one who . . . who recruited us, Fallon and me. Brown thinks he's hot shit with women and when he tried to hit on me I wasn't having any."

"But Fallon was different, huh?"

"I told you once before, she's got strange taste in men."

"You also said that about Melanie, if I remember correctly."

"She seemed to respond to him, too."

That made it a stronger likelihood that Melanie had also been used in some blue movies.

"This is starting to look more and more as if the same person killed both of them."

Her eyes widened and she said, "Do you think it was Brown?"

"I'm not jumping to conclusions, Ginger, but he does seem like the best bet, especially considering how they died."

"What about the man they arrested for killing Cross?"

"I think maybe he just happened along at the wrong time."

"You mean Brown framed him?"

"I mean *somebody* framed him," I said, correcting her. "When was the last time you saw Brown?"

"Fallon saw him last night."

"Yes, I saw him last night, too, when he brought her home. The police are looking for him to question him, and they don't seem to have had much luck. Is she seeing him willingly?"

"She was, but now I think she's just afraid of him."

"Do you think she knows where he is, or how to get in touch with him?"

"I don't know. I'd have to ask her."

"Do you think she'd tell you?"

"She's really afraid of Brown."

"What if we guarantee her protection?"

"Who's we?"

"I was thinking about the police."

"Fallon won't talk to the police, Jack. She's been busted a few times and she doesn't like cops."

"Busted for what?"

"Possession—small stuff," she was quick to add, "but enough to get her arrested. She also got arrested a couple of times for . . . hooking, but she hasn't done that in a long time."

"Is that how you got involved in the movie business, Ginger? Brown recruited Fallon, and Fallon recruited you?"

"Well, yeah. I mean, we're friends. There was a few bucks in it and she didn't really want to do it without me."

It occurred to me all of a sudden what the letters in the book probably referred to, and I wondered why I hadn't thought of it before. I decided not to bring the book up again, though. Not just then.

"Maybe we should go and talk to Fallon, Ginger. Just the two of us with no cops. Maybe you can get her to talk to me."

"She's really afraid of Brown," she said again.

"How afraid of Brown are you?"

She shrugged and said, "I'm here, ain't I? I guess we can give it a try."

\*　　\*　　\*

When Ginger went to the phone to call home and see if Fallon was there yet, Billy came over to the table.

"I know," I said before he could speak, "you're kicking us out, right?"

"The way that girl eats? I was just going to ask you to bring her here every night."

"If I did that I'd starve."

Ginger came back to the table and I introduced her to Billy. She complimented him on the food and he asked, "Would you like a drink on the house before you go?"

"Why yes, I would. Thank you."

She ordered a screwdriver and when Billy went to get it she said, "He's very nice."

"Yes, he is."

"What about Fallon?"

"She's not home yet. The fellas probably wanted to go for something to eat."

"Listen, Ginger, were Greg Foster and the others ever—"

"Involved with Alan Cross?"

"Right."

"No," she said, shaking her head, "in fact, they didn't like him very much."

"Did they know—"

"They didn't know what he was doing, and they didn't know what . . . we were doing. They just figured that we were both interested in the same guy."

"So then neither one of you is involved with any of the three of them?"

"Well . . . Fallon says she slept with Greg once, but it just never worked out. I think he still has a thing for her, but that's just my opinion. She says I'm crazy."

Billy brought Ginger her screwdriver and we stayed just long enough for her to finish it.

"Let's go back to your apartment anyway," I suggested, "we can be there when she gets back."

"What if the guys come up with her?" she asked, standing up.

"I don't think they'll be surprised to see me there, do you?"

Fallon still had not come home by the time we arrived and Ginger started to look worried.

"What could happen?" I asked. "She's with three brown belts in karate, and is a brown belt herself. Besides, why should something happen?"

"I don't know, it's just that two people I knew have been killed already, and my mother always said that things like that happen in threes."

"Do you have any coffee?" I asked, just to change the subject. Mothers will never know how the things they say stay with their children.

"I'll make a pot. Is decaffeinated all right?"

"Fine."

Ginger made the coffee, gave me a cup, and continued to putter around the small kitchenette looking for things to do that would keep her from looking at the clock.

She was putting a pot away when a key sounded in the lock and the door opened. Ginger turned violently, dropping the pot with a loud bang, and shouted at Fallon.

"Where have you been?"

"What—" Fallon started, and then stopped short when she saw me.

"We've been worried sick!"

Fallon looked at me and I said, "She's been worried sick. I've gone a few rounds with you, remember?"

"What kind of an act did you two think you were putting on?" she demanded, planting her hands on her hips.

"I thought it went over quite well," I said, looking at Ginger. "Didn't you, dear?"

"Oh, shut up!" Fallon said, slamming the door. "Is that coffee I smell?"

"Yes," Ginger said. "Do you want a cup?"

"Is it that decaffeinated shit?"

"Yes."

"Oh well, I'll have a cup anyway . . . after he leaves."

168

"I'm not planning on leaving just yet," I said, holding up my cup of coffee. "I haven't finished my cup, for one."

"And for two?"

I stood up and said, "For two, we have to talk."

"We've talked . . . and more."

"Well, this time I think we'll just talk, thank you," I said, and she frowned.

"What are you two babbling about?" Ginger asked, handing Fallon a cup of coffee.

"The last time we talked Fallon turned it into a sparring session," I said. Anything more than that she could hear about from Fallon—if indeed they hadn't already discussed it. Judging from what Ginger had told me about her, Fallon wasn't the type who balked at kissing and telling.

"What is it you want?" Fallon demanded.

"I told you, I want to talk."

"About what?"

"He wants to talk about Brown, Fal," Ginger said, "and I think you should talk to him."

"That's nonsense—"

"Stop being afraid of him."

"And that's more nonsense," Fallon said, putting her cup down on a coffee table with a bang, spilling a small portion of it.

"I'm going to take a shower," she said then, "and I'd appreciate it if you'd be gone when I came out."

She stalked into the next room. Ginger cleaned up the spill and then said, "I'll talk to her. Don't leave."

"I'm not."

Ginger went after her roommate and I could hear the sounds of their discussion even over the sound of the shower. Abruptly, when the water was turned off, the talking stopped, and Ginger came back into the room.

"I think she'll talk," she said, and went into the kitchenette.

A few moments later Fallon came out wearing a ter-rycloth robe belted at the waist, and using a towel to dry her hair.

"Ginger thinks I should talk to you," she said, sitting on the other end of the couch. "She says you think that Brown killed Cross and Melanie."

"I said it was a possibility."

"What do the police think?"

"The police are treating it as two separate cases. With Cross they think they've got their man. With Melanie's case, they're groping, but they are looking for Brown."

"To arrest him?"

"To question him."

"Then they haven't found a connection between the two murders?"

"Not that I know of, but then they aren't in the habit of confiding in private detectives."

She stopped rubbing her hair with the towel and held it in her lap.

"Can you see Brown as a killer, Fallon?" I asked.

"He's mean enough," she said without hesitation, "and strong enough."

"Why did he go after me that night, when you called me at Bogie's?"

"Why does he go after anyone? He gets mad."

"What did I do to get him mad?"

"You smiled at me and Ginger, or we smiled at you. It could have been either, take your pick."

"Does he think he owns you?"

"He doesn't own me," Ginger said. "I wouldn't let him touch me."

Fallon grinned a bit and said, "Ginger doesn't approve of some of my friends."

"Really? What about Melanie?"

"What about her?" Fallon asked with a frown.

"What kind of men friends did she have?"

"How would I know?"

"Did Brown go after her?"

"I wouldn't know that, either."

I decided to let that drop. A woman will talk about a lot of things before she'll talk about her own jealousies.

"Fallon, I want to talk to Brown. Do you know where he is?"

"No," she said immediately. "Ever since the police talked to him he hasn't gone back to his apartment."

"And you don't know where he's staying?"

"No."

"Excuse me for asking, but where have you two been . . ."

"In hotels, but we haven't . . . seen each other all that much lately."

"Do you want to see him?"

"No."

"If you did would you know how to get in touch with him?"

"No," she said, but this time it was preceded by a small moment of hesitation.

"Fallon," Ginger said.

"All right," she said. "He gave me a number, but it's an answering service."

"An answering service?" What would he be doing with an answering service? Would he go to that expense just so Fallon could call him when she wanted to?

"Fallon, has Brown taken over Cross's business?"

Fallon threw Ginger a look, and the chunky girl shrugged.

"Who's he been dealing with? Who was Cross in business with?"

"I don't know, I don't know anything about that end of the business."

I looked at Ginger and she said, "Neither do I."

"Ginger knows less about it than I do," Fallon said. "I'm sorry I ever got you into it, Gin."

"Don't worry about it," Ginger said. She walked over to where Fallon was sitting and rested her hip against the arm of the couch, putting her arm around her friend's shoulder. When Fallon leaned her head against Ginger's breast a new thought leapt into my head, and I wondered about their relationship. I also thought again about the letters in Cross's book. More and more I had the feeling that I had that part of the mystery figured out.

"Fallon, if Brown calls you, will you call me? Or if you should think of anything?"

Ginger patted her friend's shoulder and Fallon said, "Yes, all right. I'll call you."

I stood up and started for the door, and after I had gone through I wished there were some way I could look back into the room without them knowing.

I felt like a man in a trenchcoat looking for a dirty movie.

## — *thirty-one* —

I was at Hocus's office early the next morning, coffee in hand, including Sanka for his partner, Wright, who had an ulcer.

"When are you going to have that fixed?" I asked Wright while handing him the coffee.

Abruptly he dropped his hand away from his belly, which he had been unconsciously massaging, and said, "Have what fixed?"

"Never mind. When is your erstwhile partner going to get here?"

"Now," he said, looking past me.

"Making your own hours?" I asked Hocus as he grabbed the coffee from me on the way to his desk.

"That's exactly what I'm doing," he said. "It's an experiment in the department. What do you want?"

"I want to talk—check that. I want to have a dialogue about both the Cross and Saberhagen cases."

"Did you hear that?" Hocus called to his partner. "The shamus wants to have a dialogue."

"I heard," Wright said, frowning and rubbing his stomach.

172

"I hope you have something to offer—" Hocus said, "besides coffee, I mean."

"I do."

"What?"

"Information."

"About whom?"

"Cross, Melanie Saberhagen, Brown—take your pick."

Hocus tore the top off his coffee container and said, "So start at the top and work your way down."

"I want a guarantee first."

"Of what?"

"If I say anything in the next ten minutes that makes one bit of sense to you, I'd like you to go to bat for Wood with Vadala."

"That's your deal?"

"That's it."

"Sounds like I can't lose."

"Then I have your guarantee?"

He peered at me over the rim of the container and said, "What's the catch?"

"For Christ's sake—"

"Okay, okay, you have my guarantee. Shoot."

"Did you know that Cross was financing, casting, and probably putting together blue movies?"

"What?"

"And that he was a student at the institute and as such knew Melanie Saberhagen?"

"What?"

"And that he knew Brown and was in business with Brown, who recruited talent for his movies?"

"What? What?" Hocus said, sitting straight up in his chair. For a moment I thought he was putting me on, but then I realized that I had just given him three bits of information that really *were* new.

"Hocus, this establishes a connection between the Cross case and the Saberhagen case, and casts some doubt as to the guilt of Knock Wood Lee!"

"Whoa, son," Hocus said, holding up his hand like a traffic cop. "Don't get carried away."

"What do you mean?"

"You've got a connection between Cross and Brown, and I'm already looking for Brown. But as for the other stuff—"

"Come on," I said, jumping to my feet. "What more do you want—"

"Facts, evidence, something along those lines wouldn't be unwelcome."

"What kind of facts?"

"Show me something that says Cross was making fuck films, that Brown was helping him, and that the Saberhagen girl was, uh, involved. Have you got anyone who'll step forward and swear to any of that?"

I wasn't sure Fallon—or Ginger—could be talked into going that far.

"I'm not sure," I said, sitting back down heavily.

"You've brought up some interesting points, Jack," he admitted. "Was Cross in this business alone? Where did he get the money?"

"I don't think he was alone. He had to have somebody else backing him, at least initially."

"Or maybe he was just one of a few investors, and just wanted to get more actively involved. You know, personally interview the girls on the casting couch, and all that."

"I thought of that."

"Look, you want to do something really helpful?"

"What?"

"Find me Brown."

"I'll do that," I said, standing again. "Goddamn it, I'll put him right in your lap."

I started for the door and Hocus yelled out, "Hey!"

"What?"

"Don't go off half cocked and set up a showdown in Madison Square Garden. This guy ain't Max the Axe," he said, "but he ain't Big Bird, either. He's mean."

"I know that better than you, pal." I rubbed the sides of my mouth, where the bruises were fading, and left.

I stopped by the hospital to see if they were really letting Hank Po out, and found him packing his bag.

"There you are," Hank said, looking up. He was dressed and on his feet, and the bandage that had encircled his head had been reduced to one that simply covered half his forehead. "I've been calling you."

"You sprung?"

"I'm sprung," he said. He closed the Staten Island Downs tote bag that he'd been stuffing, and added, "Right now."

"Let's get a cab."

As we rode downtown, I told him everthing I'd found out since I last saw him.

"There's one thing I can't see," he said when I'd finished.

"What?"

"How can Brown continue business as usual, and still hope to duck the cops."

"And why duck the cops unless he's got something to hide?"

"That doesn't necessarily follow," Hank said. "Fallon doesn't want to talk to the cops, and does she have something to hide?"

"Maybe." I said, "And maybe Brown just ducks cops instinctively. Remember, he likes to hurt people—and Fallon, she's too afraid of him to talk to cops."

"You don't think that she came clean with you?"

"I don't think she or Ginger has been absolutely honest with me, but that might simply be out of . . . embarrassment."

"About appearing in blue movies?"

"It depends on what kind of movies they did."

"What do you mean?"

"I think," I said, taking out Cross's book, "that I've got Cross's little code figured out."

"Really?"

"Some of these should have been obvious, I think."

"Like what?"

"Like this," I said, showing him one of the entries next to Brown's name.

"SM?" he said.

"Don't say it that way. Say 'S-and-M', and what comes to mind?"

His eyebrows shot up and he said, "I get the picture. The people in the book are all people who have appeared, or are willing to appear, in Cross's movies."

"Right."

"And the letters next to each name signify the types of movies each person is willing to do."

"Right again."

"Damn," he said, "it is a trick book."

"Yeah, I guess you could call it that."

When we got to his loft on Eighteenth Street, not far from Debbie's No-Name tavern, we suspended conversation until we had paid the cab and negotiated our way up to his place.

"Should be some beer in the fridge," he said as we entered.

"At this time of the morning?"

"After the shit they gave me in the hospital, I don't care what time it is, I want a beer."

I got him one after insisting that he sit on his couch, and then shrugged and took one for myself.

"Let me see that," he said, reaching out for Cross's book with his free hand.

I gave it to him and sat in an armchair across from the couch while he perused it.

"Three W," he said. "Three-way sex, right?"

"Ménage à trois," I said, flaunting my limited knowledge of French.

"You know," he said, turning pages, "if any one of these people found out that Cross was putting their names in a book—even without last names—"

176

"One of them might have killed him for it," I finished. "That thought has just recently occurred to me."

"B?"

"Bondage," I said, hazarding a guess, and he nodded.

"Must be. BD?" he asked, trying another one.

"Black dog?"

He snapped his fingers and said, "Back door!"

"Why not 'G' for Greek?"

He leafed through it and said, "Can't find any G's, but there's a GS."

"Good sex?"

"I guess we'll never find them all out, now that he's dead," he said, still turning pages and reading intently.

"Well, at least this will give you something to do while you're convalescing."

"Here's an 'A'," he said. "If 'A' stands for anal sex, what's BD?"

"Black dog?"

He ignored me.

"'L', that's easy."

"What?"

"Lesbian, and 'H' must stand for homosexual."

"Wait a minute," I said, as a puzzle piece slid into place. It had nothing really to do with the case, but it was something I'd been very curious about, and the scene in Fallon and Ginger's apartment last night, and what Hank had just said, made it come together.

"Look at the entries for Ginger and Fallon."

He did so and said, "Fallon's a little kinkier than her roommate. Let's see, conventional, bondage, bondage, s-and-m, three-way—what the hell is this?"

"Look at Ginger's again."

He turned back to Ginger's and said, "That last one's the same, except for the last letter."

"The last letter of each has to be their initials."

"Yeah, but the 'F' is next to Ginger's name, and the 'G' is next to Fallon's. And what the hell is LOW?"

"What's 'L'?"

"We've established that. 'L' stands for lesbian."

"LOWF," I repeated for his benefit.

"I still don't get it."

"Don't you see? Both girls are willing to have lesbian sex, but only with each other!"

He got it then.

"LOWF," he said. "Lesbian only with Fallon."

"And vice versa."

Which probably explained the impression I had gotten last night just before leaving their apartment. I got that man in a trenchcoat feeling again and shook my head to dispel the thought.

"We're getting good at this," he said, picking up his beer to take a swallow, and then leafing through the book again.

"Here's a winner," he said, suddenly.

"Where?"

"Right here. This gal will do anything. She's got C, L, B, SM, 3W, A—Christ, she's got the whole alphabet here."

"What's her name?"

"Paula."

I wasn't sure I'd heard him right.

"What was that?"

"Paula."

Could it be?

"There's two of them here, too," he said. "Two Paula's."

"How'd he tell the difference?"

"I guess he could have by their coded entries," Hank said. "One's much longer than the other; but he's got a last initial next to this gal's name."

"What is it?"

"B, Paula B."

It was, I thought. It had to be.

Alan Cross's boss, Paula Bishop!

When I told Hank what I was thinking he put the book down and said thoughtfully, "Maybe that's where additional funds were coming from."

"But according to this, she was also a performer—a very versatile performer."

"She could have been both."

"Maybe the best way to find out is to ask her."

I called her office and spoke to her secretary, who told me that Miss Bishop had called and said she would not be coming in today. I asked for her home address, but the secretary refused to give it to me.

"Now what?" Hank asked after I'd hung up.

"I may not have her address," I said, leaning forward and picking up the book, "but I've got her phone number, don't I?"

## thirty-two

Paula Bishop was home when I called and although she sounded surprised to hear from me, she agreed to see me. She gave me her address on Central Park South, and I hung up.

"What's a businesswoman doing at home on a Tuesday morning?" Hank asked, trying to ease the itch his taped ribs were causing.

I looked at my watch and said, "It's almost Tuesday afternoon, but when I find out I'll let you know."

"Do that. You taking the book with you?"

"Yes. I may need it to rattle her a bit. You can have your fun with it later."

"But what am I going to do to keep from going crazy in the meantime?"

"Watch soap operas," I said, and left.

It *was* after noon when the cab dropped me in front of her building and I wondered if she'd be a good hostess and offer me lunch. The doorman knew my name and passed me through, and I took the elevator to the floor below the penthouse. I guess everyone needed something to shoot for.

I noticed something about her as soon as she let me in

and led me into the living room. She wasn't walking right. She was too stiff, and trying to hide it.

She must have had a rough weekend.

"I called your office, but they told me you weren't in today."

"And they gave you my phone number?" she asked, frowning. "I'll have to talk to—"

"No, I didn't get your phone number from your office."

"It's unlisted. You couldn't have gotten it any other way. If you're trying to protect my secretary—"

"I'm not."

"Then how did you get it?"

"I'll tell you that later. I have a few more questions to ask you, if you don't mind."

She gave a resigned shrug of her shoulders and asked, "Can I offer you some coffee?"

"Fine. Black, no sugar."

She looked very different today, not much like the businesswoman I'd seen last time. She was wearing a red brocade kimono that extended below her knees, and her hair was down around her shoulders. I watched as she walked stiffly to the kitchen and guessed that it was her back, or possibly her side. I'd walked like that a few times after a fight, when my rib were sore.

She came back with one cup of coffee for me.

"None for you?"

"I've had a few already. What were those questions you wanted to ask me?"

"I wanted to ask you again if you ever had any connection with Cross outside of your business."

"The answer is still the same."

"I thought it might be," I said, sipping the coffee. It was instant. I looked around and said, "Can we sit down?"

"I'd prefer to stand."

"Hurt too much to sit?"

"What?"

"Your ribs. They must hurt a lot."

"I wrenched my back . . . moving some furniture," she said, studying me.

"Moving furniture," I repeated.

"Yes."

"Have you seen a doctor?"

"I don't need a doctor, thank you. Could we get on with this?"

"That was the only question I really wanted to ask you. I wanted to see if your answer would be the same."

"Why wouldn't it be?"

I shrugged and said, "I just thought that maybe you would want to start telling the truth."

"I beg your pardon. Are you calling me a liar?"

"I guess I am."

"I think you should leave, Mr. Jacoby, before I call the doorman."

"Maybe you should have called him when you had to move that furniture."

She glared at me. I took Cross's book out of my pocket and showed it to her.

"What's that?"

"A book."

"I can see that," she said, but she couldn't seem to take her eyes off it. I think she might have known that things were about to fall apart.

"It's a very special book. Here, take a look at it," I said, holding it out to her. She took it and started to leaf through it tentatively.

"It's Alan Cross's book, Paula. He listed all of his actors and actresses in there. Turn to the P's and you'll see where I got your phone number."

She turned to the P's, stared at her name, and then closed her eyes.

"Damn him," she said in a whisper.

"You want to sit down?"

She bit her lower lip and nodded. I took her by the arm, walked her to the couch, and helped her to sit.

"How did it start?" I asked sitting next to her. "Did he get you to back him?"

"He was very charming, and very persuasive," she said, slowly. She looked down at the book in her hands and said, "A goddamn book. That sonofabitch!"

"Look, don't get all upset," I said, taking it from her. "Nobody has to know about this."

She got a knowing look in her eyes and said, "All right, how much do you want?"

"Oh, I'm not interested in money."

"No?" she asked, and then she got another knowing look on her face and I headed her off at the pass on that, too.

"I don't want sex, either."

"Then what do you want, Mr. Jacoby?"

"I want to know everything you know about Alan Cross's porno movie business."

"I don't know very much. He started small, using his own money."

"His own money?"

"Well, it wasn't my money."

"Did he have other investors besides you?"

"I guess so."

"Did he have someone above him, someone he worked for?"

"He never said anything . . . but I always got that impression."

"I see."

"Do you want to know how I got involved . . . how I went beyond funding . . ."

"I don't want to know about you, I want to know about him, and about a man called Brown."

"Brown," she said, and unconsciously she put her hand against her left side.

"You know Brown," I said, and it came out as a direct statement and not as a question.

"Yes."

"Did he do that? Hurt your side?"

"Yes."

182

"Do you know where I can find him, Paula?"

"Brown?"

"I *know* where Cross is."

"Yes, of course. No, I don't know where you can find Brown."

"You saw him over the weekend, right?"

"Yes, but he picked me up and he brought me home. Have you tried his apartment?"

"He hasn't been back to his apartment since the police started looking for him."

"Why are the police looking for him?"

"Because they think he might have killed Alan Cross."

"Brownie? Killed Cross?" she asked, as if realizing that she might have spent time in the company of a killer over the weekend.

"Didn't that thought ever occur to you?"

"Well . . . no."

"Doesn't Brown strike you as the violent type?"

"Of course," she said, rubbing her side.

"Then you've got to tell me where I can find him, Paula."

"I don't know, I really don't."

I sat back and put the book away in my pocket. What good was putting pressure on her if she didn't know anything that could help me?

Or did she?

"Excuse me for asking this, but did you shoot a movie this weekend?"

Looking embarrassed she said, "Yes."

"Where?"

"Where?"

"A theater, an apartment?"

"Oh, I see. No, the shootings have usually been done in a warehouse, or a loft . . ."

"Very classy."

"Don't try to make me feel dirtier than I already do."

"So, if you were shooting this weekend, that means that Brown has taken up where Cross left off, right?"

"I suppose."

She looked so down that I had to ask.

"I said I wouldn't ask, Paula, but I have to. Why do you do it?"

She couldn't meet my eyes as she answered.

"I must admit, I've wondered myself why I did it that first time. Alan flattered me, he charmed me . . . he made love to me."

"And you did it once, but why keep it up after that?"

"Once wasn't enough for Alan," she said, bitterly. "After that, he wouldn't let me refuse."

Maybe she never really wanted to stop. Why else would she keep on with it unless . . .

"Paula, was he blackmailing you?"

She bit her lower lip again and nodded.

"He said no one would see my face, just my body, but when he showed me the movie . . . there I was!"

"So you were never paid?

"I did it as a lark that first time. Alan convinced me that it would be fun, that I'd enjoy it."

I decided not to ask her if she *had* enjoyed it.

"Where did Brown take you this time?"

"To Brooklyn. I don't know exactly where, but I can guarantee you wouldn't find him there. They never used the same place twice."

"You had never been used at the same place twice," I said, "but that didn't mean it was never done."

"Maybe, but I don't know Brooklyn, so I couldn't begin to guess where it was."

"How many other people were present?"

"There was always just Cross, Brown, and a cameraman, as well as the people who were . . . performing."

"Who was there this weekend?"

"Just me and Brown. He set the camera up to work automatically."

Was Brown really taking over, or was he just trying to get some kicks for himself?

184

"Has Brown mentioned Cross since he was killed?"

"No. Do you really think he killed him?"

"I don't know, but I've got to find Brown. Somebody has to be able to give me a lead. What about the cameramen?"

"I never knew any of their names."

"That's great."

"I wish I could help you, Mr. Jacoby. I really wish I could. I would like to be free of this. If it ever got out, I'd be ruined." She turned to me suddenly and put both hands on my arm, gripping so tightly I could feel her nails right through my sleeve.

"I'll hire you, I'll pay you to get me out of this. Find the films I made and destroy them."

"How many films have you made?"

"Five, but they weren't entire features, just portions. I think they pieced them together."

And who knew how many prints of each had been made up?

"I'll pay you double your regular fee to help me, Mr. Jacoby," she said, desperately.

I almost said no, but then I realized that I had been working without a fee since Melanie's body had been found. Besides, Paula Bishop could certainly afford me.

"All right, Paula. I'll do the best I can, but you've got to help."

"Anything."

"If Brown calls you, you must call me. I have to get to Brown if I'm going to break this thing open. I've got to find out who he and Cross were working for."

"I don't think there was ever any doubt about who was in charge. Cross always treated Brown like an employee."

I stood up and she asked me to help her to her feet.

"Maybe you should have a doctor look at those ribs."

"He just punched me around a bit," she said, shaking her head. "He's done it before."

"To others as well as you."

She walked with me to the door, where I once again assured her that I would do my best.

"I hope you've told me everything, Paula," I said, just before leaving. "I can't help you if you're holding anything back."

"I'm not, I swear."

"Just make sure that if you hear from Brown, I hear from you."

"You will, I promise."

In the elevator I wondered how many others Cross had been blackmailing as well. If I knew the number, then I'd know how many more suspects for his murder I'd just come up with.

Then there was Brown. Had he taken over Cross's blackmail business as well as his movie business? If that was the case, then it was not only possible that he was the killer, but the possibility now existed that he could also turn up dead.

And what about Paula Bishop? Hadn't she just built herself up as a prime suspect for Cross's murder? Technically, however, she was now my client, and it wouldn't have been ethical for me to throw her name to Hocus to add to his list, a list that right now had only one name on it anyway: Brown.

Brown was at the top of *my* list, too. He was the key to the whole thing. I wouldn't be able to unravel this mess until I could put my hands on him, and on top of that I owed the man a few lumps, for myself and for Henry Po.

I grabbed a cab on Fifth Avenue and told the driver to take me to the corner of Mott and Hester, where I found Ray Carbone watching Knock Wood Lee's apartment.

"Hey, Jack. Checking up on me?"

"No, Ray, I'm calling you off."

"The job's done?"

"My part isn't," I said, "but your part is. I don't have the cash with me right now, Ray—"

"Hey, forget it. Pay me when you have it, that's all. You're good for it."

"I appreciate what you did, Ray."

"Anytime," Ray said. "Anytime you need help, you got my number."

We shook hands and I watched him walk toward Canal Street, hoping that I was doing the right thing. For some reason, however, I had believed Piper when he said he'd leave Lee alone. I had the feeling that he hadn't been lying when he said that he'd missed her.

I was about to leave when I looked across the street and saw Lee standing in the doorway.

I walked across and she leaned against the door frame with her arms folded, shaking her head at me.

"Taking away my babysitter, Jack?"

"You spotted him, huh?"

"If living with Wood has taught me anything, it's to keep my eyes open."

"I'm not surprised."

"I'd ask you why you pulled him off, but I'm more interested in why you put him there in the first place."

"For protection." I didn't mention the two goons who'd jumped me.

"From whom? Piper? If that's the case, I could have told you that you were wasting your money."

"Maybe, but it gave me peace of mind."

"And now why'd you pull him off?"

"I spoke to Piper and he told me he'd leave you alone."

"And you believed him?"

"Don't you?"

"He impressed you, didn't he?" she asked, with something close to pride in her voice.

"Yes, as a matter of fact, he did, and as I see it, you made an impression on him that he hasn't quite been able to shake."

She got a faraway look in her eyes and said, "Maybe."

"How are you doing?"

"More important than that, how are you doing?"

I gave her a brief rundown on how things were going, right there in the doorway. It never seemed to occur to either one of us to go upstairs.

"Then everything seems to depend on your finding this guy Brown."

"Right—which I'm not doing standing here talking to you," I said, stepping out of the doorway.

She put her hand on my left shoulder with her forefinger laid alongside my neck and said, "Thanks for the bodyguard, Jack, but it wasn't necessary. I can take care of myself."

"That's right," I said, reminding myself, "you know some karate too, don't you?"

"Yes."

"Everybody in this damned case knows karate," I said, walking away. When I got to Canal Street I stopped short and said, "Everybody but Paula," so loud that a few people walking by turned to glance at me.

Did Paula Bishop know karate? If she didn't, how could she have beaten Cross to death? She couldn't have, and she probably couldn't have beaten a younger, stronger Melanie to death, either. I didn't think that Fallon or Ginger could have killed Cross that way. In eliminating them from my suspect list, I realized for the first time that they had been on it.

More and more it looked as if Brown was the killer, and more and more it became imperative that I find him.

When I got to Bogie's, Billy gave me a St. Pauli Girl and a message.

"A girl called for you."

"Which one?"

"Fallon. She's not the one you were here with, is she?"

"No, she's the roommate. What'd she want?"

"She wanted to talk to you and sounded pretty excited about it, too."

"I'll call her from the back."

"Hey," he called as I started away from the bar.

"What?"

"When are we going to get back into a training routine?"

"This case has me beat, Billy, but when it's all over we'll get back to it."

"Well, we're not as far behind as we might have been. You did have that time at the institute."

I recalled then that Bayard had told me twice to get back to him when the case was over. I wondered how Billy would feel if I told him I was going to study with Bayard, and then chided myself for it. Billy was my friend, and he'd be pleased for me whichever way I went.

"When we do get back to it you won't be getting any more of that stuff, so enjoy it while you can."

"Right," I said, taking a swig and then rolling my eyes in mock ecstasy.

I went into the office and dialed Fallon's number.

"It's Jacoby. What's up?"

"I remembered something, and I'm not sure if it's important," she said, tentatively.

"What is it?"

"Well, it's just something that happened once when I was in the car with Brown."

"What?" I asked, wondering if I was going to have to drag it out of her.

"We were driving one day and when we stopped for a light he pointed to a window in a building and said, 'That's where all Cross's secrets are hidden.'"

"Did you question him about it?"

"Yes, but he wouldn't say anything more and I forgot about it. I just remembered it today. It's important, isn't it?"

"It is if you can remember where that building is."

"That's the only problem . . ."

"Fallon—"

"I remember what it looks like, and I think we were on the West Side driving north."

"All right, so it was Sixth Avenue, or Eighth, or Tenth, maybe—"

"I think it was Eighth or Tenth."

"Okay, tell me what the building looked like, and anything else you can think of."

She described a square, stone building about four stories high, dark, dirty brown in color. She said it looked like one of those foreign embassies you see in the movies, only there weren't any flags or flagpoles.

"What floor was he pointing to?"

"That part's easy. It was the top floor, toward the front. I think he was sorry he said anything almost as soon as the words were out of his mouth. Do you think he might be hiding out there?"

"He might, but even if he's not, there still might be some answers there for me."

"Maybe for all of us."

"Yeah, maybe for all of us," I said, thinking of her and Ginger and Paula Bishop . . . and Knock Wood Lee, most of all.

All I had to do was find the damn place!

## — thirty-three

As it turned out, the building wasn't all that hard to find, even though Fallon had steadfastly refused to go with me out of fear of Brown. I decided against renting a car, because I didn't want to be burdened with one when I finally found it, so I left Bogie's, hailed a cab, and gave instructions.

"You're kidding," the cabbie said.

"Just keep the meter running, pal. I'm not kidding. Up

190

Eighth Avenue, and then up Tenth Avenue, and we keep going until I say stop."

We started at Fourteenth Street, and when we reached Ninety-first I told him to forget Eighth and try Tenth. I found what I was looking for at Tenth and Sixty-first.

"Stop."

There it was, just as Fallon had described it, looking like some foreign consulate that had been abandoned years ago.

"Do you know what that big square building is?" I asked the cabbie.

He was a white man in his fifties, with gray hair and tired eyes. He looked at me in the mirror and said, "I think they rent space."

"Space? For what?"

"You know, storage space. They'll rent you any size room you want and you can store anything you want, as long as it don't piss or shit."

"How do you know so much about it?"

"My brother's got one."

"In there?" I asked, hopefully.

"Naw, his is in a building downtown."

"Oh."

"You gonna get out here?"

"Yes, I am."

He stopped his meter and I paid him and tipped him well, giving him a ten.

"Hey, thanks. You wanna do the East Side tomorrow?"

"No, thanks, this is good enough."

He drove off and I walked up to the front door of the building. It wasn't until I reached the doorway that I saw the metal plate mounted on the wall, explaining what the building was. It was owned by something called Space, Inc., and there was a phone number given for anyone interested in renting. There was no address given, and when I tried the glass doors I found them locked. Peering inside told me that there was no one there, not a guard, not a clerk, no one.

I stepped out of the doorway, looked up and down the block for a pay phone, and finally located one across the street.

"Space, Inc.," a woman's voice answered when I dialed the number that was on the metal plate.

"Yes, I'd like to rent some space—"

"In which building?"

"Uh, the one on Tenth Avenue and Sixty-first Street—"

"How much space would you need?"

"I'm not sure—"

"Well, I'm afraid we have none available in that building."

"Then why did you ask me how much I needed?" I asked, becoming annoyed with the constant interruptions.

"It's simply a question I'm required to ask, sir," she explained, as if she were speaking to a child.

"Look, could I have the address of your office—"

"I'm afraid it wouldn't help for you to do that, sir—"

"Would you stop interrupting me! This is a police matter!"

"Police?" she said, sounding nervous.

"I would like the address of your office so I can come down with a warrant to search your building."

"I, uh—"

"What is your name, please?"

Instead of giving me her name she rattled off the address of the offices of Space, Inc., which were located on Park Avenue South and Twenty-first Street.

"Thank you," I said, and hung up.

Now all I had to do was convince Hocus to get a warrant.

"This wasn't an easy thing to get, you know," Hocus said as we rode up the elevator to the offices of Space, Inc.

"I appreciate it."

"We normally need something more concrete to get a warrant from a judge, but I was able to use a little leverage with my captain, and he was able to talk to the judge—"

"Are you trying to tell me that your head is on the block, here?"

"No, I'm just trying to tell you that we'd better not come up empty."

"We won't."

I let Hocus handle the whole thing once we got to Space, Inc.'s office. He showed his i.d. to a secretary, who passed us through to see the manager, a little man with slick black hair who reminded me of a seal.

"You want to search the entire building?" the little man asked.

"No, not the whole building," Hocus said, "just one of the front rooms on the fourth floor."

"That floor only has one front room," the man said, "extending the width of the building. It's the rear that is broken up into compartments."

"That makes it easier, then," Hocus said. He handed the manager, Mr. Littell, the warrant and said, "The front room."

Littell read the warrant, then said, "I'll get the keys and come with you."

"I'd also like the name of the renter."

"Of course. Just give me a moment."

He went to his files and pulled out a card. He said, "It was rented to a man named Andrew Collins."

"The same initials," I said, and Hocus nodded. We were both aware of the fact that people who used phony names almost always made them up using the same initials as their real names.

"How long ago did he rent it?" Hocus asked.

Littell looked at the card again and said, "Just under six months ago."

Why did that length of time ring a bell with me?

Littell returned the card to his file and started to say,

"Shall we—" when he was cut off by the phone. "Excuse me."

He answered the phone, listened for a few moments, and then became agitated.

"Oh, my God!"

Hocus and I exchanged glances, wondering if this was going to hold us up.

"What is it?" Hocus asked.

"It's that building," he said, holding the phone down by his side.

"What about it?"

"It's on fire!"

Hocus looked at me and I said, "Shit!"

When we got there in Hocus's car the place was ablaze, and there were several fire trucks clogging the streets, battling the fire. Hocus pulled his car to the curb and when the fire chief tried to make him move he showed the man his i.d.

"All right," the uniformed man said. "Who are they?"

"They're with me," Hocus said. "This is Mister Littell, he's the manager of the building."

By not introducing me, Hocus created the illusion that I was his partner, and the fire chief accepted that.

"Just stay out of the way," he told us. "The fire marshals should be here soon."

"Do you know anything yet?" Hocus asked.

"Only that this was no accident. Excuse me."

I looked up at the fourth floor and saw flames shooting out of the windows.

"I wonder where it started," I said aloud.

Hocus looked at me, and then looked up to where I was looking.

"Well, I guess this justifies the warrant," he said.

"Big deal."

We decided to stay around as long as we could, hoping that they would get the fire under control and we'd still be able to get inside for a look.

194

Watching the firefighters doing their work reminded me of another time, when my apartment had been firebombed with my brother inside.

"Are you all right?" Hocus asked.

"Yeah, I was just thinking . . ."

"About Benny?"

I nodded.

"Look, Jack, there's no need for you to stick around. We're not gonna get in there tonight. Even if they control it we'd still have to wait for it to cool down."

"I suppose."

"Why don't you go on home?"

It was starting to get dark, which only made the flames look that much brighter and hotter.

"I think I will."

"I'll call you as soon as we find out anything."

"Thanks."

As I turned to leave, he put his hand on my shoulder and said, "It was good work finding this place, Jack."

"Yeah," I said, "good and late."

I stopped a cab on Ninth Avenue and gave him the address of Bogie's. When I got there I went right to the bar and got a St. Pauli Girl beer. It felt good and soothing on my dry throat.

"Jesus," Billy Palmer said from behind me. When I turned he was wrinkling his nose. "Where's the fire?"

"Uptown. My big break on this case just went up in smoke." I got off the stool and said, "I'll get out of here before your customers start to leave."

A few of them were already looking around to see where the smell was coming from.

"Are you all right?" Billy asked.

"Oh, yeah. I was just a spectator. I'm fine, all I need is a shower."

One of the waitresses came over to him so he patted me on the shoulder and I went through the kitchen to the office.

In the shower I wondered if the fire could possibly have been a coincidence, but then what difference would that have made? My one big lead was still gone. Papers, movie film, it all would have burned up in a blaze that size. Obviously, that must have been where Cross was storing all his gear, his movies. At least Paula Bishop could rest relatively easy. . . .

Paula Bishop? Could she have possibly had something to do with setting the fire, or even have set it herself? Had I been followed to that building today?

I got out of the shower and toweled myself dry. I'd finished my beer before getting under the water, and now I wished I had another one.

I thought about the possibility of Paula setting that fire, or hiring someone to set it, and I rejected it. I didn't think she was capable of that, but then that was a hell of a decision to come to about someone I'd only spoken to twice. Still, Eddie had always told me that one of a detective's most important assets was instinct. If indeed I could lay claim to any "detective's instincts," they were telling me that Paula Bishop had nothing to do with that fire. In her apartment, she had not seemed as cold and collected as she had in her office, and setting a fire was not the same as running a business.

Brown looked the best for this, just as he looked good for everything else. I was back to square one: find Brown.

The phone rang, but I ignored it and continued dressing, and then the intercom buzzed.

"For you, Jack," Billy said. "Hocus."

"Thanks," I said. "Hocus, what's up? Got something already?"

"We've got something, all right," he said, not sounding very happy about it.

"Well, what is it?"

"'What' isn't the question, the question is who."

"Who?"

"We've got a body, Jack. Badly burned and unrecognizable, but it's a man."

"Where was he found?" I asked, though I was afraid I already knew the answer.

"On the fourth floor, front room."

"Jesus," I said, "Brown?"

"It could be. We'll know more after an autopsy."

"Ah, Christ."

"I'll keep you posted."

"Yeah, thanks," I said, and hung up.

Square one? I thought. If the body turned out to be Brown, then I was even worse off than I had thought just moments before.

What came before square one?

## — thirty-four

Hocus called me again early in the morning, waking me up from a restless sleep. I kept dreaming that Benny was waving to me from one of the windows of that burning building, which was ridiculous, because Benny had died in my apartment. I tried to tell Benny that, but he just kept waving to me and calling my name.

"Hope I didn't wake you," Hocus said.

"I'm glad you did."

"We're going into that building this morning. I thought you might like to be in on it."

"When?"

"An hour."

"I'll be there."

When I got there he was waiting for me out front with his partner, Wright, who was rubbing his stomach.

"I hate fires," Wright said with a sour look on his face.

"The fire's out," I said.

"I know, but you never know what you're going to find."

"Anybody else up there?" I asked Hocus.

"Fire marshals."

"What are they looking for?"

"More evidence to support their declaration that the fire was suspicious."

"Aren't they sure yet?"

"They're picky fellows," Wright said. "They want to find a note from the arsonist confessing."

"Ready?" Hocus said.

"Let's go."

The elevator wasn't working so we had to walk up four flights of waterlogged steps to get to the fourth floor.

"This place looks like shit," Wright said. "We're not gonna find anything up here."

I didn't say it out loud but I agreed. The floor was ankle deep in black and gray gunk that was simply a combination of everything that had been melted down by the fire. It squished when we stepped in it, and held tight when we tried to walk.

"You fellas ought to be wearing boots," one of the two other men in the room called out. Both of them had shields pinned to their jackets, as did Hocus and Wright.

"We're not staying long," Hocus called back.

"Suit yourselves," the man said with a shrug, and went back to doing what he was doing, which seemed to be sifting through the gunk. His partner was all the way at the other end of the long room, doing the same.

"What have you found so far?" Hocus asked.

"Enough to tell us what was stored up here," the man replied.

"And what was that?"

"Film, and a lot of it. There are even remnants of projectors and cameras. Guy must have been using this place as a movie studio, or something."

"Or something is more like it," I said to Hocus in a low voice.

"Why? What do you know?"

"I don't know anything," I said, then amended the statement. "Well, I don't know much, just enough to guess that they didn't do any shooting here, just used it as storage."

"And where did they shoot?"

"All over. They used different places all the time."

"How do you know?"

"I talked to some of the . . . actors in the films."

"You wouldn't want to let me in on who they were, would you?" Hocus asked.

"You've already spoken to them," I said, "you just didn't know they were . . . performers."

"You mean some of the people we talked to from the institute were . . ."

"Yup, and Brown."

"Brown?"

"Yeah. He worked for Cross, helping to round up talent, but he wasn't above stepping in front of the camera himself."

"What about Cross and the Saberhagen girl?"

"I don't know about Cross," I said, and then hedged about Melanie. "I'm not sure about the girl."

"Well, do you know of any way we could become sure?"

"Looking at some of these films would have been a way," I said, indicating the gunk on the floor.

"Yeah," he said, dragging his toe through some of it with a morose expression on his face. "What's this?" he said suddenly, as his foot came into contact with something. He bent over and straightened up holding an object that I recognized for what it had once been.

"It looks like a videotape."

One of the fire marshals heard me and called out, "There were plenty of those around, too. That's where all this melted plastic came from."

"Videotape?" Hocus asked.

"Yeah, you know, videocassette recorder tapes." Wright said.

Hocus stared at his partner, who said, "My kid's got them."

"They must have been putting their films on videotape—" I said, and then stopped short as a thought struck me.

"What's the matter?" Hocus asked.

I thought for a moment about not telling him and checking it out myself, but I couldn't bring myself to do it to him. Besides, it would be a lot easier getting into Cross's apartment with him than without him.

"Cross's apartment," I said.

"What about it?"

"Well, you went through it just like I did," I said. "Didn't you notice anything?"

"Jacoby, if you play guessing games with me I'm gonna leave you lying face down in this shit."

"Cross had a video tape machine in his apartment," I said, holding the burned remnant up in front of his nose. "Who knows, maybe he made a habit of watching his own movies!"

"Well, what the hell are we waiting for?"

Wright stayed behind to continue to look around while Hocus and I drove to Cross's apartment building. The doorman remembered both of us and let us in with a pass key.

"Just pull the door shut when you leave, officers," he said. "It will lock by itself."

"Thank you," Hocus said. He gave me a look, but decided to let the implication in the doorman's remark pass. After all, he himself had allowed the fire chief to believe I was a cop just the night before.

"All right, where's this video tape machine?"

"Over here."

I walked over to the set of shelves against the wall and showed him the VCR with its glowing green digital clock. On the shelves surrounding the machine were all of the tapes, neatly labeled.

"Jesus," Hocus said, "there must be hundreds. What are we supposed to do, sit and watch them all? And if we find a dirty movie, what's it gonna tell us?"

"I don't know, but if we had gotten to that storage room in time and found reel-to-reel films, you would have screened them, wouldn't you?"

"Yes, C.B."

"I'll tell you what. Leave me here and I'll go through them and let you know what I find. Meanwhile, you can work on finding Brown."

"That might not be so hard, if that's him in the morgue," he said, studying me thoughtfully.

"Hocus, I've been cooperating all along, haven't I?"

"After a fashion."

"You don't have time to sit here and watch these tapes, but I do because if that's Brown in the morgue, I'm at a dead end."

He thought it over a moment, then shook his head and said, "I don't know what you expect to find, but go ahead. Call me at my office if you do find something."

"I will. Thanks."

"I'll tell the doorman you'll be up here for a while."

He stopped by the phone to make sure he remembered the number, and then left with a wave, presumably to go back to the scene of the fire for his partner.

I had seen Billy Palmer operate his machine on a few occasions, and although the buttons on this machine were not in the same place, they bore the same labels. The ones I was concerned with were Play, Fast Forward, Rewind, and Eject.

I stared at the shelves of tapes and wondered where I should start. They were all labeled, most of them with movie titles, but that didn't necessarily mean that was what was on the tape. Still, why would Cross mislabel tapes that were in his own apartment?

No, if Cross was keeping tapes of his own movies for his own private parties, they'd either be blatantly labeled or totally unlabeled. What I needed was a tape labeled "Doris Does Denver" or a tape with a blank label.

I started with the top shelf, looking *behind* the front row of tapes. For the most part that's all there was—until I got about halfway down. Behind the tapes on the center shelf were other tapes, laid flat against the back of the bookcase. I pulled out all of the front tapes and found one mystery tape for every five that were labeled. With fifty tapes to a shelf, that left me with ten, all of which I had to screen because the labels were number-coded.

I pulled an armchair around so I could sit facing the TV and stacked the tapes on the floor next to me. I leaned forward, hit the eject button, inserted the first tape, pushed the cartridge holder down, and pressed Play. I spotted a wireless remote next to the machine, and leaned back with it in my hand.

The quality of the film was really bad, and the fact that it was in black and white didn't help any. There were two women in a room in which the only furniture seemed to be a natty double bed.

The two women were Fallon and Ginger.

I watched in sort of a stunned paralysis as the girls undressed each other, carrying on a conversation that left no doubt as to what they were planning to do.

I watched for a few more minutes. As the girls stripped each other naked and fell to the bed in a hot embrace, I found myself becoming aroused. Annoyed at myself, I hit the Fast Forward button. The girls proceeded to consummate their act in comically fast motion, but I didn't find it the least bit funny. As it turned out, none of the other participants in this film were familiar to me. When it reached the end I didn't bother to rewind it, I just popped it out and inserted another one.

I went through the next three tapes without seeing anyone I recognized, and by that time my eyes were starting to ache from fatigue.

I popped in the fifth tape, but did not start it right away. Instead I went to the kitchen and washed my eyes out with cold water, then opened the refrigerator to see if there was anything to drink. I took one of several bottles of Budweiser and carried it back to the chair with me, and then started the fifth tape.

This one was a lulu.

202

I recognized Brown right off. He was stripped naked, wearing what looked like a black leather G-string, and on his hands he wore black leather gloves. He moved forward and the camera moved ahead of him to the girl on the bed: Fallon.

To make a long story short, first he kicked the shit out of her, and then he turned her over and took her from behind. All of this I saw while I fast-forwarded the action, which mercifully spared me any sound. The rest of the tape was much the same, with Brown doing the same thing to several different women. Fallon was the only one on the tape that I recognized.

I went through three more tapes without seeing anyone I knew, and then inserted the ninth tape. This one was in color and had apparently been shut off while still running the last time it was used. The action was in full swing, with two women on a bed going at each other in living color.

One woman, a slender blond, was on top of the second woman, a taller, darker lady. The camera moved closer to the bed and began to shoot from above, so the bottom woman was now easily recognizable. Although I shouldn't have been surprised, I was, to find that I was looking at the contorted face of Paula Bishop. Either she was a hell of an actress, or she was thoroughly enjoying what the other woman was doing to her.

The camera continued to move until it was showing you what Paula saw when she looked down between her widespread legs. I watched as the blond did her work, and I was holding my breath, waiting to get a look at her face, because I had an eerie feeling I knew who it would be.

The scene seemed to go on and on from that point—which demonstrated the directorial incompetency involved—but finally the blond looked up at her bed partner with a dreamy, faraway look on her face, and just as I knew it would be, it was Melanie Saberhagen.

As the film went on and the women—or woman and girl—changed positions, all I could think of was that this confirmed beyond a doubt the connection between Alan Cross and Melanie Saberhagen. As the film came to an end, the phone rang, and I answered it.

"Jacoby, are you still there?" Hocus's voice asked.

"No," I said, "this is a recording."

"Have you found out anything?"

"Yeah, I found a movie with Melanie Saberhagen in it," I said, and as I said it I started to feel sick to my stomach. I had to admit that I had become sexually excited by some of the things I had seen in some of the earlier films, but as I went from film to film, the excitement had faded and a vague sickness had replaced it. Now, after seeing the things Paula Bishop and Melanie had been doing to each other, the sick feeling was becoming worse.

"That clinches a connection," he said, "but it still doesn't mean they were killed by the same person."

"I guess finding Brown is still our only chance."

"Ah, yeah, well that's what I was calling you about."

"Brown?"

"Yeah, we just got confirmation from Dr. Maybe on the body in the fire."

"It was Brown?"

"It sure was. We just hit a stone wall, pal."

"Shit."

I hung up wondering if I had the stomach to watch the last tape, then decided that I couldn't very well leave the job nine-tenths done. I inserted the tape, then sat back and started it.

Right away I noticed something was different about this particular movie. The quality was even worse than the others had been, of the grainy, black and white type you used to see projected on a bedsheet in somebody's basement.

It was older than anything else I'd seen, and I wondered why anyone had taken the trouble to transpose an old stag movie onto videotape.

The answer eventually became clear.

I watched as a man and a woman grunted and groaned

on a small bed, and then noticed that both of them were barely out of their teens. I concentrated on the girl, trying to get a good look at her face while they rolled around on the bed, not doing a whole lot by my modern standards. They spent a lot of time in a simple missionary position, with the man on top, and finally I decided that I didn't know the girl.

The man, however, was a different story.

His face was damned familiar, but I could never quite get a good look at it, until he and the girl finally changed positions on the bed. She got down between his legs and started to give him head and when he picked up his head to look at her and watch, I had him pegged.

He was a lot younger, a lot thinner—in fact, he was damned skinny for a "porn star"—but there was no doubt about who it was.

The guy on the bed getting filmed for posterity was Leo Piper—or, as he was no doubt known then, Leo Piperneski.

Which was by no means the last surprise on that tape.

The tape was about half through when the third person entered the room. She watched the two people on the bed for a few seconds, then started walking toward the bed, shedding her clothes as she went along.

She was special, this one. Even on the grainy old film I could see that out of everyone I had seen on these ten tapes, she was different. The way she moved, as if responding to a tune only she could hear, was . . . arousing.

She was the same age as the others, had long dark hair parted down the middle, full, rounded breasts and hips, and a slim waist. She hadn't changed much in the ten or so years since the film had been shot. She was still lovely, maybe even more lovely now than she had been then.

She was still Oriental, and she was very much still Tiger Lee.

When I left the apartment, I took one of the tapes with me.

# — thirty-five

I hadn't realized how late it was until I got back to Bogie's and found it closed. I used the alleyway from Eighth Avenue to get to the back, and used my key to enter the office. I put the tape down on the desk, sat down, and stared at it.

The existence of this particular tape brought out a whole new set of possibilities.

The first possibility did not look good for Wood. If I showed this tape to Hocus—or worse, if Vadala saw it—they would feel that Wood killed Cross over it . . . and I had to admit to myself that this was a possibility. I had always wondered why Wood had given Cross so much credit when no other bookie had extended him more than ten grand, and the answer could have been the tape.

I was thinking blackmail, and that just made the case *against* Wood stronger.

Another possibility concerned Piper. I didn't know how many movies Piper had made, but I was sure that he wouldn't want any of them coming to the surface now that he had built himself a new life and a new career. Would he kill to find this tape and keep that from happening?

Bet your house he would.

There was another possibility that I didn't even want to think about, but that didn't stop me.

What about Tiger Lee, herself? What lengths would she go to to keep the tape from being seen by anyone, especially Knock Wood Lee?

I picked up the tape and dropped it in the top drawer of the desk, hoping that any other copies that might have existed had gone up in smoke in the fire. In the morning I'd give it to Billy to lock up somewhere, or maybe play purloined letter himself by labeling it "Snow White"—or more likely, "Kung Fu Cutie"—and putting it in with his own collection of tapes.

The big question on my mind as I got ready for what I knew was going to be another bad night was, whom do I approach first about the tape?

I hadn't realized that I'd fallen asleep until something woke me up.

I was lying on my back and had the presence of mind not to move. Listening intently, I soon identified the sound that had awakened me.

Someone had jimmied the lock on the door and was in the room with me.

Since the office was in the back, there were no lights at all to give the room even the ghost of a glow. I had to hope that my night vision was better than the intruder's.

Hoping that the cot wouldn't squeak as I moved—or if it did, that the intruder would think I was simply turning over in my sleep—I slid off the edge onto the floor, where I crouched, peering into the darkness.

He had to figure I was there, otherwise why try to enter so quietly? That meant he wasn't going to start searching first, he was going to try to take care of me.

Somehow, I had the feeling this was not just a simple burglary. Whoever the intruder was, he knew what he was after. Anything else would be too much of a coincidence.

I stayed as I was, listening. He wasn't moving, so I assumed he was waiting for his eyes to become accustomed to the darkness.

Crouched as I was, the pain started in my calves and began to work its way up, but finally my patience paid off. I heard his shoe slide across the floor as he moved toward the cot. He knew where it was now, but he still couldn't tell that I wasn't in it. In the dark, he'd have to get closer for that—but I had no intention of letting him get that close.

When I sprang up from my crouch my legs protested, but I turned a deaf ear. Lowering my shoulder, I caught him below the belt and propelled him backward, off balance.

I knew where the desk was, and where the lamp was on

the desk. It was one of the those desk lamps on a flexible neck, so as I heard him slam into the door, I turned on the lamp and directed it toward him.

Instinctively he brought his hands up in front of his face to shield his eyes from the glow, but in spite of that he still had to shut his eyes against the sudden light. That give me time to come around the desk, approach him, and throw a basic front kick into his stomach.

He was a skinny guy with a neck like a turkey, and whatever hot air he had in him came rushing out as he sat down on the floor gasping. A large silver flashlight lay on the floor next to him.

"Just relax, friend," I said, "your wind will come back in a minute, and then we can have a talk."

I shook him down while he was gasping for breath, and came away with a .38, which I took with me back to the desk. I sat down and waited for him to catch his breath.

"Feel better?"

Turkey Neck looked up at me with watery eyes and took a great, shuddering breath.

"Good, then we can talk."

"I ain't—" he started to say, struggling to his feet. He cleared his throat and tried again. "I ain't telling you nothing."

"No? Why not?"

That stumped him.

"Haven't we met before?" I said.

"No."

"Sure, on a dark corner. Mott and Hester. You're the one who can't keep his footing on the ice."

The embarrassed look on his face told me I was right.

"You work for Piper," I said. He started to speak, but I cut him off. "No, that's not a question, it's a statement of fact. See, we've already talked about you. What did he send you here for?"

"Stuff it."

"The tape?"

He frowned, started to speak, then stopped himself, but that was all right. He'd already told me what I wanted to know.

"All right, get out of here."

"Huh?" He looked totally confused.

"I'm tired, I want to get some sleep. I've got an early meeting in the morning."

"Who with?"

"Piper."

"You don't—"

"Yes, I do. You go back to your boss and tell him to have a car pick me up out front at ten o'clock tomorrow morning."

"Why should I?"

"Because I've got the tape, and he wants it, and that's the only chance he'll have to get it."

He studied me for a few moments, then said, "My gun."

"I'll hold onto it and give it to Piper tomorrow. He'll give it back to you . . . probably."

He hesitated, studing me further, then made up his mind and reached behind him for the door knob. He kept his eyes on me while he opened the door, then sidled over and slipped out quickly, ignoring the flashlight.

I went over and locked the door, then set some bottles up in front of it just in case he came back with a friend or two. That warning system set up, I went back to the desk, opened the top drawer, and put the gun in next to the tape.

Somehow, knowing what my next move was going to be in the morning made me feel better, and what I had told Turkey Neck turned out to be true. I *was* tired, and I did want to get some sleep.

So I shut off the lamp and did just that.

## — thirty-six

The car got there at five after ten. I guess Piper must have told the driver to let me stew a while.

"Where are we going?" I asked the driver as I got into the limo.

"I'm not supposed to say, sir," the driver said. "I'm just supposed—"

"You're just supposed to drive," I said, finishing for him. "Okay, so drive."

He took me to an apartment building on Seventy-second Street and West End Avenue.

"What now?" I asked when he pulled in front.

"You're supposed to go up to the fifteenth floor, apartment fifteen-oh-five."

"That's it?"

"Yes, sir."

"No bookstore?"

"Sir?"

"Never mind," I said. "Thanks for the ride."

"Yes, sir."

I went in and took the elevator to the fifteenth floor. Turkey Neck's gun was tucked into my belt, and felt strangely comforting there.

The tape was in a safe place and would stay there until I got all the answers I needed.

I knocked on the door of room 1505, wondering if it was another of Piper's friends' apartments. I half expected Turkey Neck to answer the door, but it was Piper himself who opened it.

"Ah, Jacoby."

"It's funny," I said, walking past him, "but you don't look the least bit embarrassed."

He closed the door and followed me in. The apartment was just as opulent as the one we'd met in earlier.

"Why should I be?"

"This belong to another friend of yours?"

He paused, then said, "No, this one's mine."

I didn't know whether to believe him or not.

"I want this conversation to be on the up and up, Jacoby," he said, moving towards a small writing desk in a corner of the room.

210

"That'll be refreshing."

He took something out of a desk drawer, walked over to me, and held it out.

"What's this?" I asked.

"The lease to this apartment. Look at it."

I took it, unfolded it, and scanned it.

"Can I offer you a drink?"

"No," I said. The name on the bottom of the lease was his: Leo Piper.

"I'm showing you that because, like I said, I want this to be on the square."

The lease could have been a phony, but I decided to give him the benefit of the doubt until I heard what he had to say.

"All right," I said, refolding the lease. He came over with his drink, took the lease, and returned it to the desk.

"Now you'll know that I'm telling you the truth," he said, turning to face me, "when I tell you that if you don't turn that tape you took out of Cross's apartment over to me, I'll kill you."

I was taken aback, and hoped that he didn't notice.

"You should be embarrassed, using a line like that." I was standing next to the phone, and memorized the number, just in case.

"I'm very serious, Jacoby. I want that tape."

"And you'll kill me if you don't get it. Tell me, what will you do then?"

"That's shouldn't worry you, since you won't be around to see it."

"How'd you know there was a tape?"

"I sent one of my men to Cross's apartment last night, but he saw you coming putting it in your pocket."

"You know what I'm wondering, Piper?"

"What?"

"I'm wondering where Alan Cross could have gotten that tape from. I mean, it's at least ten years old, and everything else he had was recent."

"All right, yeah, I gave it to him."

"And killed him when he wouldn't give it back?"

"Hell, no, I didn't kill Al," Piper said, walking to the bar to refresh his drink. "Al and I were old buddies from Brooklyn."

"Brooklyn?"

"Sure, we did some running together back then."

"Did he know Lee then?"

"No, Lee didn't know everyone I knew then."

"I see."

"Do you? Do you see that I want that tape back very badly?"

"Why didn't you go to his apartment a long time ago?"

"It was a crime scene, Jacoby. Besides, who knew Cross would be dumb enough to keep it there. I figured it would in his storage room."

"And how'd you know it wasn't . . . unless you checked just before you set the fire."

"Fire? Oh, yes, I heard about that. I wasn't anywhere near that fire, Jacoby."

"No, you wouldn't have been. You'd have had someone else do it. Wait a minute, I think this is getting clearer."

"Go ahead, then. Run with it."

He was perfectly calm, even though it was just the two of us in the room, and that was unnerving. It was as if he knew that I was no threat to him.

"Correct me if I'm wrong then—"

"Oh, absolutely—"

"You came to New York six months ago to set up shop, and one of the first things you did was approach Knock Wood Lee—"

"I knew he'd say no, but I wanted to see Tiger Lee again."

"Yeah. After he said no, though, you went back and made Lee an offer—"

"Well, I liked what I saw. If anything, she's gotten even more beautiful."

"Is this what you call letting me run with it?"

"Sorry. Continue, please."

212

"The way I see it is that you gave Cross the tape and he used it to blackmail Knock Wood Lee into extending him unlimited credit to gamble."

"Cross always was a small thinker."

"What about the movie business? Was that Cross's baby or yours?"

"Cross was dabbling in it, but when I found out, I decided to use his contacts to expand the operation and break off with the people he was dealing with. I made it pay much more."

"How did they feel about that?"

He smiled and said, "They didn't know."

"Wait a minute. You mean Cross was double-crossing the people he was working for?"

"I was always able to make Al do anything I wanted him to," Piper said, proudly. "I told him he'd be in charge of recruiting the actors and actresses, and he took to that job with great zeal."

"I'm sure he did."

"He even brought some more money into the operation by recruiting his boss."

"Paula Bishop."

"A closet sensualist, that lady," he said with a grin. "She loved it and still won't admit it."

"What about Brown?"

"That was a mistake, but then Brown had a much more assertive personality than Al. He was useful for a time, but after Al's death he became a liability."

"You had them both killed."

"I did no such thing," he said, looking at me as if I were crazy. "I wouldn't jeopardize everything I have by doing that. I was assured that Brown's death in the fire was his own fault."

"I'm sure."

"As for my friend Al, I'm sure the police have the right man for that."

"Knock Wood Lee?"

"You should talk to him, Jacoby. Get the truth from him."

"What are you talking about?"

"Look, I admit that I gave Cross that tape and hoped that it would eventually help me get rid of Knock Wood Lee and Al."

"And get Lee back in the process."

"Possibly, yes."

"You knew that Knock Wood Lee would stand for Cross's blackmail just so long."

"Yes," he said, happily, "and it came to a head that night. I was there to see it."

"You saw Wood kill Cross?"

"Not exactly," he said. "You see, I paid the doorman a large sum of money to get lost, that night. Cross had called me and told me that the Chinaman was coming over to see him. I assured him that I would be right over."

"You stayed outside."

"Yes. I got rid of the doorman, and watched Knock Wood Lee go into the building. He beat Cross to death, and then left."

"He left?"

"And went back."

"Why?"

"Here's what I figure," he said, freshening his drink again. He was still completely relaxed, as if he were simply telling a parlor story.

"The Chinaman probably lost his head, killed Cross, and cut out, but after he left he decided that he'd better go back and search the apartment for the tape."

"That's when you called the cops pretending to be Cross."

"Good man," he said, holding his drink up to me in a toast. "They got there pretty quick, too. Real good response time."

"Wood said he was looking for his money because he didn't want to mention the tape. That means that Lee doesn't know about it."

"I told her years ago that I had destroyed it, but I kept one copy for sentimental reasons."

"And you had a new one made up for Cross."

"The film died in that fire, with Brown," he said, putting his glass down, "and now the only copy is that videotape, and I want it."

He came around from behind the bar and approached me. I almost went for the gun, but decided to hold off, feeling I could get it out quickly if I needed it.

"I want it now," he said, stopping a few feet from me.

"Did Cross know who the man in the film was?"

"He knew."

"And you trusted him with it?"

Smiling he said, "He always knew better than to mess with me, Jacoby. You'd do well to remember that."

"Tell me about Melanie Saberhagen, Piper."

"Who?"

"A young blond girl that Brown and Cross used in a film. She turned up dead after Cross, although she'd been killed before him."

"I don't know anything about that," he said, shaking his head. All trace of humor faded from his face then, and he held out his hand to me.

"Give me the tape, Jacoby."

"I didn't bring it with me."

"You told my man—"

"I told him your only chance of seeing it was to agree to see me. That didn't mean I would bring it along."

"Get it, then."

"No."

His eyes went cold then, and he stared at me.

"You're a dead man, Jacoby."

"I thought that wasn't your style—"

"I either want that tape or your head," he said, and I had the sudden feeling that at that point he wasn't entirely rational.

"All right," I said, and reached for Turkey Neck's gun. My hand closed over the butt and as I eased it out of my belt

Piper moved faster than I'd ever seen anyone move before. He executed a perfect roundhouse kick, which snapped the gun from my hand, then threw a reverse kick that landed on the left side of my head.

I saw stars and hit the floor, but instinct kept me rolling just in case he wanted to follow up. I staggered to one knee, keeping my balance with one hand on the floor, and looked at him.

He was standing very still, studying me.

"Stand up," he said.

"I don't understand," I said to him, hoping that by talking to him I could give myself the chance to recover my senses completely. "Why are you worried about that tape? If you gave it to Cross, it can't be something you're especially ashamed of."

"I'm not ashamed of anything I've ever done, Jacoby, but I want that tape."

"Wait a second," I said, hauling myself to my feet. "It's Lee, isn't it? It's her you're thinking about."

"I never would have let Cross show that tape to anyone, but neither he or that Chinaman knew that. I only used it to put them at each other's throats."

"And now you want the tape back for sentimental reasons?"

"I want to destroy it."

"You really do have feelings for her, don't you?"

A muscle began to twitch in his cheek and he said, "Just give me the tape, Jacoby."

"I'm not going to do that, Piper, but—"

He came at me then and I barely avoided the kick he threw at my head. It might have decapitated me, judging from the force with which it landed on my shoulder. I went flying over an armchair into a coffee table, which collapsed beneath me, and he came after me.

"Let me explain—" I started to say, but he wasn't having any.

He rushed me and I scrambled to my feet in time to

216

keep from being stomped. I backed across the room, trying to look for the gun while keeping my eyes on him, as well.

I wanted to explain myself to him, the proposition I was going to offer, but he was past the talking stage. If I couldn't put him out of commission he was sure as hell going to beat me to death, the same way Cross had been killed.

He moved in on me and threw three quick punches. Surprising both of us, I was able to block the first two, but the third one got through and landed square in the center of my chest. For a moment I thought my heart had stopped, but as he launched another punch I ducked underneath it and hooked one to his belly. He grunted and I moved away from him, trying to get to the center of the room where I'd have more space.

I was trying to control my breathing, trying to get myself into the state of mind I'd always maintained in the ring. Piper was obviously skilled in karate, but I had been a professional fighter. Karate or no, I felt that my pro background, coupled with my own lesser karate skills, should have given me the edge.

That's all I want, I thought, just a small edge.

Piper turned to face me and recognized the fact that I had stopped running. He approached me more slowly now, and I tried to keep loose, keep moving, trying to decide how best to combine my skills.

He threw a kick, but he'd telegraphed it and I decided to try the same thing I'd used on Fallon. I ducked beneath the lethal kick and, while in the crouch, swept my left leg around to cut him off at the knees and dump him. To my surprise, it worked, but even on his butt he was dangerous. As I moved in he lashed out, snapping a kick at my belly. I was quick enough to swivel and take it on the hip, but God, did it hurt!

I staggered backward, feeling the pain shoot through my left leg. He got back to his feet and started to close in on me again slowly. I decided that the old football adage about the best defense being a good offense was the only way to go, and my decision surprised him.

As he continued to advance on me slowly I charged him, and the surprise showed on his face. I threw a few punches the way I'd been taught, but he successfully picked them all off with his forearms, and I finally decided to fall back on the old reliable. I threw a boxer's right cross that he was totally unprepared for, and the pain in my fist was sweet as it connected with the left side of his jaw. He took several off-balance steps, like a puppet whose strings have been cut, and then went down on his side.

No killer instinct, I'd been told, recently as well as during my boxing days. When you hurt your man, Benny used to say, go after him, finish him!

Piper was on his side only for a moment, and then he started to get up, but I charged him and launched a kick that caught him in the ribs. He cried out in pain and rolled with the kick to try to avoid further damage. I was about to go after him when I saw the gun on the floor.

Screw it, I thought, and picked it up. I had nothing to prove by continuing to try to take him hand to hand.

I pointed the gun at him, cocked the hammer, and said, "Move, asshole, and you're dead!"

He was in the process of getting up, and stopped with one hand still on the floor.

"Take it easy," he said, easing himself down so that he was sitting on the floor. He touched his jaw and said, "Man, you can hit."

"I used to do it for a living."

"Yeah," he said, thoughtfully, "that's right, isn't it?"

"You dumb sonofabitch, if you weren't so eager to beat me to death the way you did Cross—"

"Whoa, pal, hold on!" he said. "I told you the truth. I didn't kill Cross. I just want that tape."

"I'm not going to give it to you—"

"I'll come after it—"

"Listen for a change, dammit!" I snapped angrily, and he shut up. "I'm not giving it to you, I'm giving it to Knock Wood Lee."

218

Piper frowned.

"What do you think he'll do with it?" I asked.

"He'll probably destroy it."

"Isn't that what you want?"

"Yeah."

"Well, if that's really true, then we've got no argument, have we?"

He didn't answer right away, so to bring my point across I eased the hammer down on the gun.

"All right," he said, finally.

"You know, Piper, you annoy the shit out of me," I said, dropping my hand to my side so that the gun no longer pointed at him. "I believe you."

"Thanks. Can I get up now?"

I waved, indicating that he could.

"You believe I didn't kill Cross?"

I nodded and said, "But I don't think Knock Wood Lee did, either."

"You better talk to him about that, Jacoby."

"I intend to."

In fact, before meeting Piper's car I had called Heck Delgado and arranged to see Wood at the Tombs after my meeting with Piper.

"What happened to Brown?" I asked.

"The dumb bastard burned himself up," Piper said. "My man was supposed to handle the incendiary, but Brown wanted to do it. Next thing my guy knew, the thing blew with Brown still inside."

"So you haven't killed anyone?"

"I told you—"

"And you don't know who killed the Saberhagen girl?"

"I never even met her. Cross and Brown handled the girls."

"Are there any films left?"

"None, except the ones in Cross's apartment. They were shit, anyway. I'm upgrading my operation."

"That's what you get for dealing with amateurs."

He shrugged and said, "Cross knew the drill, but I've been in town long enough to get the hang of it now. My future products will be much better."

"I'm sure."

"Want a drink?"

"No thanks."

He walked to the bar and poured himself one, then surveyed the wreckage of his apartment and said, "Jesus, what a mess."

"I leave you to clean it up," I said, heading for the door. "Oh, one more thing."

"What?"

I tossed him the .38 and he caught it one-handed, purely by reflex.

"Give that back to Turkey Neck. Tell him he's out one flashlight, though."

"Fuck him."

"Tell me something, Piper."

"What now?"

"Tell me about Lee. Am I really supposed to believe that you wouldn't have allowed anyone to see the tape because you love her?"

He put the gun down, picked up his drink, and stared at me.

"Yes" he said finally, after a lot of deliberation. "I loved her when we were kids in Brooklyn, Jacoby, and I love her now. That's why I tried to get her back. Okay?"

Remembering that he was the one who turned her out when they were kids, I shook my head. "Man, you've got a piss-poor way of showing it."

## — thirty-seven

"All right," Knock Wood Lee said.

"All right what?" Heck asked.

220

"I kicked his ass pretty good, I admit that, but he was alive when I left the apartment."

"The first time, you mean," I said.

Wood looked at me and said, "When I went back I didn't go into the bedroom right away. I assumed he was okay. I started looking for the tape."

"You didn't look good enough."

"I guess not. I was still pretty wound up, you know? I hadn't lost my temper like that . . . hell, I don't think I ever lost my temper like that before, but when he talked about—" he stopped short of mentioning Lee's name and looked at Heck. He didn't know that I had told Heck everything when I reached his office. I'd gone there straight from Piper's, and we went right to the Tombs to face Wood.

"All right, then what happened?" I asked.

"I checked the tapes on the shelves, but I didn't have time to view them. I knew it was hopeless and I went back into the bedroom to try and force him to tell me where it was."

"And he was dead?"

"I don't know. I was about to bend over him when the cops showed up. I didn't know he was dead until they said so."

"So you killed him," Heck said.

"I hurt him pretty bad, but I don't think I killed him."

"You're saying that between the time you left and the time you went back—how long was that?"

"Fifteen, twenty minutes."

"You're saying that in that time somebody else went up there and killed him?"

"I don't know," Wood said, "all I'm saying is that I really don't think that I killed him."

Heck looked at me and I shrugged.

"You still believe Piper?" Heck asked.

"I think Piper saw what he saw and really thinks that Wood killed Cross. He doesn't know, though."

"But if he were to testify at the trial, that would clinch it," Heck said.

"I'm going to buy this one, aren't I?" Wood asked.

"I wish you had leveled with us before this, Wood," Heck said, shaking his head.

"I'm sorry, but I didn't want anyone to know about the tape, that's why I said I was looking for my money."

"Chivalrous," Heck said, "but this is one time when chivalry would have been better off dead."

Heck picked up his briefcase and prepared to leave.

"Mr. Delgado," Wood said, "I'd understand if you withdrew from the case."

"We'll talk again," Heck said, and knocked on the door for the guard.

"Jack?"

"Yeah, Wood?"

"The tape—"

"I've got the tape, Wood."

He looked relieved.

"Wood, did Cross show you the tape?"

"No," he said, shaking his head. "If he had I would have taken it away from him."

"Why'd you believe him, then?"

"Lee told me about it a long time ago, so I knew it existed, and if he knew about it, he must have had it, or at least seen it. I couldn't take the chance . . ."

"Lee doesn't know about this, does she?"

"No, and I don't want her to."

"She won't hear it from me."

"Thanks, Jack. Listen, if I don't get out—"

"Don't worry," I said, "it's as good as destroyed. I'll melt it down and bring you the remains."

"Thanks," he said again.

"Jack?" Heck called from the door.

"See you, buddy," I said, and followed Heck out.

In a cab Heck said, "What do you think?"

"I believe him."

"I believe him, too," he said. "I believe that he doesn't think he killed Cross, but Jack, he's not a doctor. The injuries he inflicted on that man *could* have killed him."

"I suppose so."

"I could go to the D.A. with the story and plea to manslaughter—"

"You'll have to talk to Wood about that."

"Why don't you talk to Piper again? As far as I can see, he's our only witness. If Wood is right, then Piper had to have seen something else."

"I'll try," I said. Having memorized the number on the phone in the apartment on Seventy-second Street, I hoped that Piper's lease had been the real thing, and I hoped he'd still be there.

I called him from my office, and was relieved to find that he was still there.

"I'm still cleaning up," he said. "Did you talk to the Chinaman?"

"Yes."

"And?"

"Piper, I need a favor."

"Is that so?"

"I want to know everything you saw that night."

There was a long silence, and then he said, "If I tell you that, Jacoby, I might be helping Knock Wood Lee."

"That's true," I said, "unless you want to look at it as helping Lee."

"You're a sonofabitch, did you know that?"

"Sure."

"All right, yeah, I did see someone else."

"When?"

"In between the time Knock Wood Lee left and came back."

"Piper, if Wood didn't kill Cross, then you might have seen the killer."

"Jacoby, there are a lot of apartments in that building this man could have gone to."

"I know that," I said, impatiently. "Who was it, Piper? Who did you see?"

"How the hell should I know? I saw a man."

Disappointed I asked. "You didn't know him?"

"He was a perfect stranger to me."

"How long was he in the building?"

"He left before the Chinaman came back," Piper said, "and he left in a hurry."

"Shit," I said. "Is that all you can tell me?"

"That's it . . . except there was something strange that I remember."

"What?"

"Well, the guy was a big man, but as he was putting his gloves on I noticed something."

"What, for Christ's sake?"

"For a big man, he had these real small hands, you know? Weird."

Yeah, I knew.

Weird.

"And I was close enough to notice that he was missing a finger," he added.

"The thumb," I said, "on the left hand."

"How did you know?"

I just knew.

— *thirty-eight* —————————————————

I gave the Detroit cab driver the address of Robert Saberhagen's building, and hoped I'd find him in.

I hadn't called ahead for an appointment.

Saberhagen agreed to see me right away after his secretary announced me, and I followed her to his office. She was the kind of woman a wife would hire to be her husband's secretary.

224

"Mr. Jacoby," he said, standing behind his desk. "I sent you a check—"

"That's not why I'm here, Mr. Saberhagen," I said, even though I hadn't yet received it.

"You haven't checked into a hotel," he said, looking at my bag.

"I don't expect to be in town that long, sir."

"Please, sit down. Can I offer you refreshments?"

"No, thank you."

"All right, then," he said, seating himself behind his desk, "perhaps you'd like to tell me why you're here."

"It's about your daughter's killer."

"You know who he is?"

"Not really," I said, "but I think you do."

He frowned and said, "I don't understand."

"I think you do, sir. There is a witness who saw you go into Alan Cross's building that night. He can identify you, and will in a lineup, if it becomes necessary."

"If that's true," he said, "why are you here, and not the police?"

"I haven't told the police yet, Mr. Saberhagen," I said, and boy, was I going to be in hot water for that one. Hocus would hit the ceiling when he heard that I acted on Piper's information without giving it to him, but what would he have done with it? Piper saw a man, so what? Who was the man, and who was to say he went to Cross's apartment?

"I came here without conferring with them, to give you the opportunity to come back with me."

He studied me for a few seconds and then said, "Why would I want to do that?"

"Because I don't think you're a murderer, sir. That is, I don't think you could kill someone and then live with it."

He folded his hands on the desk top and regarded them solemnly, blinking his eyes rapidly.

"I also don't think you were as unaffected by your daughter's death as you would have people think."

"I did love her," he said, his voice barely audible, "although I had great difficulty showing it."

"Well, it must have been difficult. I understand she blamed you for her mother's death. That couldn't have made it any easier for you."

"Her mother was a whore, but I could not—I would not have her find that out."

"So you sent her away."

"She wanted to go, and I agreed, as I told you in New York."

"Mr. Saberhagen, Cross killed your daughter, didn't he?"

He hesitated, then said, "Yes."

"How did you find out?"

"He came to my hotel. He wanted to sell me a tape, a videotape of a movie he said Melanie had made." He closed his eyes and squeezed his hands together very tightly. "And then he showed it to me."

"I know what was on the tape."

"Filth!" he said, separating his hands and bringing both fists down on the desk. "I was supposed to pay him for it that night, but when I got there the door was open and he was on the floor in the bedroom. He had been badly beaten, and he wanted me to call an ambulance."

He stopped, opened his hands, and examined the palms. I decided not to push him.

"I guess he thought I wasn't going to, because he started babbling. He told me how he hadn't meant to kill Melanie. He told me that he loved her, but that she was going to leave him."

Alan Cross loved Melanie Saberhagen? Wouldn't that be ironic if it was true? Cross the pussyhound falling for a young, confused girl he'd recruited for porno movies. I didn't believe it for a minute. I thought it infinitely more likely that Melanie had wised up and not only wanted to leave, but wanted to blow the whistle on Cross. Maybe he slapped her around a couple of times and maybe the little girl who had been studying karate for years had decided to fight back. Cross might not have intended to kill her, but people have been known to get killed even during sparring sessions, when contact is forbidden. This would have been nothing like a sparring session . . .

Anyway, they were both dead, so who would ever know the truth?

"I couldn't believe my ears," he said, "and then I couldn't believe my eyes, because the next thing I knew my hands were over his mouth and nose, cutting off his air, and he was too weak to fight me." He looked at me through tortured eyes and said, "I am not a physical man."

"The circumstances were extraordinary."

"Yes, they were," he said, "they were. I knew I had killed him, and I left quickly. That night I tried to think what to do, and the next day I hired you to find Melanie. It was the only thing I could think to do. Then I came home and waited for you to call me and tell me that you found her body."

"Which I did."

"I tried to seem unaffected by her death."

"You succeeded admirably," I said, remembering the distaste I'd felt for him at the morgue.

"I did not want to seem as if I had a motive, just in case . . ."

"Apparently you thought it out very thoroughly."

"Yes, but you were right a moment ago, Mr. Jacoby, when you said that I couldn't just forget . . . killing someone. I remember that, and I still feel the shame of denying loving my daughter." He stared at me and said, "Would you believe me if I said that I've been hoping you—or someone—would come for me?"

"Sure, I'd believe you, Mr. Saberhagen."

He nodded, then picked up his phone and buzzed his secretary.

"Miss Hall, would you please get me two tickets on the next flight to New York?" He listened a moment, then said, "First class, of course."

Of course.

# — thirty-nine

Lee was out when I went to Wood's place to give him the tape.

"You don't know how I appreciate this, Jack," he said, holding it tightly in both hands as if he was afraid I'd try to take it back. "I can't thank you enough for everything you did."

"Let's talk, Wood."

"About what? A fee? Hell, man, I'll pay you as much as—"

"Not a fee, Wood. I want to know what happened between you and Cross."

He stared at me for a few moments, tapping the tape against the knuckles of one hand.

"I lost it, Jack," he said, finally. "For the first time in my life I really lost control. Cross was making remarks about Lee—" he stopped there and started pacing the room. I knew he was going to tell me something that he normally wouldn't.

"I love that woman more than anything, Jack. I think you know that." I did. "When he started talking about her I couldn't stop myself. I started beating on him and I couldn't stop. He tried to fight back but he was no match. Dammit it, Jack, I wanted to kill him!"

"You didn't," I said. "Saberhagen took care of that for you."

"Yeah, but I'm the one that made it happen. I'm not proud of that, you know, but I really think that if it all happened again, I'd do it the same way." He looked down at the tape and said, "I'd never let anyone hurt her."

I was about to say something when we heard a key in the door.

"It's Lee," he said, with something akin to panic on his normally placid face. "Stall her while I stash this?"

"Sure," I said. I was enjoying this side of Wood, a side I was not normally privy to. I could picture him running

228

around the apartment trying to find someplace to hide the tape, for which he had suffered through a lot.

I went to stall Lee for as long as he needed.

With the case over I finally had time to do something I'd been wanting to do—spend time with Alison. She got a Sunday night off from Billy, but as it turned out we spent it at Bogie's, eating dinner and listening to a guest speaker at one of Billy and Karen's "Sinister Sundays." The speaker was an author named Mallory, who was also signing copies of his book *Kill Their Darlings*.

Alison wanted to hear all about the case. I told her how Hocus had hit the ceiling when I returned from Detroit with Saberhagen, because I had one without telling him first. He had calmed down when all the facts became known—and that was when Vadala hit the ceiling. But in spite of the way *he* felt about Wood—and me—Vadala was a good cop and he was glad to have been saved from sending an innocent man to jail for life.

I didn't tell her that after Hocus had calmed down, I'd asked him check with Vice to see who was doing business in porno movies. My plan had been to give whoever it was a call and whisper "Piper" in his ear, but when I found out that the "man" was Cagey Carl himself, I decided to forget it. If Piper was taking a bite out of Carl Jr.'s action, I wished him luck. They'd butt heads eventually anyway, and without my help.

As for Robert Saberhagen—well, Heck had himself another client.

"Did you take a fee from your friend Wood?" Alison asked.

"He sent me a check, but I sent it back to him in pieces."

"That was nice of you."

"Not really. As it turns out, I also got a check from Paula Bishop as a token of her appreciation. That one I cashed."

"It sounds like you did a wonderful job, Jack."

"There was a lot of luck involved."

She put her hand on mine and said, "I think you're being modest."

She was a nice girl, maybe the kind I wouldn't have minded spending some time with.

"How about helping me out with this?" I asked, showing her the real estate section of *The New York Times*.

"What's that for?"

"I think it's time I found an apartment of my own and got out of Billy and Karen's back room."

She made a face and at that point Karen came walking over, smiling her matchmaker smile. When she saw the newspaper her expression changed.

"Since when do you read the *Times*?"

"Since I started looking for an apartment—"

"That's nonsense—"

"No it's not," I argued. "It's time I found my own place."

"But we like having you around," Karen said, "don't we, Alison?"

Alison looked at me and said, "Very much."

"I'll still be around," I said. "I'm, uh, going to have to give up my office on Fifth Avenue. Can't handle the rent anymore."

It was true. I was sorry to have to give it up, since that had been the only office Eddie Waters had ever had, but Fifth Avenue rent was just too much for me to make every month.

"That means I'll need some place to use as an office from time to time. Think Billy would agree to that?"

Karen smiled her lovely smile and said, "Why not? If we let you sleep there, we'll let you do anything—well, almost anything."

Somebody called Karen's name and she said, "See you two later," and hurried off.

"Well," Alison said, taking part of the real estate section, "Since that's settled I guess we'd better start finding you an apartment."

"Yes," I said, staring at her while she frowned over the paper, "I guess we'd better."